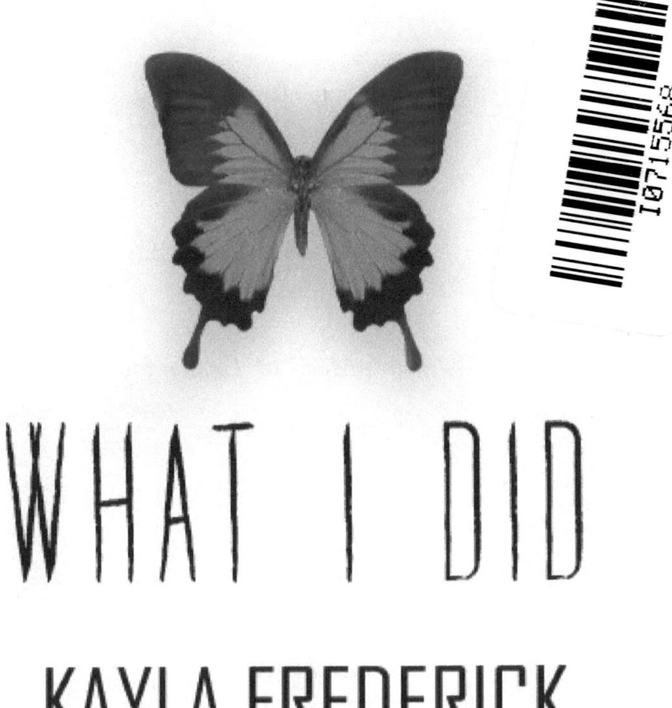

WHAT I DID

KAYLA FREDERICK

<u>*Also by Kayla Frederick*</u>

~ Memento Mori: 13 Tales of Horror

~ The Residency

~After the Devil

~Flirting with Death

~Voices

~Dead by Morning

What I Did

Kayla Frederick

This is a work of fiction. All the characters and events portrayed in this novel are either products of the author's imagination or are used fictitiously.

What I Did

Cover by Valdas Miskinis
Edited by Claudia Englert

ISBN: 978-1-950530-34-2
First Edition July 2024
Library of Congress Control Number: 2024914218

"We only have but one story. All novels, all poetry, are built on the never-ending contest in ourselves of good and evil."
~John Steinbeck, *East of Eden*

Chapter One

CHIN IN HAND, I rested my elbows on my knees, leaning forward as the killer on the television jumped from the shadows. The fake screams and blood were the highlight of the past hour, but I was dangerously close to yawning. The actress onscreen did the typical horror movie cliché and fell over nothing, overexaggerating her tumble to the ground. I groaned, wishing the killer would end her already. He walked toward her, and she held her hands up over her face as if that would save her.

Laughing, I plopped a handful of popcorn into my mouth.

"Everything alright?" Mom asked from the kitchen table.

I glanced over my shoulder, forcing the slightest hint of a pleasant smile. It was Friday night, and I was tucked under a blanket with snacks and a horror movie. What could be wrong? "Of course."

When her eyes moved to the TV, it was at the same time that the knife sliced through the air. Her nose wrinkled, and I recognized the hint of judgement in her eyes, a little twinkle that told me exactly what she thought of my choice of entertainment. She had never approved of my love of horror but believed too strongly in me "finding my own identity" to do anything about it.

"Be careful about dropping too much of that popcorn," Mom said, standing from her seat. "The rats are back again."

"That's wonderful," I said, looking at the tiny yellow crumbs I'd already dropped.

"I'm going to get an exterminator in here eventually, but I can't afford it this week," she continued, either not noticing the mess or choosing the path of least resistance and not mentioning it.

"If we already have them, I don't think a few crumbs will make a difference," I pointed out and shoved another handful of the buttery snack in my mouth, making extra sure to drop a few more pieces.

Mom sighed, already beaten down by her day of monotony to argue. "Just be careful when you walk into the kitchen, okay? I'm not using the conventional traps because apparently, it's not fixing the situation. I'm going to try glue boards. Don't step on it or it'll peel the skin off your foot."

I pictured the skin slipping away, leaving all the raw meat exposed. Maybe if this movie had tried something like that, it would've been interesting. I held up my finger and thumb in an okay sign. "Gotcha."

The sound of her ripping open the package was louder than it should've been as I turned back to the movie. I cranked up the volume, watching fake blood spread from the fake corpse. "Terrible special effects!"

The sound of ruffling plastic stopped. "I don't know why you watch that stuff."

Something about Mom's passive-aggressive comments

made me love these movies more. Though, really, I preferred the authentic videos. I never told anyone about watching those though. That part of me had been born accidentally. I'd been aimlessly scrolling through social media when a leaked video of a woman's beheading showed up in my timeline. The video started, but I hadn't read the caption, only realizing what it was after it was over.

I sat for a while, replaying the film in my head and processing what it meant. My stomach should've flopped. I should've been sickened, horrified, *something* other than intrigued. I clicked replay, maybe seven or eight times, before I'd had enough. I couldn't wrap my brain around the fact that I had literally seen someone *die*.

Horror movies drew out the death scenes, giving them theatrics and suspense, but real life wasn't like that. For all the fake movies I'd ever seen, the beheading seemed somehow faker. There was some jeering from the surrounding crowd, a swing of a sharp blade, a thud, a tiny spray of blood, and the woman was *dead*. Snuffed out in a three-minute clip. It stayed with me, and I thought about it at the most inconvenient times.

I didn't know what that said about me, or maybe I didn't *like* what it suggested. Either way, it had left me with the thought that human life was both strangely fragile and persistent. Every snuff film I watched proved it more.

I need to stop this, I'd told myself, but somehow, watching them got me through the day. It was like an awful addiction. What did that fascination mean? What kind of a person loved violence and gore? No one I knew. Not my mom or my best friend, Keaton. I was different from them and not the good kind of different.

When I thought about it, I couldn't remember a time that I *ever* truly felt as if I belonged. When I was little, I used to lie in the backyard, feeling the grass beneath my hands as I stared up at the sun, wondering when the aliens who had dropped me off would take me home. Surely me being here among all these humans who were so unlike me was an awful mistake.

Of course, I didn't tell my mother this, or anyone for that matter, because I was sure it was a foolproof way of getting myself sent to an asylum. Mom had gone to one for a few months when I was little. Not that it helped.

On a whim, I once told Mom about seeing the world as a series of grays, and she told me I was depressed. This didn't feel like that. It wasn't *sadness*. This emptiness was different. This felt like a void, a gaping hole that needed to be filled by something I had yet to discover.

I didn't know how serial killers came to the inevitable conclusion it was their destiny to bring harm to others, but something in me started to suspect I was on that path, and I didn't know how to get off it…or if I wanted to. Understanding other people—their wants, their needs, their goals—was never something I could do. The basic ability other people have to connect to one another was mysteriously absent in me.

Bundy spoke often of a "malignant being" who drove him to kill. Berkowitz heard voices. Hell, even the Zodiac claimed to have headaches that could only be cured by killing. Those serial killers all believed something in them *drove* them to do what they did. Maybe they were bullshit defense strategies to keep them from facing the death penalty, but it didn't stop me from wondering, what if they weren't?

What if the difference between killers and normal people wasn't their intelligence or family background or genetics, but some entity, a dark part of their own subconscious that takes over?

Chapter Two

LEAVING THE APARTMENT was never a choice I willingly made. I left to go to work and school—because I had to—and on the rare occasion when Mom was in a mood and would kick me out. Sometimes, I would go out for Keaton's sake, but like me, she was inherently an introvert.

It had been a few days since I'd last heard from her, and while it wasn't unusual for me to go no contact, it was odd for her. She was the type to check in daily in case anything drastically changed in my life in the span of twenty-four hours.

I pulled out my phone, staring at her name, and considered texting her, typing out a message before I deleted it. Lately, she wasn't the same Keaton I knew. She had developed a crush on the cashier at the multiplex and that was all she could think to talk about. At first, I had tried to be supportive of my friend, going with her as she debated whether to come right out and tell the girl her feelings. She never did, of course, and it didn't take me long to figure out why she *really* wanted me to go. She was using me to see if the other girl was jealous. The first time I had suspected Keaton's true motives was when we were in the lobby of the theater, and she had started laughing hysterically for no reason as she grabbed my hand.

While I liked Keaton, I didn't like being touched, and I certainly didn't like being part of someone else's game. Not that I had anything better to do, but it wasn't what I considered to be a good time. Keaton never apologized for using me, so, I hadn't gone back with her.

I slung my backpack over my shoulder and went out the door to start my day. As my upstairs neighbor, it wasn't uncommon to see Keaton around the building. I glanced up the stairs but saw no one. The lobby downstairs was void of life too.

I pulled my headphones out, sticking them in my ears as I passed the parking lot. Mom's shiny red Sedan was parked in one of the spots near the exit. I could've taken it instead of the bus, but I didn't trust myself.

The thing about my darkness was that it didn't only affect the way I thought about the world, it turned me against myself just as often. Recently, I'd had days when I found myself driving and wondered what it'd be like to swerve the car into oncoming traffic. It didn't take too many instances of those thoughts for me to decide that driving wasn't for me.

I plopped down on the hard red bench at the bus stop, studying the other three people in the bus shelter. They kept their distance, and I relaxed as I waited. Sometimes, people *didn't* understand the concept of personal space. That was why I started carrying two pocketknives. One in my pocket, and one clipped into the cup of my bra, just in case.

When the bus came, I avoided eye contact with the others and slipped into the first empty seat I passed. Eye contact led to conversation, and I didn't want that. I never wanted that.

Keaton was the closest thing to a BFF I had ever had, and while I cared about her, if she suddenly stopped talking to me, I wouldn't pursue the situation. We would never talk again. Mom had noticed that about me, how easy it was for me to cut people off, and unlike my comment about a gray world, she had seen my lack of any real attachment as a red flag and immediately took me to a therapist.

He used a lot of phrases—anxiety, agoraphobia, Borderline Personality Disorder, possible psychosis—you name it, I was probably diagnosed with it. Mom had been devastated, but the labels did nothing to me. I was the same person I had been before Dr. Reggie had given his two cents. Mom tried to force me to follow his plan, and up until I turned eighteen, I went along with it.

Then I told her no more. It hadn't made me better, and it never would.

I am who I am.

Day by day, she witnessed me withdraw further from society but didn't understand my reasons for doing so. I tried to reassure her it wasn't out of sadness, that the truth was, the actions came from feeling nothing at all. Maybe that was worse than sadness, I don't know, but Mom wasn't happy for that explanation either.

I gave up. She was going to think what she was going to think.

When the bus approached the intersection I needed, I rose from my seat with my head down. This crossroad was about a block away from where I worked, a medium-sized grocery store in the middle of town called Grocer's Way. Nothing too fancy, but it was large enough that I gathered no attention from my coworkers when I walked through the door. Though I suspected if the store *was* smaller, that would still be the case. I didn't have many friends. Like high school all over again.

Fortunately, real life treated me slightly better than high school had. At least I wasn't bullied here…for the most part. There was only one coworker who gave me problems, but I didn't see him right now. Samuel was a stocker so I couldn't tell if he was here or not until I did a lap through the store.

I don't know if "ex" would be the right word to describe him since we had only gone on one date, but that was the extent of our history. When I'd first started working here, I thought Samuel was attractive, charming, *decent*. He had asked me out, and I had agreed with little knowledge about him. When I found out he was a "Netflix and Chill" type guy, I said, *no thanks*, and left. I had never been the kind to jump into bed with a guy, and I wasn't about to start now. Needless to say, he didn't take the rejection well. His affection burned away to hostility, and it had been that way ever since.

I had to stay on guard, waiting for whatever nonsense he had cooked up for the day. On his off days, I could relax, but he was an ass kisser which meant he often came in on times when he wasn't scheduled too. The walk to my locker in the employee lounge was quiet. I set my backpack inside my assigned blue box and got my name badge out. Putting myself together, I walked toward my register, seeing who I had to work with today.

There were two girls, Harlow and Carmine. They were

friends outside of work, and Harlow was close to my wannabe-ex. I plastered my best *see-I'm-human-too* smile on and did what I could to get through the shift. The first few hours breezed by in the way that minimum wage dead-end jobs tend to do.

"Hey," a voice said from behind me. My work bestie, Oscar. He was on the shorter side, his curly brown hair making up some of his height. He blinked his big brown eyes. *Bestie* might be a strong word. We were *acquaintances* at most since we only talked at work. And lately, even that seemed rare. Our shifts were opposite, him working mornings and me in the afternoon so only a few hours of our time overlapped, if any at all.

"How's it going?" I asked.

"It's…going," he said and glanced at my register. "Lunch time yet?"

"Yeah, just about." I signed off and stepped out of the cubicle. "Anything in mind?"

He glanced across the store to the connected restaurant called Burger Joint. It was a little place that sold burgers and chicken strips. Nothing fancy, but I'd grown a taste for them.

"Works for me."

He studied my profile once or twice as we walked as if he wanted to speak, but no words came out. I pretended not to notice, hiding my eyes by pulling out my wallet to see how much money I had on hand.

We ordered separately but sat at the same table. I took a bite of my burger, wondering what I was really eating. I had seen some disturbing reports about fast food in the past. I set down my food and narrowed my eyes at Oscar. He sat hunched, elbows on the table, and stared at the unwrapped lump on his plate as if he expected it to dance for him.

"You can't eat telepathically, you know," I told him.

He raked his fingers through his hair. "Yeah, I know. I'm…out of sorts, I guess."

I took another bite, studying him as I chewed—the bags under his eyes, the white shirt with the dirty collar. There was *something* wrong with him. He looked as if he hadn't eaten or slept properly in a few days, but I didn't know how to approach the situation, didn't know if I *should*. I was shit at giving advice.

"What's wrong?" I asked.

He stared at me as if he debated telling me the truth. "Things are…going to be different soon," he stated, jutting out his chin. "They're going to be better."

I swirled my tongue across my bottom teeth to remove a piece of lettuce that had gotten stuck. "That's good, right?"

Oscar looked down at the table again, his spark gone. "Yeah."

I was confused, certain I had done something to spur the odd reaction. He sounded almost…*disappointed,* as if I hadn't reacted the way he wanted. We said nothing for the rest of the meal, and as I finished my food, I stared at Oscar's *still* untouched plate, wondering why he bought anything if he didn't want it.

"Are you *sure* you're okay?" I asked, crumpling my empty wrapper.

"Yep," he answered and cleared his throat. "Yeah." Oscar finally unwrapped his burger, but it was to take two bird-like bites before he set it down again.

"Are you full?"

"Doesn't matter," he replied, nearly tossing away the entire tray as we went back to work.

Chapter Three

THAT NIGHT, KEATON must've realized how long we had gone without speaking because her name appeared on my phone. I debated answering it, not exactly wanting to leave the house again for the day. I ignored her first call, staring as it went to voicemail. A minute later, my phone started to ring again. Knowing she wouldn't give up if I ignored her, I held the phone to my ear.

"Hello?" I said uncertainly, almost cautiously.

"Hey," Keaton said. "Plans for tonight?"

I already knew where this conversation was going. "You outta know me better than that by now." Every time she asked, I never had plans, and this fact had remained true for years.

"I do, but I wanted to be sure your calendar was empty 'cuz I want you to come out with me tonight to see a movie."

I stared at my blanket and wondered why I had answered the phone. Hadn't I already known this would be the conversation?

"Please."

"You never apologized for what happened last time."

"You're right," she said after a brief pause. "I'm sorry. Now what do you say?"

"Trixie gonna be there?"

"Dude, you don't know?" she asked, voice animated.

"Don't know what?" I asked, hardly interested by the gossip. Sometimes, it felt as if Keaton didn't know me at all.

"She got fired last week. It's okay though. It happened when I was there so I ended up getting her number from the whole ordeal," she said, and by the tone of her voice, I could tell she was smiling.

"Well, that worked out well for you, didn't it?" I said. I had the inkling Keaton may have had a hand in getting Trixie fired, but she would never admit it, and I would never ask.

"Yeah, but enough about that. We haven't spent much time together in days. I want to go to the movies to chill. You know, me and you? That new horror flick is out."

"You're gonna have to be specific."

"Come on, Jessie, hang out with me," Keaton whined. "We don't have to see a movie. We can go get something to eat or get a coffee or *I don't know*. Walk around the park?"

"Could you have any cheesier ideas?" I laughed but considered it. Going out for a bit could be a good thing. The longer I stayed indoors, the more I thought about Oscar in the Burger Joint. The weird reaction to my questions and his cryptic: *It'll be better soon.* "Fine, fine. We can do something."

"Great, be down in a minute," she said, ending the call without a goodbye.

I set the phone down. In my messy t-shirt and shorts, I wasn't dressed to go anywhere, but by the time I convinced myself to stand up, there was a knock at the door. I threw on a clean sweatshirt and leggings before I answered it.

Keaton beamed at me. By nature, she was an unconventional dresser, appearing more like a skater boy with short white-blonde hair and baggy clothes than a girl. In fact, the first time I met her, I thought she *was* a boy until she talked. I adored her aesthetic.

"If it wasn't for me, you would be a hermit," she declared.

"Still practically am."

"The world could end, and you still wouldn't leave your house, would you?" Keaton joked as I slipped out of the apartment, listening to the familiar click behind me as the door closed.

"What would be the use in that? There'd be nowhere to go anyway."

Keaton punched my arm lightly. "Smart ass."

"Less people, more peace," I replied.

"Amen to that," Keaton agreed, rolling her big blue eyes as we crossed through the apartment lobby. "So, what've you been up to the past few days?"

"Oh, big things," I replied, thinking of Mom's declaration of the rats. "Wild things."

"You've been home watching horror movies, amiright?"

"Yep," I said, tucking a lock of my dirty blonde hair behind my ear. "How are things going for you and Trixie?"

Keaton stuck her hands into the pockets of her oversized black trip shorts. "I mean, we're not a couple yet if that's what you're asking. We're talking."

Outside the lobby, the sky was darkening. The blue-purple of the night contrasted by the dim streetlamps as we walked through the parking lot. At this point in the conversation, other people would've asked follow-up questions or offered some helpful insight about themselves. I did neither. I really didn't want to know more. Her love life was none of my business.

We drove in silence, but that was the thing with Keaton. She didn't mind, she never did. I couldn't make heads or tails of her sometimes. Maybe it was why I had trusted her from the moment we met. She was an outsider like me. Or maybe it was because she was the only person I could truly be myself with. She didn't try to diagnose me. She accepted me.

Keaton was my haven. The only one I had.

Through many years of awkward social interactions, I had learned that dark humor made a lot of people uncomfortable, and sometimes, angry. Like my horror movies, Mom hated any dark joke I made, but Keaton? She laughed with me, and I wondered if she'd still be laughing if she knew that half my jokes were grounded on real feelings.

Chapter Four

NIGHTS OUT WITH Keaton reminded me that regardless of how much of an outsider I thought I was, at heart, I was still human. Nothing and no one else made me feel like I mattered. Especially not my job. Well, not the job so much as a certain someone *at* the job.

The next morning, I kept my head down as I made my usual trip to work. My commute went by without incident, and when I hit the door of Grocer's Way, I scanned my surroundings for signs of Samuel. He never had two days off in a row which meant he was here *somewhere*. Eyes and ears peeled, I made it to the employee lounge before his nonsense began. A piece of paper had been taped to my locker that said, "Stuck up bitch." Angrily, I ripped it off, crumpling it in my fist as I twisted the code into my lock and opened the door.

"Jessie," Samuel sneered as he entered the break room. He brushed past me, ramming his shoulder into mine. He was a big guy, and I was sure the contact would leave a bruise later.

"You forgot your trash," I called after him, throwing the paper at the back of his head before I pulled my name badge from my locker and slammed the door with a *clang*.

He watched me, unfazed. Perhaps the worst part of his

ugly personality was the fact that he had an attractive veneer on top. Chocolate brown hair, green eyes, and a slender face. The paper landed at his feet, and he scooped it up. I was almost positive he would stick it to my locker after I left, but I wasn't going to stay to give him the chance to say anything else.

Trembling with rage, I walked back out to the sales floor. When I took my place behind the register, I hoped it wasn't obvious. Harlow glanced at me from the nearby register, offering me a small smile, which I ignored.

At work, I tried to be professional, to keep my head down, and speak only when necessary. I had learned that was the best way to get through my days without getting in trouble. It was the only thing I could do. I had tried to report Samuel's bullying to my boss, Mr. Waters, but it hadn't gone down well. Samuel had charmed his way out of the situation, and Mr. Waters had looked at me with sympathy as if he assumed I was completely batshit crazy for having a bad thought about his star employee.

And I wasn't the type to make the same mistake twice. Instead of trying again to fix the situation, I let it go, which *did* hurt a bit, if I was being honest. When I was a kid, I had imagined I would grow up to be some big important person with a big important job, but now that I was practically an adult, I barely made it in the most basic job industry.

And it sucked.

I started to ring up my first customer of the day. The meaningless work was something to focus on, something to distract me. I hated every minute of it, but I reminded myself that at least I was being paid to hate it. The day was easy until a man in a fedora made it to the front of my line. He leered at me the entire time I rung up his things, and I pretended not to notice as I told him his total.

He pulled out his wallet, opened it, then paused. "You'd be much prettier if you smiled," he said, staring at me as if the rude comment would somehow make me listen.

I stared back, deadpanned. The part of me interested in normality for the sake of my job told me to play along, but the rest of me fully understood and supported Aileen Wuornos' choice of victims. If I ever did snap, it'd probably be thanks to a guy like this. I glanced toward the aisle, where Samuel was knelt putting cans in a perfect row on the shelf. Or *him*.

After a full minute of silence and still no smile, the man huffed and swiped his card. When his transaction finished, he grabbed his bags and stormed off. I offered him the middle finger as I watched him go.

"Looks like you could use a break," Oscar said from behind me.

"Are you on break?"

"I took mine earlier," he said, and put his hands in his pockets, avoiding eye contact.

I frowned, feeling as if whatever he'd wanted to say yesterday was still on his mind and now this was a game of chicken to see who would break first. "Oh, okay," I said at last. When it was clear Oscar wasn't going to say anything else, I added, "Well, let me know if you want me to grab you something. Some chips or water or whatever."

"Thanks, but I'm good," Oscar said and smiled, but it didn't touch his eyes. "Never change."

I didn't leave as he took my place at the register. Red flags were everywhere, and I was blinded by them, ready to charge like a bull in a fight to figure this out. "Oscar, what's going on?"

He ignored me, waving a customer to the register. "And how are you today?" he asked her as he started to ring her up.

"Huh," I muttered, baffled. I wanted to keep asking him questions, but it was clear he wasn't going to answer. I made eye contact with Samuel on accident before veering off in a different direction when I realized how close he was. Had Samuel heard what Oscar had said? I couldn't tell.

I went to the deli section, browsing for something small to eat. When I was on break alone, I didn't like to go out for lunch. I'd buy something in the store and eat it in the break room. Today, I grabbed a sandwich and glanced toward Oscar's line, debating trying one more time to get him to open up.

I did exactly that. As I rounded the shelves, I could hear someone speaking.

"It's not that hard. They can train monkeys to do your job. Just ring it up."

Samuel.

I stepped around the candy rack to see Samuel standing by Oscar's register. Oscar waved his wand over the bottle, frowning. "It's not my fault. The register's frozen," Oscar said calmly and set the wand down to poke something on the screen.

"Yeah okay," Samuel rolled his eyes. "I think you're just stupid."

Anger washed over me, and I stormed up to him. "Leave him alone. It's not your break time anyway, so why are you even over here harassing him?"

Oscar stopped, watching the exchange.

Samuel opened his mouth but walked away to disappear into the store when he spotted Mr. Waters standing at the end of one of the aisles.

"He's such a dick," I said as I threw my sandwich on the belt. Then I reconsidered. "Wait if your register isn't working, I'll go to Harlow's."

Oscar smiled. "My register isn't frozen. It's fine. I wanted to give him a hard time."

"I love it."

Oscar scanned the sandwich then looked at Samuel's discarded drink. "Want a lemonade?" he asked, holding it up.

I shrugged. "Sure. Hate to see it go to waste."

Oscar told me my total, and I swiped my card. "Have a good lunch," he said.

"Thanks." I grabbed my food and took two steps away from the register.

Only when he started ringing up his next customer did I remember what I'd wanted to say to him. *But he seemed fine,* I told myself and made my way to the break room, content with the knowledge that I'd tried.

When I passed my locker, I almost expected to see another note taped there, but there wasn't one. The break room was a quaint room with white walls and a blue floor. Across one wall were a series of vending machines for snacks and drinks. Another wall had a counter with a sink and a microwave. The rest of the space had about six white tables spaced out, starting from the place the line of lockers ended.

I sat at the nearest table, ready to eat when I heard footsteps and realized Samuel had followed me. Bracing for a fight, I balled my hands into a fist as he approached and lifted my chin to glare at him.

"So what is it?" he asked. "*He's* good enough for you to date and I'm not?"

I scoffed, hardly able to believe we were having this conversation. "Date? Who said anything about dating? We're *friends.*" I made a show of taking a sip of the lemonade he'd been unable to buy.

"I don't get it. I mean we go on one date, and—"

"And what? You assume you have some ownership over me now, is that it?"

"You are simple."

"You know what's really simple? Leaving someone alone. Obviously, I want nothing to do with you."

Samuel tilted his head back to exaggerate the sound of his laughter. "Maybe this is fun for me. What will you do?"

I flared my nostrils. At six foot two, he had the advantage here, but that didn't stop me from thinking about grabbing his hair and smashing his face into the table.

"Exactly," he said, taking my silence as a point for his argument. "You should be grateful that someone like me is even interested in you. Smart girls wouldn't waste such an opportunity."

That was a direct insult, but I couldn't find the words to argue. I stared into his eyes, going into the dark places in my brain, the same ones I usually tried to avoid. Keaton told me once that when I shut down, my eyes change from blue to black, and I could imagine they're as black as coal right now.

Or maybe not because he had the audacity to *grin*. For now, he wasn't afraid of me, but if he kept pushing, I was sure we would both regret the results.

Chapter Five

FTER THE ENCOUNTER with Samuel, my nerves were on edge for the rest of the day which was unfortunate because I couldn't go home and hide like I wanted. Twice a week, I took classes at the university in town for a degree in forensics. It fascinated me in the same dark way that the beheading video had. While I knew this was also a decision Mom wasn't happy about, she was glad for the idea of me doing *something* with my life.

She had never gone to college, dropping out sometime before she graduated high school. Minimum wage jobs were the best she could get, and she had made it vehemently clear that she wanted better for me. Or she wanted me to stop living on her couch.

I wasn't sure which.

On the way to campus, I texted Keaton to tell her what had happened at work. She was the only one I told about Samuel, the only one who knew how much I endured. I didn't tell Mom because I didn't know how she'd react.

My phone buzzed with a response from Keaton: a series of knife emojis. I laughed at first but then felt hollow because somewhere in the back of my mind, his words keep replaying—
"*What will you do?*"

I tucked my phone away with that question at the front of my mind. I hated to admit it, but I didn't know *what* I would do. If his taunts continued to escalate, there would come a time where I would have to step up my game and do *something*, but what? How far would I let him push me before I let the darkness decide his fate?

My phone buzzed again, and I saw another text from Keaton. It said, *You've got to stop letting him get the best of you.*

She was right, but it was impossible to stop my brain from replaying his words over and over on a loop, making me angrier each time.

As I walked through the door to class, I pushed the thoughts away. Samuel had no place here. While I generally hated leaving the house, I didn't mind when it came to college. Here, I didn't stand out for my outside-the-box thinking and fascination with the morbid. Unlike high school, where I had felt invisible to teachers and classmates alike, in college, the professors warmed to me…more than my classmates at least.

When Professor Parks began to speak, I wrote his every word, but diligent note taking only occupied me for so long before I started to operate on autopilot. The problem? It left my brain free to wander. When that happened, it would take effort to wrangle it back into place. Today was one of those days.

I kept thinking back to the note Samuel had taped on my locker. I envisioned myself stalking up to him, demanding to know what was wrong with him, and shoving the paper down his throat. I started to smile down at my notebook. As soon as I realized it, I cleared the emotion away, hoping no one else had noticed. I didn't want to explain where the expression had come from.

I shoved a fistful of hair from my face and went to work jotting down a new paragraph. In the desk beside me sat an average man in his twenties named Mark Something. He jabbed me in the shoulder. It wasn't often that someone talked to me.

"Do you have an extra pencil I could borrow?" he asked.

I stared at him, the hopeful rise of his eyebrows and tiny curve of his lips. In my mind's eye, I could see myself dig into my bag, pull out a sharpened pencil, and shove it right through his eye.

My hand trembled with the urge. It was as if the darkness in my head tried to take control of me sometimes, the urges powerful enough that I wasn't sure I could break the spell if I wanted to.

"Jessica?" Mark asked as if he wasn't sure I had heard him.

"Oh, yeah, sure," I said finally, reaching into my bag. Careful of the image in my head, I tossed it onto his desk.

His forehead scrunched. "Thanks?"

He'd interpreted my move as rudeness, but I thought it would've been much ruder to stab him. He eyed me strangely for the rest of class, and I pretended not to notice. I tried to comfort myself with the knowledge that he would most likely never ask to borrow another pencil.

When the end of class came, I packed up fast enough to be the first one out the door. After the awkward interaction with Mark, I was glad to go to my next class though the note on the door said it had been moved. The class would begin in the auditorium instead.

My shoulders slumped.

Every quarter we had active shooter training to make sure we'd know how to react if a dangerous situation were to arise on campus. A girl had been murdered in her dorm the year before, and the school had emphasized everything safety related.

I thought about going home. We wouldn't get into much of a lecture today anyway since the seminar took up about an hour. My alternative though would be going home to an empty apartment. That itself wasn't such a bad idea, but when Mom got home and saw I made it before her, she would riddle me with questions about my day.

Staying it is.

Yawning, I stuck to the shadows, steering clear of the larger groups of people as I made my way across campus. I kept my head down, relieved when I walked into the dark auditorium. Keeping an eye on my feet, I listened to the hushed conversation of my classmates around me and sought out a seat that was both the farthest from everyone and the closest to the door. A banner with the words "Active Shooter Preparedness" had been hung across the front of the stage. I stared at the looping writing, wondering why they'd print it in red ink.

A man who looked a little older than me jumped up onto the stage and tapped on the microphone, sending the sound of distinct thumping through the auditorium. "Hello, everyone. I'm here to talk to you about something that's becoming more and more common. Active shooting situations have been on the rise over the past few years…"

I zoned out. The lecture was exactly the same as the other three times I had been forced to attend. Resting my chin in my hand, I stared at him as he walked to each end of the stage, making intense eye contact with those seated there.

"If you ever find yourself caught in an active situation, remember the acronym ADD."

The ADD process was simple. A person had three choices to make when faced with danger. One, they could avoid the attacker, also known as running for your life. Two, they could deny the attacker entrance to their location—hiding for your life. Or three, defend yourself.

The last option was the one that made me think. In a life-or-death situation, everyone would be out to save themselves. First instinct would naturally be to run, but the thought of fighting back was interesting. It would be an excuse to unleash the demons inside me to see how it felt without anyone thinking twice about it.

Chapter Six

BY THE END of the day, I was exhausted. I didn't usually fall asleep on the bus because I had heard too many horror stories of what happened if you let your guard down, but today, it didn't matter. I snorted awake when the bus came to a halt at my stop, earning a dirty look from the lady beside me.

I hurried through the lobby and up the stairs, glancing toward Keaton's apartment before unlocking the door to my own and going inside. Mom was in the living room with the television on, but at the sound of the door, she looked over the back of the couch.

She must've noticed the look on my face because the first thing she said was, "What's wrong?"

I locked the door before staring at her, not knowing quite how to answer. It had been hours since the confrontation with Samuel, and I was too good at bottling things up for her to know I had ever been upset. Part of me wondered if Keaton had paid a visit.

Keaton wouldn't do that, I reminded myself.

Keaton wouldn't do anything that would betray my trust. Besides, If Mom knew anything about Samuel, she would hassle me about him until I came clean and told her everything. In a weird way, I felt like if I told her, Samuel would have penetrated his way into every aspect of my life.

"Long day," I mumbled, throwing my backpack onto the floor to hide my dark expression from Mom. "We had active shooter training again today."

Mom tsked as she turned back toward the television. "Such a shame these things. Humanity is really falling apart."

"Tell me about it," I said and moved to my room where I planned to stay for the rest of the night.

I closed the door and sat on my bed before I pulled out my phone. I stared at the last message in the text thread with Keaton. *Why do you let him get the best of you?*

I deleted it deciding that out of sight, out of mind would work the best when it came to him.

You busy? I texted her, hoping for some human interaction besides the voices in my head.

I set the phone down, staring at the screen. I expected it to light up a minute after I texted her because Keaton was usually on top of everything. Minutes crept by, and I started to think that maybe she had already gone to bed when her reply finally came back.

What's up?

She was obviously busy. I thought about not answering, worried about bothering her, but did it anyway. *Just wanted to see if you could chill tonight.*

Again, Keaton didn't write back right away. I tossed the phone down, glaring at it as if the sheer force of my anger alone could elicit a response.

When Mom opened my door, I was still frowning at it. She caught the expression, and her eyes twinkled as if she thought about asking me again what was wrong but decided against it. "I'm heading out," she said. "Text me if you need anything, okay?"

I glanced toward my window, to the darkness outside. I didn't want to know where she could be going at this time of night. Mom worked about twenty hours a week as a waitress downtown to keep her benefits from the state. While it wasn't uncommon for her to work the night shift, it was when she had already worked a full day.

"Okay," I said, patiently waiting for the door to close before I got up. I waited for the sound of a car door before I jumped across my room, rushing into hers.

She had the master bedroom so it was larger than my room, but her bed still took up a majority of the space. At the foot of her bed was a dresser and beside it was a tiny end table covered in papers and wadded up tissues. I made sure I didn't disturb anything as I pawed through the belongings on top of the table. Nothing. I rifled through the drawers, eventually producing the reason for my search—an empty prescription bottle.

It wasn't her name on the label. I clenched it in my fist. At least I knew where she was going. Angrily, I tossed the bottle back into the drawer and slammed it shut, shaking the entire table enough to discard a few papers to the floor. I didn't bother to pick them up as I went back to my room.

Every time Mom started to get better, she relapsed again. It was a vicious cycle, and I hated being caught up in it. Hated that I was fundamentally useless in helping her. Quite a few times, I wondered if Mom had started popping pills *because* of me.

There was still no response from Keaton, and now, I was glad. I didn't want to tell her about Mom, didn't want to tell her that right now, I essentially had no faith of any kind in humanity.

When Keaton's response did come in, it was a one-word response. *Ya.*

Judging from how sparse and noncommittal her texts were, it was obvious she wasn't really thinking about me. She was most likely out with Trixie, and I was an annoying fly, buzzing in on her fun.

You're annoying her, my anxiety whispered to me. I tried to push it out, but it got louder.

Never mind, I texted. I stared at the passive aggressive message for a full minute before hitting send and throwing the phone for the final time that night.

I reclined back onto my bed, covering my eyes with the backs of my hands to keep myself from crying. With the anger fizzling away, the loneliness was creeping in, and I hated it. One time, I thought about giving myself a lobotomy to see if it would damage my brain enough to not feel a thing because emotions were torture.

You're pathetic, bothering her all the time, an ugly voice insisted.

I told myself that wasn't true, but how did I know it wasn't? Keaton could've secretly hated me, and the only reason she kept an eye on me was because Mom paid her to do so.

I wouldn't put it past either of them.

Go to sleep, I told myself. It was the only foolproof way to put myself out of my own misery.

But first, more fuel on the fire, I thought and reached for my laptop.

I was in a secret group, one filled with people like me, people touched by the darkness. Strangers united by a mutual love of horror and gore. Maybe it was the secrecy of it, or the fact that I had found a place where I could be myself…I didn't know, but the group cheered me up. I had heard that exposure to this kind of content was the kind of thing that could morph someone like me into a serial killer because it desensitized us to violence, but honestly, I didn't believe it. I think I was already damaged and that was *why* I wanted to see those horrible things to begin with.

I started to read an article about a girl who supposedly escaped the grasp of a serial killer when an IM popped up on my screen. I expected it to be from Keaton since, if she had texted me back, I hadn't seen it.

Instead, the message was from an anonymous profile and said three words: *I see you.*

I didn't have many enemies simply because I never interacted with humans. There's only one person who would have the gull or motive to try and scare me like this—Samuel.

Snarling, I wrote back the words *You're an ass.*

I hopped up, going over to my window to peer at the ground through the cracks in the blinds. I didn't see anyone, and normally, I would've been concerned at such an ominous message, but I wasn't. My blinds were closed, the door locked. I was on the second floor. The only other way into the apartment would be through the fire escape, but the silver staircase was empty.

Huffing, I let go of the blinds, listening to them crash together before I stormed out of my room, pacing to get the anger to go away. I wanted to confront Samuel, to make him stop this once and for all, but it came to me that in the grand scheme of things, there wasn't much I could do.

What will you do?

I surveyed outside the living room windows too but still saw no movement below. This was Samuel trying to get under my skin, and it was working. Most likely, he had never been here. He was at home, laughing at himself for getting a response.

Why am I so gullible?

I had already spent a large part of my anger on Mom and now whatever was left evaporated. I was alone again. I hopped into bed, pulling the blankets up to my shoulder and put my head underneath my pillow.

Maybe tomorrow, things would be better.

I'M NOT AN optimist, and there are many reasons why. I might've been able to get myself to go to sleep on the pretense of a better morning, but it was all a lie. I didn't know when Mom had come home, but she was sprawled out on the couch in the morning, a bottle of wine spilled across the wooden floorboards in the living room.

I pinched the bridge of my nose. This was my *mother,* probably the person I was supposed to love the most in the world, and yet, I felt nothing of the sort. I wanted to hit her, to make her feel *my* pain, but it wouldn't do any good.

It would only make the rift between us deeper.

I put two fingers to the curve of her neck, picking up the faint pulse. When I pulled my hand away, the urge to slap her was still there, but I didn't act on it. I went to the kitchen to get something to clean her mess and made quick work of wiping up the wine.

Squeak.

What was that? I thought and paused with the trash can still open.

Squeak.

I followed the sound right to Mom's glue board in the corner of the kitchen. The trap had been empty last night, but now, there was a tiny animal stuck in it. An idea came to me. If Samuel really was keeping an eye on me, maybe I could use this mouse to make a point.

It's going to die anyway, I rationalized.

From my research, most of the famous serial killers—Bundy, Radar, Dahmer—had a list of commonalities. They were white males, charming, above average intelligence, and they started small, working on animals before eventually escalating to their ideal targets.

Where did that leave me? I'm white, sure, but as a female, I was an exception to the rule. Female serial killers are a rarity. For some reason, they don't go on killing sprees as often as their male counterparts, or maybe they're better at not getting caught.

With the exception of insects and spiders, I had never killed anything. The thought of hurting animals made my stomach twist in ways that it did not when I had similar thoughts with humans.

Forgetting about Mom and her mess of alcohol and pills, I went toward the mouse. As my shadow draped across it, it squeaked and tried to run, jerking violently on its immobile limbs. The closer I got, the harder its little body squirmed. Would it get desperate enough to tear chunks of its feet away to escape? I picked up the board by the corner to avoid accidentally touching any of the glue. A tiny spark of fear lit up the mouse's beady black eyes, and its whole body shivered in its failed attempts to escape.

The more I stared at it, the sorrier I felt for the creature. Maybe because it was already trapped or because it was so small and helpless, I didn't know, but the thought of doing more to it seemed cruel.

It wasn't this mouse's fault that my life was like this. It was innocent.

I went outside, senses on high alert for signs of Samuel in the crisp dawn air. There was a forest across the street from my apartment, and as I approached the line of trees, I patted my pocket to make sure my knife was there in case anyone was watching.

Did I really think Samuel would set up camp outside of my apartment all night? No, but I didn't really *know* what lengths he would go to get under my skin either. I believed strongly in a *better safe than sorry* mentality. It had gotten me this far in life; it had to be worth something.

I set the glue board down by the trunk of the first tree, watching as the mouse tried again to free itself. It wouldn't, of course, and if it did, it'd probably wish it was dead. It was doomed to that anyway. At the very least, out here the mouse could still make a meal for a hungry animal…granted the predator who ate it didn't also find itself trapped.

Chapter Seven

I WENT BACK inside the apartment, throwing myself into bed to try and once again block out the world. Somehow, I fell asleep, and the next time I woke up, it was close to noon. My night had been plagued with nightmares, but this wasn't a new phenomenon. My sleep paralysis fits always ended with monsters and demons holding me down, trying to kill me.

As I got ready for work, I thought about going to the doctor for sleeping pills but feared it would only sharpen the fits. I pulled my uniform on and eyed my laptop, wondering if Samuel had written anything else during the night. I opened it, checking to see if the IM thread from last night was still there. There was no response but a tiny "read" had appeared underneath my message. I thought about that all the way to work. According to the time, he had read it about a minute after I sent it.

I got on the bus and plopped down in my usual seat, pretending to be normal. When I got to work, I didn't want to show any signs of a rough night. I didn't want Samuel to know how badly he had rattled me, but I had the suspicion he knew anyway. That was why he hadn't bothered to write anything back.

He didn't need to.

Forget about it, I told myself as soon as I reached the store.

I wiped the thoughts away, gluing on a fake smile as I passed Harlow and Carmine. Samuel was in the employee lounge, talking and laughing with his friends at a table near my locker. When he spotted me, his laughter got louder.

What a poor attempt to get my attention.

I kept my eyes straight ahead. There was nothing taped to my locker today, and I counted that as a win until I opened it. Inside sat a picture of me in my room from the night before. Except in this one, I was *sleeping.* I grabbed the photo from the tape with such force that a tiny tear formed. Fuming, I threw my bag into the locker and slammed the door. I nearly *flew* across the break room, not caring that I approached Samuel's entire table of friends as well as himself. He stood up as I neared him.

"Good morning, Jessica," he said, subtly walking a few steps away from his friends as if he didn't want them to hear what I had to say.

I mirrored his steps, slapping the picture to his chest. "What is this?"

"A picture," he responded with a smirk.

"No shit," I said, clenching my teeth to keep my voice down. It didn't work well.

Samuel plucked the picture from my fingers, smiling at it. "See how relaxed you are! Might wanna be careful leaving your mouth open like that or you might eat *all* the spiders inside the grungy apartment you call home."

"You think this is funny? I could take this to the police."

Samuel's smile got bigger, and he tilted his head to the

side as if he was truly proud of himself. "You could, but who would believe it came from me?"

I tried not to flinch from the comment. If I couldn't get Mr. Waters' to believe me over him, the police definitely wouldn't give me the time of day. "What the fuck do you want? Why the anonymous IM messages? The threats? *This?*" I smacked my hand on the picture hard enough to make a little clap sound.

"Just making a point."

"Which would be what? That you're a psychopath? I've *known* that," I said pointedly.

"It takes one to know one, right?"

"You're insane."

"Yeah, and so are you. I think you could do with being knocked down a peg. You walk around this place like you're too good for everyone." His gaze went to the picture again. "But it looks like you're perfectly human to me."

"I don't know how you did this, but if you do it again, I'm going to report it to the police. Do you understand?" I asked, jabbing my finger toward him. I teetered on the edge of a blackout. If I hadn't been concerned about keeping my job, I probably would've let it consume me. Maybe *it* would know how to handle Samuel.

"Terrifying," he said, unfazed. "Is that all?"

I glanced sideways to see our coworkers still watching and made sure to put space between us. Engaging further wouldn't do me any good because he *wanted* me to react. These people only knew what happened here before their eyes. They didn't know my and Samuel's history. He was trying to get me to react so he could tell them all later, *See I knew she was crazy.*

I backed away, step by step, until I was out of the break room. I didn't take the picture with me, and I only realized that after I made it to the front of the store. What was it about some guys, scratch that, some *humans,* who felt as if they were entitled to everything? I wished I could go back in time to stay in bed the day Samuel had asked me out.

My life would be much different now.

Getting my game face on was tough on a normal day. Today, when my day had started on such a stressful note, it was nearly impossible. I hurried to the bathroom and into the first stall, reveling in the silence as I tried to get myself together. Frustrated tears welled in the corners of my eyes, and I scolded myself. Samuel wasn't worth *tears,* but they ran anyway, and I stayed hidden until they were done. The last thing I wanted was for *him* to see me cry. To know that deep down, he bothered me *immensely.*

When the worst of the storm subsided, I emerged from my hiding place, positive I would be reprimanded for staying away from the register for so long. I splashed water on my face and headed back out to the floor, but the bad mood was deep in my bones. I told myself I had to be nice for the sake of my job, but I couldn't do it. I curled my lip every time someone approached, dreading the thought of an interaction. To some degree, I did that every day, but today, it was worse. It was as if that dark part was growing, engulfing everything else. I admired the serial killers who kept their demons in check with an upbeat charisma. When mine were tapped, my reaction was to shut out the world.

An old lady left my line in a huff, talking about *terrible customer service,* but I couldn't be bothered to respond. I kept looking for Oscar. His humor was the antidote I needed. He would make me feel better. A few hours passed, but he never appeared. When Mr. Waters walked by, I called out to him.

"Sir, does Oscar work today?" I asked.

Mr. Waters offered a small sympathetic smile. "He called this morning. Said he wasn't feeling too good, and he wouldn't be in today."

"Oh."

"Ready for your break?" he asked.

I bobbed my head, trying not to be too put out by the information.

"Go ahead and take it."

"Thank you," I replied, stepping away from the register.

My stomach rumbled with hunger, but as I ran a list of options through my head, none of them sounded good. On average, I didn't eat a lot. At most, I thrived on one meal a day. I wasn't worried about my weight. It took too much effort to feed myself as much as I should. I decided to skip lunch and eat whatever food Mom decided to cook when I got home. And she *would* cook. The first week after relapse was always full of her trying to be super mother as if the guilt was hard for her to contend with.

Crack.

I froze, glancing over my shoulder. That sounded like a gunshot. *That can't be,* I thought, staring blindly into the aisles as if I thought the answer would appear. Nothing changed, and I kept walking, thinking someone had dropped a pallet.

Crack.

A scream.

One of my coworkers ran past me, into the employee lounge screaming, "He's got a gun!" followed by more sharp bursts of sound.

There was an active shooter here and now. For all my plotting during the seminars, my initial reaction was nothing. Pandemonium reigned around me—gunshots, screams, and thump of bodies—but I was motionless.

You have to move, I told myself, but my body didn't want to obey.

The front door was too far away through the danger zone of screaming people. The back door was a possibility, but it depended on where the shooter was going. If he was toward the grocery side of the store, it might be too late to go that way.

I accepted the idea that maybe I *wasn't* going to be able to run. *I should hide.* Glancing around, I ducked into the room nearest to the employee lounge. Mr. Waters' office. It was tiny with a computer, a fax machine, and a trash can. I pushed the door, but it halted, leaving a crack open.

I'm so dead, I thought and tried to push the desk in front of it. It wouldn't move. The sounds of gunfire drew closer, and my heartbeat more erratic. I was almost out of time, and I was trapped like a rat. I switched the light off, hiding in the crook of the door. It wasn't much shelter, but I hoped it would be enough. I put my hands over my ears, but I could still hear it all.

Gunshots, screams, pleading, anguish, footsteps, then silence.

The longer I listened, the higher my adrenaline spiked

until I thought it would shut down my brain completely. People talk a lot about fight or flight, but in extreme stress, the body can go a different route. It prepares itself for death.

Panic crept up my chest, lodging itself in my throat until I couldn't breathe. I moved into fight mode. Patting my pocket, I felt for the knife, thinking of the matching one in my bra. If the shooter got in range, I could fight back. If I wanted to survive, I would have to.

There was no guarantee I would win, but I could *try*.

Guns beat knives, I reminded myself.

I tried not to think of that too true fact as the store went completely silent again. I knew better than to peek my head out. Until the police got here, it wasn't over yet. A gunshot rang out, accompanied by the sound of a falling body. I exhaled, closing my eyes as I realized the shooter was at the end of the hall. I dared a glance through the tiny crack to see the monster responsible for this.

The figure inched past, floppy hair sparking familiarity— *Oscar.*

He crept along, automatic rifle held up with the readiness to shoot at a second's notice. He was cloaked in all black, eyes focused straight ahead. There was a look had never seen there before. I barely recognized him.

I remembered back to the day I'd started working here. There were a handful of us called in for orientation. Me, Oscar, and a few nameless others who had quit not long after being hired.

Mr. Waters had said we were all going to be cashiers, but he wanted to give us a tour of the entire store and introduce us to people working in all the different departments in an attempt to have a more *family-like* vibe to his business.

One of the guys who worked in the back room, I couldn't remember his name because he'd quit a week after I started, had looked Oscar up and down.

"You going to be working back here?" he asked and turned to Mr. Waters. "No offense, but he's all skin and bones."

Mr. Waters had said, "No, he's going to be a cashier."

"Good," the backroom stocker had said, visibly relieved. Then turned to Oscar and smirked. "You wouldn't make it back here, kid."

For the rest of the tour, Oscar had been sullen. "No one ever takes me seriously."

I had the feeling something like this had happened to him before, but I didn't press the issue. "I wouldn't stress about it. He seems like a dick anyway," I told him.

The tour ended ten minutes later and orientation broke for lunch. We ate together in the Burger Joint, and that had been our norm ever since.

No one ever takes me seriously.

They will now, I thought as I ducked back into my hiding place.

Another shot, and I closed my eyes. Would he shoot *me?* Footsteps announced his location. He'd passed the door to the office and was on his way to the employee lounge.

If I was quick, I could pop open the door and make a run for it.

Or, the voice in my head urged.

Or nothing, I argued back and grabbed the handle,

preparing myself to run. I peered through the crack and saw the back of his head. He was close, but not too close. My bottom lip trembled as I thought of my friend beneath the monster. The person I knew and didn't know at all. He had been funny and full of life at one point...how had he been reduced to this?

He made his own choices, I reminded myself, trying to work up the nerve to make the plunge into the hallway. I couldn't move. All I could think about was how happy he'd been the first time I had decided to eat lunch with him, grateful to have at least me to call his friend. And I had taken that for granted. Taken *him* for granted. He had shown me time and time again that he was there for me, but I never considered myself to be close to him like I was to Keaton.

I might die today, I thought, but I couldn't come to terms with that information as a fact, as an actuality. As I stared at Oscar's curly black hair, I thought, *this is my friend. He won't hurt me.*

He pulled the trigger with a sharp pop, the bullet penetrating the door of the employee lounge, and I wasn't sure anymore. Before today, I had never thought Oscar could hurt *anyone.* He wasn't the kind to resort to violence. I had seen that firsthand, thanks to Samuel.

This is my chance. I can escape.

I didn't move as the darkness redirected my thoughts to my training, about the third choice, my own urges, and came to a new decision. *This could be the answer I've been after.*

No, I told myself, eyeing the empty hallway. *Not him.*

I could run. Now. To safety.

What about everyone in the lounge?

They wouldn't be so lucky. I had a choice to make. Run and save myself or kill my friend and save my coworkers?

I thought about Oscar's future. The short hour best he probably had to live. Most likely, he would kill himself after this—spree killers usually did—and if he didn't, he would be led to the jail cell where he'd rot for the rest of his life.

Four steps separated us, but he didn't know I was here. I risked a step out of the office, only one. It wasn't much, but it felt significant. This next minute of my life would be an important one or the last one. Another step and this time, the floor squeaked. Oscar was close, but the barrel of the gun was closer as he turned to face me. I didn't look at it. I stared at Oscar, seeking something familiar. When we made eye contact, something in me ached because I found it.

This was my *friend.*

"Get out of here, Jessie," he said, voice so hoarse it was hard to distinguish his words. It sounded as if he was on the verge of crying, and I wished he would. More than anything, I wished he would put the gun down and surrender himself to whatever fate the police would bestow upon him.

He did neither of those. The gun raised slightly higher, shielding his face behind it. I didn't have a choice then but to look at the gun so close to my eye that it could poke me if I got any closer.

"Please," he said.

The emotion was fading, and my friend was going with it. I said nothing as he aimed the gun right at my forehead. Fingers shaking, I pulled my knife out of my pocket, flicking out the blade with a practiced twist of the wrist.

His eyes landed on it. "Come with me."

I shook my head. "I can't do that. You know I can't."

Oscar bowed his head, a tear streaked his cheek. He studied the knife again before he slowly lowered the gun. I closed the distance, wrapping him in a hug. When I pulled away, his eyes stared into mine, my heartbeat loud enough to cause the blood to thunder in my ears.

"I know," he said and took one hand off the gun to wrap around my fist with the knife. "Thank you."

I closed my eyes as we pressed the sharp tip into the skin on the side of his neck. Together, we dragged the blade across his throat, the silver leaving a blast of crimson. I didn't open my eyes until he let go. He reached up, fingers covered in the slick of his own blood and collapsed to his knees before he fell, lying in a giant puddle of red.

I felt nothing as I stared at the scene. There was a gaping hole where my feelings should be as if someone had opened the lid of the container where they were stored and let them escape. All I could think of were the movies I had seen—weren't people supposed to die instantly when their throats were cut?

Oscar did not.

He gasped and choked, clawing at his disconnected skin as if he thought he could somehow fix it that way. Throughout his struggle, his eyes stayed on mine. If he tried to tell me something in those last moments, I had no idea. I stared at him, not moving closer or farther away. I stayed like that until the light left his eyes.

Then, time was meaningless.

I dropped to my knees, blade still in my hand until

someone came to find me. The police I thought. I was in such a daze; it was hard for me to be sure.

"Weapon on the ground!" a man ordered, gun pointed at me.

I snapped out of it then. It's easy when a two-hundred-and-fifty-pound man points a gun at you. I obeyed, setting the knife in the puddle of blood which I had knelt in without being aware of.

Chapter Eight

THE ENTIRE CAR ride to the police station wasn't something I could remember. Between the near death situation and taking someone's life, my mind was shot. I kept picturing Oscar's eyes, the gentle *please* as he begged me to go, to leave him to his own self-destructive tendencies.

He would've let me live, I thought over and over again.

Paired with the gasping, choking sounds of his last few minutes, it was like a terrible lullaby, soothing me and enraging my demons at the same time. Before I knew it, we made it to the police station. It wasn't a glamorous building, tiny and made almost entirely out of brick. I had never been inside it before for all my years in this town. Being led inside in handcuffs was its own experience.

I tried to reel my mind back in by thinking about what my future had to offer me. In all the true crime books I had read, there was plenty about the basic rundown of police interviews and procedures. One section I wasn't that familiar with, ironically, happened to be self-defense and standing your ground laws.

The officers led me past the reception desk. I still had blood on me, probably more than I was aware of, and the looks

I gained were not simple passing glances. The officer behind me, I think she introduced herself as Officer Stone in the car, took me to a quiet room. She sat me at a table before slipping into the other side, staring at me. If it was a trick to unnerve me, it worked. I stared back with only a fifth of the confidence I usually had. Everything else was in the void with whatever emotions I should've felt.

"Can I get you something to drink? Some water perhaps?" she asked.

"No, thank you." I couldn't imagine ever eating again.

"I know today must've been hard," she began. "But I need you to run me through what happened."

"Today…" I started and paused to wipe my face. A fresh streak of red stained my sleeve. "It started normal. I went to work. My boss told me to take a break, and when I went to the employee lounge, I heard shots. There were screams, and I just kind of had this awful feeling in my gut. I had training at college the other day about active shooters so I panicked, and I hid in my boss' office since it was the closest room to me."

"And then what happened?"

"The door doesn't close all the way so I could still kind of see out. That's how I saw it was Oscar…I-I couldn't believe it."

"When you realized it was someone you knew, did you try to say anything?"

I forced my mind to break through the haze to sort through what had happened. All I could remember was Oscar's defeat as he lowered the gun.

"Not at first."

"When he saw you, did he try to shoot?"

"He pointed the gun at me and told me to go. He made it clear that if I didn't, he would shoot me."

"So, you…killed him?" Officer Stone put her hands together on the table, staring at me as if she were trying to figure something out.

"I didn't know what to do. If I didn't leave, he would've shot me. If I *did*, he would've gone to the employee lounge and shot everyone in there."

"Mmhmm," she said, writing down an elaborate list on her notepad. "Now you said you *recognized* Oscar."

"Yeah. He was my *favorite* coworker. We ate lunch together a lot."

"Did he ever mention wanting to harm himself or anyone else?"

"Are you asking if I knew if he planned this?" I asked, clenching my jaw. I was still *wearing* my trauma which made the notion extra offensive.

Officer Stone stared.

"No, he didn't say a thing," I added, trying to keep myself from getting upset. "He's been…*reserved* the past few days."

"Reserved?"

"He barely ate, wouldn't talk much, and the last time I saw him—well, the last time I saw him before *today*—he made this weird comment. He told me to never change. When I asked him if he was okay, he shook it off."

When her pen stopped, and she said nothing, I asked, "Am I going to jail?"

Officer Stone gathered her supplies and stood up. "I am truly sorry about what you've experienced today. Please excuse me."

She left, door closing behind her with a click. I didn't like that she left without answering my question, but maybe, she didn't know what the plan of action was yet. I would bet money she was going to compare my testimony to the statements gathered from other witnesses.

I didn't know why I was nervous. I hadn't lied to her, and I didn't *plan* on lying to her. What happened had been out of my control. They didn't know that though. They suspected I was in on the shooting with Oscar. Officer Stone's questions made that clear.

I settled into the seat, staring at the silver handcuffs around my wrists. There was blood on the edge of my sleeve, and I thought about the confrontation with Oscar. Before today, I never wondered if Mr. Waters had set up surveillance cameras, but now I did. Did one overlook the hall?

If that camera existed, and they watched the footage, they would see that the confrontation between me and Oscar had been more than him pointing a gun and me reacting in self-defense. They'd see that Oscar *lowered* his gun. They'd see the hug, the *tears*. It would be enough to support their theory that I had been in on the shooting.

Closing my eyes, I tried to regain control over myself. There was no proof I did anything. I swallowed hard, wondering what Samuel would tell the police if they asked him about me. Would he tell them the truth or would he take the opportunity to implicate me for a crime I didn't commit?

It doesn't matter. It'll be his word against everyone else's, I told myself as a way of consolation.

It didn't work.

This game I was playing was dangerous. In the end, it didn't really matter if I was involved or not. Whatever story they would be able to sell the best would be the one they would settle on.

It seemed like hours passed before Officer Stone came back. When she did, she had a grim expression I didn't like at all. "Oscar has been pronounced dead."

I had already known what I'd done, known the odds of him surviving were slim to none, but hearing it made my stomach slosh.

Please, he had said, and really, I wasn't sure what the plea was for. Was it for me to leave or to end his life? I'd never know.

I locked my gaze on hers. "What's going to happen to me?" I demanded, a little more force in my voice this time than the first time I had asked her.

"Right now, nothing," she said. "From what we've gathered, Oscar was the sole shooter. You acted out of self-defense and eliminated a dangerous situation."

"So, I'm free to go?"

"For the time being, it appears that way. However, we're going to compile some more testimony, and we'll meet with you again in a few days. In the meantime, don't leave town. Go home and get some rest."

Chapter Nine

WALKING OUT OF the station wasn't something I wanted to experience again. Reporters waited to bombard me with lights and questions as soon as I stepped outside. My first attempt to leave resulted in such chaos that I had to have an officer escort me out the second time. Mom came to pick me up, and I had never been happier to see that ugly red car than I was in that moment.

Mom didn't drive away pedal to the medal like I had hoped she would. She pulled me into her arms, covering me in hugs and kisses—something she hadn't done in years. "Oh, my beautiful daughter," she said, squeezing me with a tightness that had me fearing she was trying to kill me.

Hesitantly, I hugged her back. I didn't know if it was the pills making her emotional or the fact that I could've died. I wasn't going to ask, part of me guessing that not knowing would be better for my mental health in the long run. When she finally let go of me, she stared at the blood on my shirt.

"Are you hurt?" she asked.

My eyes went to the window, to a reporter who had nearly pressed himself against the glass to watch us. "No. Can we please go home?"

"Of course."

Once the car began to move, and the chaos fell behind us, I let myself relax. I wished Mom would keep driving and never stop. I wasn't a fan of change, but wanderlust flashed through me as familiar sights and buildings rushed by. I didn't want to live in this town anymore, this place that would always be studded with the horrible memories of what had happened.

When we made it to the apartment, the group of reporters was worse. There was no way to avoid them, and avoid the attention that came with them.

"They're everywhere," I said.

"Come on," Mom said and switched the engine off.

She got out of the car, but I stayed in my seat. I stared at the dashboard, contemplating alternate ways to get into the building, but every route was blocked.

Mom pulled her jacket off and tossed it to me. "Here."

I took it, holding it over my head as a makeshift shield. Underneath it, I felt hot and ridiculous, but it helped us get through the crowd. I could still hear the shouted questions, but they were muffled beneath Mom's demands for the reporters to give us space and to leave me alone. Today, I loved her. Pills or no pills, she was showing up as my mother.

Keaton met us halfway up the stairs and gave me the same kind of attention.

"Jess!" she cooed, causing me to nearly drop Mom's jacket as she pulled me into her arms. "When I saw the news, I was so scared! You're a hero!"

In my head, I vehemently disagreed. Out loud, I said nothing, patiently waiting for her to release me. She knew little about Oscar, about what he had meant to me, and a few hours after killing him wasn't the time to explain.

"Let's get you inside," Mom said, opening the door for us.

"Thank you," Keaton said.

Relief settled in my gut once we were inside the secluded safety of the apartment, but it didn't last long. Next would come the truly tough part. The part where I would have to continue my day, continue my *life*, as if the shooting hadn't happened.

"What did you two want for dinner?" Mom asked, going straight for the kitchen.

I didn't respond. I stared at my sleeves and saw the situation as someone who wasn't me must've seen it. The smell of drying blood made me gag, and I couldn't believe I hadn't smelt it sooner.

Keaton must've had the same thought. "You should shower."

That was easy to agree to.

I went to the bathroom and closed the door. The tiny space reminded me of Mr. Waters' office. When I closed my eyes, I could've sworn I heard the gunshots. Lost in thought, I bent over the tub, hardly feeling the water when I tried to test the temperature.

I slipped out of my clothes and stood naked in the bathroom. Some of the blood had soaked through my clothes and left dried sticky patches across my arms and chest. That was enough to get me to step into the water. The swishing sound of the curtain brought me back to focus, and I stared at the basin of the tub, watching as Oscar's blood washed away with the water. I went into a sort of trance, unable to look away until there were no hints of red left. I got out of the shower and grabbed the towel off the rack, wrapping it around myself.

"Got you some clothes," Keaton said, cracking the door open enough to pass me a stack of pajamas.

"Thank you," I replied, taking them. I had been so eager to be clean that I hadn't bothered to pick any clothes out first. As an afterthought, I said, "Wait."

I set the fresh clothes on the sink and looked at the old ones laid out across the floor, splattered with dried blood. I gathered them and hurried back to Keaton. "Make these disappear," I told her, thrusting the bundle into her arms, and closed the door before she could argue.

I made sure to avoid my reflection as I got dressed, uninterested in seeing the person who would look back at me. Drying my hair one more time, I tossed the towel down and wandered out to the living room. Keaton was in the kitchen, most likely finishing up my request.

"How're you feeling?" she asked.

I didn't answer as I made my way to my room. I made the mistake of glancing at the muted television as I passed it. Mom had left the news on, and it was covering the shooting. I wasn't surprised at this, of course, but I *was* surprised to find out that it had been covered live. The part of me being put into a cop car was playing on a loop. My name and picture had been announced. At first, I was a suspected accomplice which changed to me being the hero who took down the gunman.

I didn't feel like a hero.

I *wasn't* a hero.

The betrayal in Oscar's dying brown eyes told me I was

an opportunistic monster at best. A monster, who as it turned out, wasn't as big of a monster as she thought.

"You don't need to watch that," Keaton said, realizing where my attention was.

She turned the news off before she led me to my room, the clatter of pots and pans from Mom fading into the background. Keaton closed the door as I sat on the edge of the bed.

"So, I know you're not touchy feely or anything, but how *are* you? What you went through…" She trailed off, running her fingers through her short-bleached hair. "You uh…man…"

I knew what she wanted me to say. *I killed someone.*

"It was Hell," I said, blurting out what I thought was the most appropriate response when in reality, I still couldn't quite decide *how* I felt. How I *should* feel.

"I bet," she replied and sat beside me. "Did you know him?"

My bottom lip trembled, and I couldn't hold myself together. "Yes."

Keaton pulled me into her arms, and I buried my face into the crook of her neck, drawing in the scent of her perfume as I sobbed. I let it soothe me until I drifted off to sleep.

***

WHEN I WOKE, Keaton was gone. Mom said she had gone home shortly before I'd woken. So, I sat at the kitchen table, staring at the food on my plate. I took a small bite. It was good, but the idea of eating was not. Mom's eyes never left me. It was as if the concern from earlier had faded away, and now she wasn't sure what to think of me. Or maybe she had reflected on what I had done and realized I was a monster.

I pushed away from the table and went to my room, feet heavy as if they were made of lead. When I settled down among my blankets, I glanced at the laptop beside me. I might've been at Ground Zero when the shooting went down, but I still had questions. Who all had Oscar killed? How many fatalities *were* there?

I pulled the tiny computer toward me. The chat with anonymous was still up, and it had a new message—*I knew there was something wrong with you, but to kill your friend in cold blood? Damn. Maybe I* should *be scared of you.*

The message had a link attached. I told myself not to engage, that it would be worse for Samuel if I straight up ignored him, but my curiosity won out. What was in the link? Considering the source was Samuel, there was a good chance it was a virus, but I wasn't one to back down from a challenge.

Sure I would regret my decision, I clicked on it. It pulled up another website, a thread of random people talking about the shooting. Posts ranged from people giving their thoughts and prayers for the victims to others asking for details. The newest thread at the top caught my attention. It was labeled "Jessica Mills isn't a Hero."

My throat constricted. It was as if someone had scooped out my brain and translated it to binary code for everyone to read. I *really* didn't want to know what this said because I was sure Samuel had created it, but I couldn't stop myself from clicking on it. Against my better judgement, I started to read, scrolling through the posts, one after another. There was a post about my statement with the police and a picture of me and Oscar.

"She didn't have to kill him," someone wrote. *"He could've been talked down. He liked her. She could've used that to take the gun. She never took the gun."*

Someone else came to my defense. *"She was in a life or death situation. It wasn't as if she could think rationally. She probably couldn't remember her own name right then."*

"Violence is never the answer."

"Don't forget, he pointed the gun at her."

"So she says! That's not proof."

"What would you have done if you were her?"

"Talk to him. Distract him. GRAB. THE. GUN. Cutting his throat? That seemed like too much. For all we know, she planned the shooting with him, and killed him at the last minute to play innocent. She was friends with him, right? The killer?"

It wasn't funny, but I laughed until I cried. They were right, and it was for that reason that I didn't know how to accept what I did. Things could've been different. Oscar could've lived. He would've been in prison, but he would've been *alive*.

Thank you.

Hell of a choice for last words, Oscar.

Chapter Ten

IT WAS THE worst thing I could do but I spent hours on that website. I scrolled in search of input from Samuel but couldn't find anything. There were stories from some of my other coworkers though. One of the stockers in particular stuck with me.

My friend was hiding beside me. I was less than a foot away when his head exploded. He was dead, and I was left hiding with pieces of him all over me. I don't know why I wasn't shot too. Maybe he hadn't seen me. Or maybe he wanted me to live with the memory of what he had done. I'll never know.

I kept reading, hoping to get the bad taste out of my mouth. I don't know why I'd hoped I'd find someone speaking up for Oscar. They wouldn't. What he had done wasn't excusable, but it was hard for me to remember my friend as a monster.

I scrolled so long I passed out on my computer.

When my eyes opened, I was hiding in Mr. Waters' office, gunshots in the background. I flexed my hands, studying the creases in my palms as they opened and closed. Was I dreaming? It all looked real. *Too* real.

I bolted out of hiding, and Oscar appeared. I was so happy to see him with life in his eyes that I sprang toward him with open arms. The gun swiveled to me. He was cold, feral. Before I could change my mind, he pulled the trigger. The blast of the gun made my teeth rattle as a blossom of red soaked through my shirt.

I gasped awake, wild with panic until I realized I was in the safety of my room. Groaning at the pain in my spine, I pushed away my computer. It had died during the night. My first move when I got out of bed was to plug it in, the black screen powering up to a blue one. I yawned and rubbed my eyes before I crawled back in bed. When I opened my eyes again, it was noon. The sound of my phone ringing beside my head pulled me from my near coma.

I squinted against the light to read Mr. Waters' name on the caller ID. I debated answering it, wondering what he was going to say, and if it would be like any of the comments I had read online. I almost didn't answer it, but at the last second, I gave in.

"Hello?" I croaked.

"Hi, Jessica, is this a bad time?"

I didn't know what he thought I was doing or had to do, but I replied, "No. What's up?"

"I wanted to check in and see how you were doing. After everything, I've been uh…making my rounds. Calling to see how everyone is and wanted to let you all know that I'm going to close the store for a little while."

He didn't have to say it, but I had the suspicion that his phone call was for more than that. He wanted to see which of his employees were still *alive*. I thought about hanging up. I didn't know how to answer the question, and I didn't want to pretend. My mouth was determined to disobey me, and I said, "As well as to be expected."

"Right. It's still shocking what happened. A real tragedy."

"Yeah," I said, flatly.

"Well, I'll let you get some rest," he said, sounding as if he was about to hang up.

"Wait!" I blurted out. The silence on the line made me unsure if I was too late. "Did…did Oscar say anything weird to you the last week he worked?"

"Weird how?"

"Just…strange?" I asked and squeezed my eyes shut. I didn't know why I was doing this, why I was dragging out this phone call or the pain with it. These were the kind of questions I shouldn't ask, the kind that could be seen wrong, taken out of context and used against me later, but I couldn't help it. Some part of me was bothered by the fact that I hadn't been able to tell how close to breaking my friend was until he was already past the point of saving.

No one else noticed either.

"Not that I can recall," he said. "I'm sorry."

I swallowed away my feelings and asked, "How long is the store going to be closed for?"

"Until things calm down a bit. We lost a lot of good people, and this will give everyone the chance to grieve."

"Thank you," I said then paused, wanting to ask about the possibility of a camera in the hallway leading to the employee lounge, but I stopped myself. I had already asked enough questions. Besides, no one had said anything about it. I wouldn't either. I counted down from five and hung up.

With no work and today happening to be one of the days I had no classes at college, I wasn't sure what to do with myself. If I could've chosen anything, it would've been to sleep the rest of the day, but my eyes didn't want to close. I was surprised I had slept as much as I had since it hadn't come easy. Every time I closed my eyes, there was blood, a river of the substance narrated with screams. Oscar's tiny little "please" then his dying gasps.

I got out of bed for the sole purpose of having something to focus on besides the carnage in my brain. I used to *like* the fucked-up things I thought about, but now, they made me sick. Desperate to keep it all away, I wandered out to the kitchen to make a sad breakfast of oatmeal.

I don't know why I had assumed Mom would be up before me, that she would make me breakfast and ask how I was feeling. That was what moms did, and my mom, well, she was part-time. She had done the role of concerned caregiver yesterday. Today, she must've thought it would be fine to phone it in.

Curiously, I wandered to her room to see if she was home. Mom was slumped across her mattress, mouth wide open as she slept. The empty vodka bottle on the table gave me all the answers I needed. I narrowed my eyes at her, though I didn't know if it was out of anger or a desire to keep myself from crying and whisked away to go back to the kitchen. My oatmeal was already plenty cold by then. I picked at it sparingly, comparing it to lumpy vomit.

"What are you doing?" Mom asked when she finally stumbled into the kitchen.

"Eating breakfast," I said, tapping the spoon against the side of the bowl.

"You hate oatmeal," she said as she plodded over to the coffee maker. "I was going to cook."

"It was here."

Mom glanced at the clock then back at me. "You should've woken me." Her eyes moved to the corner of the room. "Did you move my mouse traps?"

My blood started to boil. She noticed everything around the house *but* me. Partly, I wondered if I ran away how long it would take her to notice that I was gone. I dropped the spoon to the table with a clatter. "Hard to do when you're blacked out, *Mom*." I stood up so fast the chair scraped the floor.

"Don't take that tone with me," she said, slamming her fist to the counter.

"Why not?"

"Because I'm your *mother*."

"That's why you need the pills, huh?" I asked, kicking the leg of the chair to scoot it out of my way as I took a step closer to her. "Because you're my mother."

She went silent, staring down at the counter.

"Didn't think I knew, really?"

"Jessica, I—"

"No, Mom," I said, walking out of the kitchen. "I needed you to be here for me today, and you did this. You can't ever think about me."

"Where are you going?"

I didn't answer as I went into my room, slamming the door behind me because we both knew I *had* nowhere to go. I kicked the dresser next to my bed, sending pain up into my ankle that I only noticed when I took my next step. I pulled the blinds shut and let myself fall on the bed, lying in the darkness. I stared up at the ceiling, listening to the sound of the cars outside and Mom storming around the apartment on the other side of my door.

A little bit of light managed to stream through the blinds, and I glared at it. I hated the sun. If I had the ability to be completely nocturnal, I would do that. I wasn't like other people, people who crave the sunlight, the warmth and company it brings with it. As an introvert, my social interaction battery drained quickly. Even more quickly in the sunlight. Being alone with time to think was the only time that it charged. With nowhere to go, it would be able to charge for a while. The problem was that batteries that charged too much tended to die quicker...or explode.

***

BEING AN INDOOR person was a good thing because outside, I was a pariah. I had *thought* going out for coffee would be a good idea. I only made it a block away from home before I realized what a mistake I had made. First, there were reporters *everywhere*. Getting out of the building itself was a hazard filled with microphones and shouted questions.

Once I got past them, I'd thought I was in the clear. And

I was. For about five minutes at least.

People were not kind. They openly stared. One woman crossed the street to avoid me. Easy enough to say I never got the coffee. The woman had been the last straw for my already frayed nerves. I balled my hands into fists and went back home, once again fighting through the reporters.

"Jess!"

"Can I ask you about Oscar?"

"Were you involved in the shooting?"

I ignored them all as I went inside, the clatter of the door behind me a wonderful relief. Inside the apartment, my day didn't get much better. Mom's foul attitude leeched out of her pores, surrounding her. She sat at the table, sipping from a mug of coffee, but at the sound of the door, she rose and threw her cup into the sink, brown liquid splashing all over the counter before she stormed down the hall to her room.

I said nothing.

Once again, I was in a predicament of not knowing what to do with myself. On instinct, I plodded to my room. Mom was still mad, and she would most likely be this way all day. I wouldn't mind honestly, as long as she continued to go out of her way to avoid me.

I needed to take my mind off all my worries and do something fun. But what *was* fun anymore? I picked up my computer and navigated to the gore group, but I didn't look at any of the posts. I stared at the banner at the top of the screen.

The Gorehounds of Albany.

The back of my head played through the shooting, and my stomach turned. Gore wasn't so fascinating when you had to deal with it up close. A wave of disgust washed over me when I thought of how much time I'd wasted on this site. How had I considered this an enjoyable past time?

What's wrong with me?

Desperate to get rid of the ick, I clicked the little icon in the corner. A drop-down menu appeared, and I clicked *leave group*.

I'd seen enough gore to last me a lifetime.

With my last link to any kind of social connection severed, I felt lonely. Keaton hadn't checked up on me since I had fallen asleep in her arms. It hadn't been but twelve hours, but the paranoid part of my brain was already ready to convince me she hated me.

Stop it, I told myself.

An IM pinged to life on my screen. Of course. Currently, Samuel seemed to be the only person who hadn't faded away. I hadn't responded to the message he sent the day of the shooting. I had blocked that account. This message was from a brand new one.

Can't handle the truth? He'd written.

I stared at the black lines on the white until the question lost all meaning. I had no motivation to do anything else. I didn't want to engage, and he obviously wasn't the type to take no for an answer. I stared at my hands, flexing them, my brain flashing back to the sensation of blood in the creases of my palms.

Right when I was about to close the computer and call it quits on torturing myself for the day, a new message pinged in the thread. Samuel had sent me a JPEG. I stared at it warily, knowing that from him there was a 50/50 chance it was either something horrifying or a dick pic though really, that was one in the same.

I chewed gently on one of my fingernails as I clicked it, squeezing my eyes shut when it began to load. Working up the courage, I opened my eyes and gasped, shooting up so fast I nearly sent my computer flying to the floor.

It was a picture of Oscar. More specifically, a picture of Oscar's *body*.

I wanted to throw up. Shock, rage, despair? I didn't know what to go with. I chose disgust after my stomach decided it'd had enough and upchucked my terrible oatmeal. It looked the same coming out as it had going in, and I vowed to never eat oatmeal again. Groaning, I wiped my mouth with the back of my hand.

Tentatively, I glanced toward the computer again where the image was still proudly dominating my screen. Hurriedly, I clicked the little 'X' in the corner, closing it out and deleting the file, scrubbing all traces of it off my computer.

How had he gotten that picture? Better yet, *why* did he have it?

Distracted by Samuel's newest exploits, I barely heard the knock on the apartment door. After a minute of continued banging, I jumped up, eager to find any distractions from the fresh reminder of Oscar's final moments. Peering through the peephole, I expected to see Officer Stone, but it was Keaton and Trixie.

I opened the door, eyes on the floor. Keaton was used to seeing me in this state, but Trixie wasn't. She was practically a stranger, and she was about to see more of me than she wanted or needed to.

"You okay, dude?" Keaton asked, putting her finger under my chin to lift my face.

I forced a smile as we locked eyes. "I'm fine."

"Hi, Jess," Trixie said, giving me a quick polite hug.

I returned it, easing a bit. I was glad to see that she hadn't resorted to treating me like I had the plague. Most likely, Keaton had something to do with that, and I was grateful. I studied Trixie as I pulled away. She was what I imagined Keaton would look like if she emphasized her femininity rather than hid it. Trixie had waist length bleach blonde hair with blue and red highlights. She was dainty and pretty with a spaghetti strap top that showed off a line of creamy skin above her jeans.

"Come in," I said, realizing there were reporters in the lobby staring up the stairs at us. "Who let them in the building?" I asked as soon as Trixie and Keaton were inside the apartment.

"No one," Keaton said, shoving her hands into her pockets. "They've taken it upon themselves."

"And that's the real tragedy," Trixie said, snapping her purple gum. "You're trying to heal, yet all they want to do is relive it. It's sickening."

I went to sit on the couch, finding the movement easier than thinking of a response.

"Where's your mom?" Keaton asked, sitting beside me.

"In her room. She's been in there all day," I said, scratching the back of my head.

Keaton sent a dirty look toward the hall. "Why?"

I didn't want to tell Keaton about the pills, about the fight we'd had this morning…at least not with Trixie here.

Maybe if it were just me and Keaton, that would be different.

"If you want us to go, we can," Keaton offered, patting one of my hands gently. "I understand. I just wanted to see how you were doing, but if you're not up for company yet, that's okay too."

"No, no, it's not that," I said. Problem was, I didn't know what to do with the company. I was sure Keaton and Trixie didn't want to sit here staring at me. They wanted to talk, but I didn't know what to say, how to let out my demons without sending them screaming.

Keaton must've sensed this because she said, "How're you coping today?"

"I…don't know. Everything feels…different and the same. Like I've stepped into some kind of alternate universe."

"Understandable," Trixie said, sitting in the armchair across the room. She leaned forward, resting her elbows on her knees as she stared at us. "In all likelihood, you haven't really, like, processed what happened yet."

"Yeah," I said though I doubted that was it. The problem was that I had broken this down forward and backward enough times that it was almost obsessive, and I *still* couldn't wrap my mind around it.

"Have you seen Samuel since it happened?" Keaton asked.

My eyes jumped to her, and for a paranoid second, I wondered if he had sent the picture of Oscar to her too. "No, why?"

"You have the look on you that you have whenever he does something stupid."

"Huh. Well, he uh…" I regretted the bit of a sentence as soon as I saw the look on Keaton's face. She wouldn't let me back out now.

"What he do?"

"He made this thread online saying he thinks I was in on the shooting, and he's got a whole bunch of people agreeing with him."

"That's bullshit," Trixie said.

"Couldn't have said it better myself," Keaton said then scoffed. "Of all people, he should be *grateful*. He was in the break room from what I've heard. If you hadn't done what you did. *Phew.*"

I thought of Oscar's desperate *please*. He had hated Samuel as much as I did. Was that the whole purpose of his plan? Had *Samuel* been his target?

"I didn't know that," I admitted and wondered if that knowledge would've changed my decision. If I had *known* Samuel was one of those people hiding, would I have simply run when Oscar told me to and left him to his carnage?

I'll never know.

"What's the website?" Keaton asked, searching for my laptop.

"Don't worry about it," I said. "He'll get bored soon enough."

Keaton didn't listen. She snagged my laptop from the room and plopped down on the couch beside me. The website and IM thread were still pulled up.

"What's this?" she asked and clicked on the JPEG of Oscar's body before I could stop her. "Oh my God!" she gasped, holding a hand to her mouth.

She was a tough as nails tomboy. I wasn't used to seeing her shaken by anything. Trixie shot to her feet in concern.

"Is that…I mean…who…"

I didn't answer Keaton's half questions as I closed out the picture. Intrigued by the scent of drama, Trixie came around the back of the couch, studying the computer screen.

"What was it?" she asked.

Keaton scrolled through the IMs, searching for the answer I wouldn't give. "This is him, isn't it? Samuel? Can't put his name on his bullshit."

I vowed to do a hard drive scrub after Keaton and Trixie left. Not only that, I would block Samuel's newest account as well as delete the picture so I would never have to see it again.

"I can't believe he would send you that," Keaton said.

"I know," I said, though at this point, I wasn't surprised. Samuel had no *low*, no limit to his depravity.

"And he says *you're* fucked up?" She shook her head as if she couldn't believe what had happened.

I couldn't either.

Trixie's eyes were wide, becoming wider with the fact that she still didn't know exactly what we were talking about. "What was the picture?"

"Gruesome," Keaton replied, not giving more details.

Trixie took the hint and didn't ask again. I stayed quiet as Keaton wrote "Fuck off" and blocked Samuel's newest account

I didn't point out it would do no good. He'd have a new one tomorrow, possibly tonight. I was sure Keaton already knew that too, but for the time being, she was doing what she could to protect me, and I appreciated it. I sent a scathing glance to the hallway that led to Mom's room. At least I had *someone* to protect me.

"This thread is crap," Keaton said, going through the posts on Samuel's website. "Like this person said, you were in a life or death situation. What you did stopped the killings."

"He didn't have to die though, they're right about that."

Keaton huffed. "You have a good heart, Jess, but think about it. This guy did this knowing he would most likely be shot down by the police. He was old enough to know better, to understand the consequences, but he still made his choice. I know he was your friend, but you don't have to defend him anymore."

The words didn't make me feel better, but the conviction Keaton had while closing the laptop did.

Chapter Eleven

THE REST OF the day after Keaton and Trixie left was quiet. Mom and I never made up for our fight, and I went without eating dinner. My stomach rioted with the absence of food, but I was used to going hungry. The feeling of emptiness, of *pain,* that came with starvation was a tiny reminder that despite everything, I was still *alive.* If Mom *had* bothered to cook something, I probably wouldn't have eaten it anyway. And not out of spite either. I felt generally unwell, and I couldn't tell if it was all in my head or if I was coming down with something.

Stress is good for that.

Half the night, I laid in bed staring at my dark ceiling. For a little while, I'd had my computer open next to me, waiting for Samuel's newest IM thread to ping, but no new message came. The chat threads were more than enough to keep me fully loathing myself. Would things ever go back to normal or would I always be that girl who was friends with a killer?

That possible second shooter?

I stopped dead in my reading when I realized the picture of Oscar that Samuel had PM'd me had made its way there too. The second I saw it, I reported the website and forced myself to go to sleep. Sleep usually cured everything for me—headaches, sour moods, boredom, you name it.

It didn't work its magic this time.

When morning came again, I was determined to try going outside one more time, to show that I wasn't going to be beaten down. It wouldn't be a fun trip, but as I slid my shoes on, I tried to convince myself it would be worth it.

I won't hide my face, I thought as I slipped out of the apartment. *I'll make them see me.*

I jogged down the steps and into the lobby, mentally preparing myself before pushing through the reporters stationed outside. The morning group was smaller than the one that formed midday. They mobbed me the best they could, trying to create a ring around me to make escape impossible, but I was practiced at this now, and I ducked through them with ease. With one obstacle down, my confidence started to rise. I crossed the street, zigzagging across town.

So far so good, I told myself.

I stopped at a crosswalk, waiting on the signal to go. There was a puddle near the curb, and I eyed it, waiting for someone to splash me. No one did, and I started to think maybe, just maybe, things would be okay.

Before the light turned green, someone screamed "murderer!" from the passenger side of a passing car.

My blood went cold. Before the insult, no one had picked me out as anything more than an average city girl but now everyone stared. They kept their distance, but my adrenaline spiked as if I was in real danger. Dizziness hit me, and I clamped my eyes tight, willing myself to not pass out. *I made it far enough. Abort mission.*

I surveyed the distance I had made it from home, ready to call it quits. Their eyes burned holes into the back of my head as I retreated, but thankfully they didn't call me more nasty names.

Anxiously, I flexed my hands in and out of fists, trying to distract myself as I rounded onto the block with my apartment building. I noticed the reporters first. Then a familiar figure among the crowd who stood out because he *didn't* belong. Samuel. The reporters had drawn the attention of some of my neighbors so Samuel, standing in the mouth of the alley beside the apartment, didn't stand out.

As I stared at the back of his head, I debated between confronting him and slipping past without him noticing. The morning, and previous night, had been tough on me, and I wasn't sure how much more I could take so I watched him. Samuel inched closer to the building, resting his hand on the railing at the bottom of the fire escape. Remembering the picture he had given me, my vision went red. Had I been right to assume it was how he got close enough to take it?

If he were willing to go that far, what would stop him from going further? From popping out the screen over my bedroom window and *coming in?* I rubbed the goosebumps away, eyes narrowing to slits.

Enough is enough, I decided.

"What are you doing here?" I hissed, stalking up to him without the hesitation I would've used if we had been at work. Here, I didn't have to restrict myself.

He jumped at the sound of my voice but hid it behind a wide smile. He looked almost...*thankful.* "Why, I wanted to see how my good buddy was doing today."

Several nearby reporters scuttled closer at the scent of possible drama. I grabbed him by the wrist, trying to pull him away before they could ask any questions.

For a moment, he stood his ground. "See? She's violent," he said to them before he allowed me to pull him halfway down the alley and out of their immediate sight.

When we were what I considered to be a safe distance away, I let go. "What do you want?"

"I really did want to see how you were doing," he said, innocently.

I saw right through the act. "You are full of shit. You don't care how I'm doing. You're up to something. What is it?"

Now it was his turn to gauge how far away the reporters were. When he turned back to me, his face twisted as if he had licked a lemon. He dug in his pocket, pulling something out. "I wanted to give you this," he said, slapping the picture to my chest the way I had done to him in the break room.

I didn't look at it, positive it was the one of Oscar. "If this is that picture of Oscar…"

"You'll what? Kill me?" he asked and batted his eyes.

"I wouldn't joke like that in front of them," I said, hoping at least one of the reporters had heard his comment.

"Whatever. It's not that anyway."

I snatched the picture, part of me convinced he was lying. The picture was of me, Trixie, and Keaton from the day before. A shot of us in the living room, huddled around my computer. "This is going to help a lot when I file for your restraining order."

Samuel laughed. "Remember the other day in the break room? When you said I'd regret whatever I do to you? I haven't yet, and you…you keep making it easier. It's almost like you enjoy the torment."

"Is that really what you think?"

"I don't know what to think, honestly," he admitted. "You don't bother to tell anyone about our little interactions, and at first, I had to wonder why. Then, the shooting happened, and it occurred to me that you haven't sought out help because you're hiding something. You don't want to risk it being exposed."

I sneered at him. "Really? Is that what you think? Because I think you're doing all this because of your wounded pride."

Samuel bared his teeth and lunged to grab my wrist. "You little bit—"

I didn't like to be touched, whether that be hugs from family and friends or grabs from Samuel's sausage-fingers. Out of reflex, I wrenched my free hand back, launching my palm forward with enough force to crack his nose. Blood dripped down his chin, and I pulled away, trying to shake off the pain radiating up my wrist.

The reporters who already had an eye on the scene peeked down the alley, and that was that. As soon as they saw the blood on Samuel's face and the matching smear across my wrist, they lifted their camera to take a picture.

Then I realized the extent of my mistake, the trap I had fallen into. Samuel had done this to support his thesis, and I had given him exactly what he wanted. As the reporters started to come toward us, screaming questions and snapping pictures, I rushed out before escape became impossible, saying nothing to anyone. I hurried upstairs to the apartment and nearly dove under my pillows and blankets, hiding from the world.

Stupid, stupid, stupid! I screamed inside my head.

How long would it be before tonight's spectacle appeared on the news?

Chapter Twelve

TWO HOURS.

Walking across campus later that day, I heard people talking about the incident with Samuel before I caught a glimpse of the story on the TV in the cafeteria. Samuel stood beside the reporter, hand up to cover his bloody nose though he left enough room for the smallest trickle of blood to make it through his fingers.

"You say she attacked you?" the reporter asked him.

Samuel sniffled as if he was overwhelmed by the entire ordeal. "Yeah, I wanted to check up on her, and I don't know what happened. Jess, if you're watching this. I'm sorry if I said something to offend you. I only want to be your friend."

I didn't want to hear anymore. I tried to shrug it off, thinking of the laugh Keaton and I would have over it later on. Other people didn't think it was funny. If I thought I was a pariah before, it was nothing compared to now. I might as well have had a flesh-eating disease for the way everyone made a show of staying away from me.

When I went up to the counter to pick up a wrapped sandwich, the girl who had been standing there shouldered her bag and threw down the handful of items she had already picked up, storming off.

Whatever, I thought, trying to not let the hurt show as I paid for my food.

She was a stranger, someone who didn't matter to me in the slightest. Yet, I couldn't push the feelings of rejection away. I scanned the cafeteria, trying to pick a table that had the least amount of people. I approached a table of three. They looked at one another, and like the girl, made a show of storming away.

"I give up," I muttered to no one as I threw my backpack to the floor.

To have a table to myself here was truly a feat since there were only five in the entire place. The other four were packed full, but no one dared sit with me. I unwrapped the sandwich, eating without tasting it. Eating by myself wasn't new—if anything, it was like reliving my high school days. The feeling was made realer when Keaton appeared. She visited me on campus occasionally, but it wasn't something she'd done in a while. Though real emotions escaped me most of the time, I couldn't help but give her a grateful hug. The other people in the cafeteria stared her down, and I was glad she didn't go to school here. She would've been outcasted for this, for *me*, and she deserved better than that.

"You're not worried about being on the news?" I asked her, trying to downplay my own humanity as I sat back down.

"Oh, but every little girl's dream is to be a television star!" She laughed and rolled her eyes.

I laughed with her because it was a good joke—we, as misfits had no idea what regular girls and women wanted. We weren't cut from the same cloth.

"But seriously, they could put my picture everywhere,

and it wouldn't make a difference. You remember I was right by your side when the police dropped you off and there were tons of reporters. They know me. That hasn't changed. I'll be here no matter what." She paused, twitching her nose. "On that note, I heard you gave it good to Samuel today in quote—" she lifted her hands to make air quotes as she spoke, "—a violent assault."

This was bad, hell *terrible,* but it showed that at least I wasn't afraid of him. And hey, he would never be able to escape the fact he had been beaten up by a girl. No more tough man bravado in front of his friends.

"I had my reasons," I said at last as I set my juice back on my tray.

Keaton cupped her chin in her hand. "I don't doubt that."

I bent over to grab my backpack, slipping out the photograph Samuel had given me before I slapped it on the table. Keaton's features shifted, her eyes going from wide to slits. The hand that had cradled her chin thumped to the table, and she picked up the photograph by the corner.

"Where'd you get this?" she asked.

"Samuel gave it to me. He was outside the apartments this morning. He's been following me."

"So, the IMs weren't the end of it," she said, tapping her fingers on the table.

"Nope," I replied, popping the *P*. "This isn't the first picture he's taken without me knowing either."

"And he had all those reporters fooled into thinking he was the victim. He cried a little too. Like man, what drugs is he on?"

"Hella good ones, I would assume. I mean he tricked me into hitting him. He knew all the reporters would be there, and he baited me."

"Then why did you run? Why not stay and give your side of the story? Tell them it was Samuel's fault?"

"I know how it looked. It's no secret what he's been saying about me. I think everyone in town has visited his website at least once, and I had blood literally on my hand."

"Yeah, but you had a good reason."

"Come on, Keaton," I said, glancing down at the picture. "They don't care about a good reason. They care about a good *story*. Besides, who's going to believe me? He knew what he was doing. This doesn't look like a candid stalker photo. This could be professional grade. They would've said I was trying to cover my ass."

"Depends. What was the other picture of?"

"Me in my bedroom. He got a picture of me sleeping from the fire escape, I think."

Keaton stretched her eyes wide. "How long ago did this happen?"

It took me a minute to remember. Ever since the shooting, time had slowed down. A few days felt like a few months. "He gave me the picture a few hours before the shooting."

"He's a dumbass. *That* picture will prove he's crazier than he lets on. Take it to the police."

"Yeah, it would but…I don't have it. I threw it at Samuel when I found out, and after everything with Oscar, I forgot about it until today."

I didn't want them to, but my eyes betrayed me and welled with tears. Keaton tsked and pulled me into her arms, stroking my hair. "This sucks, Jess, but he's doing the most. Give him time, and he'll hang himself with his own rope. I promise you that. Just wait."

When she pulled away, I lifted my hand to wipe my dewy eyes, embarrassed again for my own humanity. "Yeah, but he's going to try and make sure I hang with him."

"You're not in this alone. You've got me. Now that I know what he's capable of, I'm gonna keep an eye out for him. I go in and out a lot more than you. If I catch him around the apartment again, I'll have a conversation with him one on one." She punctuated her point by cracking all her knuckles.

"Impressive."

She smiled then went straight back to seriousness. "But I'm gonna be honest with you. I don't think he followed you to get these pictures. Has he…sent you any links or anything in those creepy PMs?"

"A few times," I said uneasily. "Where are you going with this?"

"I think he sent some spyware and hacked your webcam to get these."

I stared at the picture of me, Trixie, and Keaton again and felt sick. He certainly had the technological know-how to pull it off.

If he never came to the apartment before, why come now? I thought, remembering how fascinated he'd been with the fire escape.

He's escalating.

Before I could follow that train of thought, I spotted someone approaching the table. She was thin and wiry with pink spectacles that slid down her long nose more often than they were in place. My academic advisor, Chelsea. I had never seen her outside her office before, and I didn't know what to think of seeing her now. Other people in the cafeteria watched her too, and when they realized she was headed toward me, they whispered excitedly about the possible upcoming drama.

"I gotta go," I said to Keaton. "Thanks again for coming to see me. I really needed the pick-me-up."

"'S no trouble," she replied and held her arms out.

I got up, hugging Keaton tighter than I had ever held anyone before. I reveled in the moment, and she flashed me the peace sign before she walked away, hands in her pockets.

I acknowledged Chelsea. "Hi, Mrs. Morris."

"Miss Mills, I was wondering if you had a moment to talk?" she asked, clutching the purple folder in her hands a little tighter.

"Of course," I said, trying to see if there was a label on it or any indication of what was about to happen. "What's this about?"

Chelsea slipped into the seat across from me, and I collected plastic bits of my trash from the table.

"First, I wanted to check in, and see how you're doing," she said, gently lying the folder down.

"I'm fine," I said immediately. Too fast.

Her eyebrows arched in suspicion, the thick lines looking like alarmed caterpillars.

"It's tough, but I'm going day by day," I added.

"What you went through was something I'll never be able to imagine," she said, holding a hand to her heart.

I said nothing, waiting for her to continue.

"Well, considering everything you went through, the Dean wanted me to talk to you about possibly taking some time off."

"Is this about the news today?" I blurted out, flabbergasted by the situation. School was all I had left. The only reason I left the apartment.

Samuel is gonna take this from you too.

Chelsea's eyes went wide. "No, no. It's nothing like that. We believe you could use the time to grieve and…process what's happened."

My nose twitched. I didn't like how calm she was being, how rational. I wanted to be angry, but her calmness made it difficult. Not impossible though. I grabbed my bag, tossing it over my shoulder as I stood up. "You want to get rid of me because the publicity will be bad for your school," I said, putting two and two together. I shot venomous glances to the tables around me. "As if it's not bad enough that the news has me eating here alone like a leper."

"Jessica," Chelsea said, in way of protest. I waited for her to continue, to finish telling me why I was wrong, but she didn't.

I rapped my knuckles twice on the table. "You know what? Time off sounds great. Thanks," I said and walked away, ignoring her calls for me to come back.

What was the point of fighting anymore? I never won.

Chapter Thirteen

THE SILENCE WALKING home was loud, *deafening*. In my paranoia, the looks from passing people were worse, and I had the thought that someone would throw something at me. What was stopping them?

By the time I burst through the door into the apartment, I was panting for air. It was chaos outside, but inside? It was peaceful. Mom wasn't hiding in her room. She was owning up to the minimum requirements of her life. She was at work, and she would be until at least midnight.

The alone time was exactly what I needed.

I sat on the couch, thinking about what to do with the evening ahead of me. My pile of horror DVDs were perched on the shelf beneath the TV on the entertainment center. Usually, I would've dove right in, but today, I didn't touch them. I didn't need to. If I wanted a horror story, all I had to do was close my eyes, and I'd see Oscar.

I lifted my hands, digging the heels into my eyes until it hurt as I tried to change my line of thinking. When he'd been alive, I never thought of Oscar this much, and I was ashamed of myself for it. Maybe if I had, he wouldn't have been driven to do what he did.

It's not your fault, I told myself, but it didn't change a thing.

I had known something was wrong with him, but I let it go. It *was* my fault. Maybe they were right to say I was the second shooter because I hadn't tried to change the outcome. The only difference between us was while I pondered the thought of my darkness, playing with it like a cat with a mouse, he had run with his. I hadn't been able to kill the mouse when I wanted to, but he had slaughtered seven human beings.

Would've been eight if I hadn't done the final one for him.

Plucking out my phone, I pulled up Samuel's website, scrolling through the new threads and waited for the newest IM. It bothered me that he was the only person who really saw me for what I was.

Keaton didn't see it. Mom didn't see it.

But *he* did.

To make it worse, I missed Oscar. This had been the longest I'd gone without talking to him, and I had to keep reminding myself that I would never talk to him again.

Before this, I had never lost anyone I was close to. For all my obsession with carnage and death, I'd never been to a funeral. Though my father wasn't around, he was still alive somewhere. At least as far as I knew.

I threw my backpack to the floor, my shoes a moment behind and reclined on the couch, staring up at the ceiling. I could've gone to sleep if my brain wasn't determined to torture me.

To fill the silence, I tried putting on the news again,

admittedly afraid of what I would see. The shooting was the top story, but the story about me and Samuel from earlier didn't make another appearance. Either way, I was relieved. Maybe they realized how petty it had been or maybe they didn't see any use in airing it more than once. I went to turn the TV back off when the reporter said, "There will be a vigil tonight in honor of the lives lost."

Dumbfounded, I kept watching, realizing *this* was why the report from earlier hadn't re-aired. I jotted down the details onto a nearby pad of paper, facing a new dilemma.

A vigil.

Was this something I should go to or something I would be better off avoiding altogether? On one hand, it would give me a chance to reflect, grieve, and get myself out there to show my support for Oscar's victims. Something I imagined normal people would do. On the other hand, I was sure there would be reporters there—far more than the many who had been camped outside my apartment since the shooting. Also, I was more than sure Samuel would make an appearance.

I wonder if he knows about it, I thought. When I opened my laptop, which I had left on the table beside the couch, a new IM waited.

Don't think about it, bitch.

My mood shifted. I didn't want to cry. I *laughed.* Who did Samuel think he was to make such a demand? I tossed my laptop aside without responding.

Ruffling my hair, I got up, pulled the entire container of ice cream and a bottle of red wine out of the fridge, and settled back onto the couch. This would be a good night to lose myself in someone else's creation. Settled into my nook where I would most likely be for the rest of the night, I turned the TV on and went to Netflix to scroll through the movies. I took a swig from my bottle and set it down. The tiny buzz of alcohol didn't help much. I was still annoyed, aggravated, sad, frustrated…an emotional casserole.

When Mom came in from work, she stopped at the sight of me. I winced, wondering what was about to happen. This would be the first time she'd spoken to me since our fight, if she said anything at all. She set her things down on the kitchen table before sitting on the couch beside me.

She's acknowledging my existence, I thought and barely avoided making a face.

Why had I decided on secluding myself in the apartment instead of going to spend the night at Keaton's? It would've been a hell of a lot better than whatever was about to happen.

"What're you watching?" she asked at last, studying me as I continued to scroll through options.

"Nothing at the moment," I replied, tone as bitter as the last time we talked.

Mom waited for me to scroll past *Sinister* before she said, "I thought that was your favorite movie?"

"It is," I replied. I wanted something funny, something to distract me from thoughts of Oscar, Samuel, and the vigil.

"For what it's worth, I'm sorry," Mom said.

I could hear the hurt in her voice, and I squeezed my eyes shut. I wanted to believe she really was. That she wanted to stop, that she wanted to be *better,* but this was a song and dance we had done hundreds of times before, always ending with the same results—her blacked out in bed or on the couch, a mess of alcohol and pills around her.

"I don't want to hear that, Mom," I said, slamming the remote to the couch beside me.

She tucked her lip into her teeth, biting so hard she looked as if she was about to start crying. "I understand."

"I don't want *apologies*. I want to understand *why*. If you're really sorry, you'd stop. If you were sorry, you'd stick with the program. You were how far into Narcotics Anonymous?" I asked. "Now you have to start all over again."

"Everyone makes mistakes," she said weakly.

"This isn't like buying the wrong thing from the grocery store," I said bitterly. "If you really want to get better, you have to have dedication. Discipline. It's been *years*, Mom. I would've expected mistakes and accidents when I was little, but…" The words lodged themselves in my throat.

"But?" she prompted, knowing full well that the next words out of my mouth were going to be anything but kind.

"But not now. You should've been better by now."

"You're right," she said, folding her hands in her lap. "You're absolutely right, and there's nothing I can say to excuse my behavior."

"No, there's not," I agreed, picking the remote back up to continue my aimless scrolling.

Mom pouted. "How are you doing with…everything that's happened?"

I took another swig from the bottle of wine. "Does it matter?"

"Yes, Jess, honey, it does."

I cut her a sideways glare.

"I might be terrible at this whole mother thing, but you have to know I do my best."

It's a sorry best, I thought, sticking my tongue in my cheek to keep myself from saying the words out loud.

"No matter what, I don't want you to forget that I love you."

She looked so sad that I forced myself to say, "I know that," even though I didn't. Not really. I kept thinking of how alone I had felt the morning after the shooting when I woke up to a blacked-out mother. If anyone had the right to be blacked out that day, it would've been me.

"Are you going to answer my question?" she asked, tucking a strand of my wild hair behind my ear.

This was what I wanted, right? For my mother to at least *pretend* to be interested in me. I would play along. For now. It wasn't as if I had anything better to do. She'd get bored of the ruse soon anyway.

"At first, I was fine, but now, it's like…I can't go anywhere without people judging. I don't understand. I thought what I did was helping people. It's not like I wanted to kill my friend, but no one thinks about that. They look at me and see some type of monster."

"I'm sure you're thinking too much into it," she said. "You've always had a bad habit of that."

I rolled my eyes. "Mom, I know what I'm talking about. Today, Chelsea, my academic advisor, basically told me to stay away from campus for a while."

"Does she have the authority to make that call? You've

paid good money to attend those classes."

I didn't mention I hadn't paid a dime because scholarships had gotten me in there. Now wasn't the time to argue the details. I chose to move the conversation forward instead. "Word came from the Dean himself. I'm bad publicity apparently."

"I'm sorry," Mom said. I hated her. And I hated her sympathy because it was nothing but a band-aid. Mom had learned she could do anything she wanted, and she would get away with it as long as she slapped the *sorry* band-aid on it later. "Honey, you aren't a monster. You have a dark sense of humor, but I know you. You would never hurt someone for the sake of hurting them. You were caught in a terrible situation, and you had to make a tough call."

I bit my tongue. Literally *bit* it to keep myself from snarling. Mom was the last person to know who I truly was. I shielded a lot of myself from her, partially because I was scared she would turn harder to her vices, while the other part worried she would up her judgements of me. She didn't know how much I hated Samuel, how much I *wanted* to hurt him. How many times I had wondered what murder would feel like before I had actually done the deed.

"Mom, what if I told you I've had the fear that I would hurt someone one day?"

Mom's lips eased from their solemn line, and she almost looked compassionate. Immediately, I found myself searching her eyes for a familiar sign of a glaze. Naturally, she wasn't a caring person, it was the pills that made her empathetic or sympathetic or whatever the hell you have to be to care about your daughter.

"You're not the kind. You're an intelligent young woman with passion," Mom said.

I wanted to laugh, but a crushing sadness knocked the urge away, and I reflected on her words. Was that honestly how she saw me? If that was the case, how did everyone else see me? Keaton? Trixie? Samuel? They all had different opinions of me. Different even from how I saw myself.

Which image was the real me—her version or mine?

"You don't understand," I told her. What was the best way to approach this without sounding like a psychopath? Maybe that was the only way. "You noticed I moved your trap, well, I never told you *why*."

"Well, why did you?"

"I wanted to kill the mouse."

Mom stared straight ahead, mouth puckering like a fish. "Did you?"

I swiped a lock of hair from my eyes before I said, "No, I put it out by the woods."

She smiled a quick, clipped grin and patted me on the shoulder. "See? That's my point. You had every opportunity to hurt that creature, but you didn't."

"No, I left it to continue suffering instead."

Mom wilted, this act already weighing on her. "Why are you so stubborn?"

"I learned it from my mother," I said and picked up the bottle of wine, gulping it down until the back of my throat was raw and my stomach warm with alcohol.

"Word around the diner is that there's going to be a vigil

tonight."

Silence as I capped the bottle, setting it back on the floor. What a way to kick me when I was already down.

"You should go."

My eyes stayed on the bottle. "I don't know if that's such a good idea."

"Why not? There would have been many more names to mourn if you hadn't done what you did. You saved those people. There's no shame in that."

"If you say so," I said. Half the people I had saved were the same ones dragging my name through the mud on Samuel's website.

"Something to think about," Mom said and squeezed my knee as she stood up.

When she walked away, it felt as if a giant weight had been lifted. I listened to her rustling around the kitchen but kept my eyes on the TV. My first reaction was to ignore her advice and continue my browsing. I had already made myself a little nest of blankets and snacks, I didn't want to leave. Then the intrusive thoughts came. What would my absence say to those who thought I had been in cahoots with Oscar?

It doesn't matter what other people think, I chastised myself.

I should only go if I wanted to, and I didn't. All the people who died, with the exception of Oscar, had been strangers. I thought of Samuel's show for the cameras earlier and his warning. No doubt he'd try something if I showed up. Maybe that was why he had taken the time to bait me—he wanted to be sure I *would* show up.

I can't imagine why she wouldn't be here, he would say and the

people in his chat thread would eat it up.
That got me off the couch.
Spite was one hell of a motivator.

Chapter Fourteen

MY ENTIRE REASON for going to the vigil was to make a point, but I couldn't remember what that point was as I approached the parking lot. The group gathered was too large for one lot and people spilled out onto the grass and the adjoining parking lot next door. My anxiety skyrocketed, and I swayed on my feet, nearly bumping into Keaton.

Keaton set a hand on me, steadying me before she let go. She showed no signs of nervousness as she surveyed the seven crosses buried in flowers visible through the gaps in the crowd. People hugged one another, talking through tears. I glanced at Keaton, daring myself to be hopeful. If there were this many people here, who would really notice me?

I'd gone out of my way to *not* stand out. Keaton had coached me through my decision of what to wear—black clothes, baseball cap flipped backwards with all my blonde hair tucked underneath, and a pocketknife…to be on the safe side.

As Keaton inched me toward the group, I started to dissociate. The world around me grew hazy, and I waved my hand in front of my face, examining the way it passed with unreal slowness. I struggled to remember it was *my* hand. Life had an unreal quality, my surroundings detached like I was stuck in a lucid dream, and there was no waking up.

It was easier for the darkness to take over, and it did the job well. Too well maybe. I could believe I was someone else and somewhere else. I was *ready* for this, ready for Samuel to try something stupid. Ready for someone to confront me and tell me I didn't belong here. I glanced at Keaton again, her odd mixture of feminine and masculine, and wondered if maybe she felt like this sometimes too.

When we joined the crowd, no one looked our way. Between the number of people and my choice of outfit, I didn't stand out. My coworkers tucked together on the other side of the parking lot didn't recognize me. I could've smiled I was so relieved. Keaton slipped her hand into mine, giving me a comforting squeeze as we listened to the tearful stories people shared with one another.

"See? You're fine," she said as we walked through the crowd.

"You were right," I admitted sheepishly. I glanced over my shoulder, scanning all the nearby people again to make sure I was in the clear.

"Did you know any of them?" Keaton asked, and it took me a minute to realize she was gesturing to the crosses.

I stared at them, shaking my head. Three of the seven had been my coworkers, the other four random customers.

Keaton pulled her hand free, using it to wrangle her blonde bangs from her eyes. She gestured with her chin, and I followed her gaze to a girl giving a soulful eulogy about her cousin who had been the second one to die.

A few people lit some candles, circling them around the floral arrangements in a way that reminded me of a Pagan ceremony. I wasn't usually one for flowers, but the red and white roses were a beautiful touch. After the last person had spoken their piece, all seven of Oscar's victims were accounted for. Someone released a handful of balloons—seven to be exact— but I thought how wrong the whole thing was as my eyes followed them up into the sky.

Eight people died that day.

Eight.

Oscar *and* his seven victims.

I came back from my dissociation then, painful, and sudden. I didn't want to be here anymore. I had made a mistake thinking this would be a good idea. I started to back away.

"Where are you going?" Keaton asked.

I didn't answer. I turned away, desperate to escape when I ran into the person I least wanted to see—Samuel. Literally, I bowled directly into him. I pushed away as soon as I realized my mistake. He held his hands out and between them and the crowd, I couldn't escape.

"Look who decided to crash the party," he said. Keaton caught up to me as he studied me from head to toe before glancing at Keaton and back to me. "Going butch too, are you?"

Keaton smiled, the dangerous one I'd seen her wear before punching her bullies in high school. "You must be the infamous Samuel I've heard about."

"One and only," he said with a smirk and a bow as if he thought Keaton was flirting with him.

He's got his head stuck so far up his ass all he can see is his own bullshit.

"Let me ask you a question," she said, tilting her head slightly. "You think talkin' like that makes you cool?"

"Oh, I wasn't talking to you," Samuel said dismissively, waving a hand at her as if that would make her disappear and snagged the baseball cap off my head. My blonde hair tumbled out around my shoulders, but I didn't try to get it back. My identity was compromised. Samuel spun it once on the tip of his finger, gloating.

"But you could take pictures of me?" she demanded.

Samuel laughed, eyes twinkling. "I guess I should be flattered you're telling your friends about me."

"You be whatever you want to be," I sneered, studying my hat hanging limply from his finger. I thought about snatching it back but recoiled. It was soiled by his touch, and I didn't want it back.

"If you think you're gonna intimidate her or me, you're wrong," Keaton told him. "I'd watch yourself if I was you."

"Or what? What exactly will either of you do?" He looked from her to me then laughed so loud he caught a few people's attention.

I cast my eyes to the ground, not wanting to be seen. If they heard his laugh, had they heard his comment too?

"Come on," Keaton said, grabbing my arm as if she sensed how close I was to shutdown. "He's an asshole."

I didn't protest as she started to lead me away. We made it through the grass and to the edge of the road when he said, "Yeah, you should leave. You didn't have any business here to begin with."

Keaton turned back to him. "If it wasn't for her, your sorry ass would be dead."

"Yeah? Count those crosses. I think there's one missing because guess what? *That's* how much we care for *killers*. Even ones with pretty faces."

My gaze dropped not because he hurt my feelings, but because somehow, he had managed to speak my internal thoughts out loud for everyone to hear. I was a survivor, but I wasn't welcome here.

Just as Oscar's memorial wasn't.

"Let's just go," I said, pushing past Keaton and Samuel before either could say anything else.

"Gladly," Keaton replied, sizing up Samuel a moment longer before she followed me.

KEATON WALKED ME home, both of us strangely silent the entire time. She offered to come in with me, but I wanted to be alone. We said our goodbyes, and I hurried inside the apartment. Mom appeared in the front room as soon as the door closed as if she had been waiting for me. I wished I had the power to make myself transform into someone else, *somewhere* else. I couldn't deal with Mom's theatrics after what I had gone through today. I wanted to sleep. To disappear.

"How'd it go?" she asked.

I stared at her hopeful eyes and general innocence and all desire to tell the truth slipped away. Mom hadn't lived in the real world in a long time. There was no use in having her start now. That was why she was stuck on the pills. Those were *her* escape from the life she created.

"It was fine," I lied.

"Really now?"

"Keaton came with me, so it wasn't bad."

"Good. In a year from now, you'll be glad you went."

"Sure," I said, wishing I could be on that same level of delusion.

I opened my mouth, ready to call her on it, when I closed it. What was the point of arguing? She wouldn't understand. No one *really* understood. She would numb herself to the truth anyway.

I went to my room, slamming the door behind me in case she tried following me. I leaned against it, wondering if Mom took the time to print out lists of cliché things to tell me every time we interacted or if it was all adlibbed.

I took off my shoes and whipped them across the room before I jumped into bed, burying my face in the pillows to let out a muffled scream. It wasn't Mom I was upset about. It was Samuel and the way he managed to make me feel…*small*…like I didn't belong.

I already knew there'd be an IM waiting for me before I opened my laptop. When I worked up the nerve to power my computer on, I was right. An anonymous profile had connected to me.

Can't fight your own battles anymore? the message asked.

You made it both our fight when you decided to take that picture of us, I shot back.

I closed my laptop wondering how much evidence I needed to strike up a harassment charge against him. After the incident in the alley, it would take a lot to convince anyone he was actually the perpetrator. The anonymous IMs all came from different accounts, different I.P. addresses. There was no way to prove it was all him. That was why he did what he did. He knew that I couldn't fight back, and if I did, he had plans for turning that against me too.

I felt helpless. Trapped in my life.

If this was how Samuel had made Oscar feel, I could almost understand why he had felt his only true escape was death.

Chapter Fifteen

I DIDN'T TRY to leave the apartment again. There was no desire, no need. Keaton checked in on me a few times over the course of the next week to make sure I wasn't dead. I wasn't sure what the difference was. I had basically become another piece of furniture in the apartment. We passed the point where it seemed Mom had more of a life than me, and that was saying something.

Keaton told me I had a life outside of work and school, but I didn't believe it. I had no hobbies, no other friends. Nothing to live for, per se. When Keaton had the time, she'd drop in to eat dinner with me and Mom. Tension was still pretty high between me and my parental figure, but at least we could tolerate to be in the same room as one another. That was progress. I knew how this would go, the same as it always did— she would continue to pretend things were the same as they had been until that became the norm again.

I didn't forget about the pills, of course, I never did, but sometimes, it was easier to go with the flow. To pretend they didn't exist. It made life tolerable at least. The days that Keaton came over for dinner gave me some sort of purpose. I put everything I had into the meals, and when she left, I would clean the kitchen and go right back to my lair to be part of the darkness.

The internet went quiet.

The popularity of Samuel's thread began to die. Ever since the incident at the vigil, he hadn't sent me any I.M.s, and I had to wonder if Keaton really had kept him away from me. Or if he had other reasons entirely.

I made a mental note to talk to Keaton about it the next time she stopped by. I could text her, of course, but this seemed more like an in-person conversation. For a little bit, I sat thinking about and appreciating Keaton. She was sacrificing a lot for me. She should be out enjoying her life with her beautiful girlfriend, but instead, she took time out of her day every day to take care of her fucked up friend.

That was dedication.

Loyalty.

I breathed easy with the thought that like Mom and her pills, the entire situation with Oscar and the shooting would be in the past. It would never be forgotten, of course, but it would get easier to live with in time.

The morning of the funeral for Oscar's first victim, it was like all the progress was lost. The chat thread boomed with more quotes, questions, *thoughts and prayers,* and more emojis people thought were praying hands but were really high fives. Someone had started a conversation theorizing who would show up to each of the funerals. They were right in assuming I wouldn't go to any of them. If I had been out of place at the vigil, I would be *really* unwelcome in the intimacy of a funeral.

I sat on the couch as Mom got ready for work. She glanced at the news then me. I expected her to say something, to suggest I should go to this funeral, but she didn't.

"Have a good day," she called as she tossed her bag over her shoulder and went out the door.

I wondered if she knew the irony of her words or if she had said them because she knew I *wouldn't* have a good day. I didn't know how anymore. I kept my eyes on the television, the news on repeat. The information about the funeral played at the top of every hour. I shook my head, wondering if all the funerals would be such a big deal or if only the first one would attract this much attention.

There was another funeral that was sure to light up the threads, the news stations, and everywhere else where people lurked—Oscar's. No one had mentioned a thing about him, and it sucked. That was the one funeral I *wanted* to go to. He was the only one I couldn't let go of, but I didn't know his family, and I had no idea how to reach out. Oscar's mother had done a soulful apology for the actions of her son, and since then, none of his family had been on the news.

They had gone out of their way to disconnect themselves from him and what he had done.

I didn't blame them for disappearing.

Over the course of the next few days, each victim had their funeral on a different day, which made the entire week something out of a horror movie. The town was sad. Really sad, but by time the weekend came, the buzz was all but gone. I had the nagging suspicion that the families of the lost had planned out their funerals like that on purpose to ensure that they kept the attention of the public for as long as they could.

Keaton had dressed up to sneak into one to see if

Samuel would show up, but he didn't go to them either. There were some borders he wouldn't cross after all. That or he had watched me enough to know that those were things I wasn't planning on going to. I was pleased when Keaton told me of his absence, but when I really thought about it, it only cemented the fear that he was planning a whole new shot against me.

"Have you seen him hanging around?" I asked her.

"Nope."

"He hasn't said anything to me since the vigil," I'd admitted. It was strange to have an entire day go by without communication, let alone a week.

"That's good then. Maybe he finally got bored," she had said and promptly changed the subject.

The optimism lifted my spirits, but my gut weighted them down again. I couldn't shake the feeling that something was wrong, that I was in danger somehow. I pushed it away, burying it in its usual place beneath thoughts of Oscar. From what I could tell, he was still at the funeral home, frozen in the freezer. He stayed there two weeks.

His family had abandoned him. I could understand their decision, but at the same time, it didn't seem fair. I wanted to scream at them, to make them see sense. The reason he had done what he did was because the people who were supposed to be there for him hadn't been.

If no one claimed his body, what were the rules about who could? I would scrape up the money somehow to bury him if it came to it. I hadn't been there for him when he needed me, and that was guilt I would always carry. The least I could do would be to be there for him now.

I closed my eyes, imagining what the news would say if it came to that. Would there be outrage, or would I simply be filling the dirt into my own grave?

Chapter Sixteen

TWO DAYS AFTER the last of his victims' funerals. That was when Oscar's ceremony was. The news coverage made me sick—a biased thing, every other word "alleged" or "killer." I wanted to slap the reporter, but it was a secondary thought to what else the news showed. Besides his mother, I had never seen any of Oscar's family before. Today was the first real glimpse I got. They were crying, huddling together in an attempt to hide their faces from the camera. They didn't want this attention.

I feel you, I thought.

Those glimpses of his family were everywhere and the focus of hate online, especially in Samuel's threads.

These are the people responsible for evil, someone had captioned the picture.

I clenched my hands into such tight fists that my nails drew blood from my palms. I felt bad for them, probably worse because of what I had done. If I had convinced Oscar to turn himself in, his family wouldn't have had to try to plan a funeral in the limelight.

They wouldn't be the lightning rod for public hate.

The day of the memorial, reporters stormed the cemetery, disclosing the location of Oscar's final resting place to the world. I wouldn't be surprised if his grave was vandalized by the time night came.

I jotted down the address and googled directions before I hurried to put my shoes on. I was a mess as I ran outside, but it didn't matter. The entire world had already seen me at my lowest.

The reporters outside the apartment ate me up as I struggled to get through them. I didn't let them stop me. I was on a mission. When I made it to the cemetery, the press was there too. They had been "polite" enough to shut off their cameras, but they still shouted questions at everyone who passed the gate.

"You outta be ashamed of yourselves!" I yelled over my shoulder.

They didn't hear me though, their attention focused on the front door of the columbarium as they waited for either someone to enter or exit. I noticed this and made a wide U around the building to approach the back door.

Cemeteries had an air of peace about them, and even in the middle of this chaotic time, that held true. I focused on the feeling of the air going in and out of my lungs as I peered through the glass door. There were two women inside, staring at the names on the wall halfway down the hall. I recognized Oscar's mother from the news, but the other woman was a mystery. Oscar's mother was on her knees, head bowed to cry. The other woman, a heavy-set gal, stood behind her, hand on her shoulder.

I slipped inside, closing the door quietly behind me before I ducked behind a huge potted plant to keep out of sight.

At home, I had been sure this was a good idea, but now that I was in the thick of it, I wasn't. What if they screamed at me? What if they hit me?

I should go home, the tiny warning bell in my head sounded.

I silenced it and took two steps forward. They didn't notice me. Beginning to relax only slightly, I took two more strides and finally, Oscar's mother, a petite thing with light-brown skin and deep brown hair, looked at me through wide eyes as if she assumed I'd bring her harm.

Recognition stretched her eyes wide and an odd mixture of sadness and anger crossed her features. She was on her feet before I could react. I took two steps back with the assumption it would be to strike me. She matched the steps and pulled me into her arms. I didn't hug her back because I didn't know what *to* do. I had been sure this woman would hate me.

"I don't blame you," she said, making sure I heard every word.

I had to pull away. "You don't?" I asked, staring this woman directly in the eyes to make sure I didn't misunderstand whatever she said next.

"No, you…did what you had to do. My Oscar he…he was troubled…and you set him free."

I bit my lip to keep my eyes from welling with tears.

Set him free.

That sounded like a gift, a blessing, a *pleasantry*. Oscar's dying gasps played in my head, telling me it had been anything but. "I'm sorry," I said, choking on the air I used to say them with. I couldn't breathe, and I thought how inconvenient it would be for me to have a panic attack right now.

"Ever since Molly, he's had a tough time."

Molly. The name sounded familiar, and I tossed it around inside my head, trying to put a face to the name.

Oscar's mother touched a niche below Oscar's. *Molly Rodriguez,* it said. *1992-2018*

Then it clicked. The girl who had been murdered on campus last year.

"I didn't realize he had a sister," I said, dumbfounded. How much tragedy could one family take?

Oscar's mother's face pinched with pain. "Why are you here?" the bigger woman asked. Her voice was flat, monotone. The sound of a person who had spent so much time feeling that they were no longer capable of it.

"I saw on the news that Oscar's memorial was today and I…came to pay my respects," I said, glancing at the golden plaque on the wall.

Oscar Rodriguez. I touched the corner of it, and in the back of my mind, I could almost picture Oscar beside me, resting his hand on my shoulder.

It'll be okay, Jessie, he whispered in my ear. I closed my eyes, trying to keep the tears in.

"You cared about him," Oscar's mother stated.

It wasn't often that I let anyone see me cry, but in this case, I made sure she saw the tear streak my cheek.

"He talked about you all the time."

All of this would leave me with mental scars for the rest of my life, but over time, details would be forgotten until a few sparse memories remained. Those words out of Oscar's mom's mouth would be one of the minute details I would remember years down the road.

"I'm going to miss him," I replied.

She hugged me again, and this time, I didn't fight to break free. She smelt like Oscar, and it soothed me. When we broke apart, we didn't say goodbye. I looked at Oscar's niche again, and without explaining myself, I started to walk away.

She called after me, "Thank you."

I knew why without asking. The moment Oscar died, everyone had stopped seeing him for the person he had been. They only saw him for the monster he had become on that last day. I couldn't do that. There were too many memories of the before times.

As I walked toward the door, I paused and turned back to see Oscar's family. I whispered my last goodbye to Oscar before pushing the door open and slipping outside.

Chapter Seventeen

I TOLD NO one about the run in with Oscar's family and what I had learned about his sister. Mostly because I wasn't sure how I felt about it.

The next day, I contemplated going back to Oscar's memorial place to mourn him in peace, and to see how his niche was holding up after a night alone, but it would do no good. No matter what, that place would also hold memories of the encounter with Oscar's family. As much as I wanted to belong there, I didn't.

It's all wrong.

I shut myself in the apartment with only the news stations for company. It had become habit. I expected another story about Oscar's, but an accident on the freeway took the news coverage instead. Not that I was happy for a massive accident, but I was relieved to have something else take the spotlight for a while. Keaton said there were still one or two reporters stationed outside the building, but interest in the shooting was finally starting to wane.

I thought about my life going back to normal as I dozed on the couch. What *was* normal now? Did it exist? Knocking at the door woke me up, and I jumped up, opening the door to

Keaton.

"You look better today," she said as she came inside, sitting on the couch.

"I *feel* better," I replied, sitting down beside her. I didn't have it in me to tell her why though.

Her face twisted, and I had the idea she wasn't visiting to visit. "I've got some news."

"Good or bad?" Whenever she started a statement like that, it was usually *bad* news.

"They opened the store today."

I downplayed it, pretending that I had already known, but inside, I was hurt. They opened the store and didn't tell me? What did this mean? Was I fired? I had been sure I would've been one of the first that Mr. Waters called. I never considered the possibility that he didn't *want* me back.

"Oh, yeah, I go in later on in the week," I said quickly. Too quickly.

Keaton narrowed her eyes. "Are you okay?"

"I'm fine. I...I think I need a nap, okay?"

She put on a small smile, and I couldn't tell if it was real or not. "Okay. I'll stop back in later."

I waited for her to leave the apartment before I holed myself in my room. Why would Mr. Waters not call me back? I had been one of his best employees. Despite my reluctance to socialize, I had won employee of the month several times.

I opened my laptop, determined to find out *when* the store had reopened and realized that my online immunity disappeared too. Samuel had left a new IM for me: *Ha, ha, loser. Serves you right.*

How did he know?

Life was truly unfair, and now, I was beginning to see it. Mom was home, but I had seen her cart the bottle of red wine into her room about an hour before Keaton's visit. With any luck, she'd be out cold right now.

I could've cried if my body had any interest in obeying me. I almost wished I would because afterward, I would be numb.

I never went to sleep, and when Keaton came back a couple hours later, she called me on it. "It's not healthy what you're doing to yourself. We should go out. Play laser tag or something."

I cast her looks over the top of my laptop as I searched through my emails. Leaving was the last thing I wanted, but I agreed for the sake of avoiding an argument. "Yeah, maybe."

"What are you looking at over there?" she asked, plopping down beside me.

"Going through my email," I replied, selecting a bunch of them to move to my trash folder.

"Those aren't from Samuel, are they?"

"No. I still haven't heard from him," I lied. "They're emails from reporters wanting interviews about what happened."

Keaton grasped my hand before I could press the button to delete them. "Hold on."

"What? Why?"

"You should do one. Tell your side of the story."

I couldn't believe she'd make the suggestion. "That's the worst idea I've ever heard."

"Why? There's still a lot of speculation. An interview

would give you a chance to say your piece, to clear the air. It would let you get your story out there. That way people have a chance to see you without Samuel's filter."

She was right, of course, but the thought of being in a cozy little room under a spotlight with layers of makeup made my skin crawl. The questions wouldn't be easy. They would be like a dozen needles being jabbed into the spaces between my ribs, but I would be *seen*.

"Plus, the money wouldn't be bad either," she said after skimming through the contents of one of the emails.

"I don't know, Keaton. What if they're really hard questions?"

"I can help you practice if you want," she offered.

"You really think this is a good idea?"

"I don't know either way but not everyone gets chances like this. You wanted the world to know what a piece of garbage Samuel was, and there's no better opportunity than this."

My face didn't change expression as I hit the reply button.

Keaton leaned forward as I started to type, reading my every word. "I know you're not *thrilled* to do this," she said before I could hit send, "but you got to make them think you've got *some* interest."

"Why?" I asked, not caring what interpretation they had of me. "They sent *me* an email, remember?"

"Yeah, but these are the people responsible for deciding what parts of your interview go public and which don't."

Indecision wavered in the pit of my stomach again. Didn't it make more sense to air the entire thing? "Why break it up?"

"Not saying they will, but if they do, it'd be in your best interest to stay on their good side."

"Yeah, I guess."

Keaton curled her fingers, and I passed her the laptop. In a few quick strokes, she typed up a perfectly professional response before hitting send.

I stared at the little *message sent successfully* icon. "What now?"

"We wait," she said and closed the laptop.

"Okay," I replied, part of me hoping I *never* got a response.

A knocked sounded at the door, and Keaton blinked. "Well, that was fast."

"I doubt it's them," I said, moving to get up.

Keaton waved me to sit back down, and I obeyed as she trotted over to the door. She pulled it open a crack like she was ready to slam it closed. A second later, she opened the door all the way, revealing a detective on the other side. My heart did the weird little skip it did when I assumed a situation would go horribly wrong. Officer Stone had said to expect a visit in a few days, but it had been *weeks*.

"Good afternoon, Jess," the woman said, sitting in the armchair Keaton had been in. She had straight black hair that framed her pale face, her steel-colored eyes her most prominent feature as she pinned me with her stare. "My name is Detective Morgan. I'm here to follow up on the events from a few weeks ago."

I glanced toward the door, but Keaton had taken the

opportunity to slip away. Whatever happened next, I would have to face alone.

"Afternoon," I said stiffly.

"How are you today?" she asked.

"Better," I said, keeping my eyes away from hers.

"That's good," she said, pulling her lips to the side as the silence grew awkward. "I've got some good news for you. You've officially been cleared as a suspect. From everything we gathered, Oscar acted alone."

I said nothing again. The word *alone* resonated with something in me, bouncing around the inside my head. I thought of his tiny niche in the columbarium, one section up from his sister.

Alone. That was my future too.

Chapter Eighteen

AFTER THE VIGIL and the funerals and the interaction with Oscar's relatives, I had never felt closer to death than I did that next morning. Emotions had always been difficult to understand, but now it was as if they had a physical weight. They settled into my stomach like rocks, weighing me down every time I tried to move.

I should've been happy that I was officially cleared as a suspect, but it wasn't an emotion I could use. I was ready to surrender and make a vow to never leave the apartment again. In the ironic story of my life, that was the moment the responsibilities I had been avoiding came back to bite me on the ass. When I saw Mr. Waters' name pop up on my caller ID, my first instinct was to ignore the call.

This was probably a pity call explaining why I hadn't been asked to come back, and I was in no mood to listen. They didn't want me? That was fine, I could find another job. I eyed it until it stopped ringing, and my phone beeped, announcing the presence of a new voicemail.

Damn.

My curiosity urged me to open it against the part of my brain that told me to delete it.

"Hi, Jess, it's Mr. Waters. I wanted to see if you were ready to come back to work. Talk to you soon."

"Oh," I said to no one, feeling dumb for my choice to not answer.

I dialed him back. "Mr. Waters, you called?"

"Jess, hi. Yes. How are you?"

"Fine," I said, mentally willing him to move the conversation forward.

"That's good. I don't know if you've heard, but the store has reopened. If you're ready, I would love to see if you could come in for the evening shift tonight."

"Yeah, that's fine," I said.

"Are you sure?" he asked. "If it's too soon, I don't mind giving you a few more days."

"Don't need them. See you in a few hours," I said, and hung up the phone before he could try to make me change my mind. For some reason beyond my understanding, I was *excited* to go back, to show Samuel that once again, he hadn't beaten me.

My first move was to screenshot the call. I opened my I.M. chat, sending the picture to the last anonymous account. *Suck on that.* The tiny *read* appeared instantly, but the response never came. I grinned like a jackass though if I was being honest, I hadn't *wanted* my job back. If I refused the offer and quit, however, it would be handing Samuel a victory on a silver platter.

And I would never let that happen.

Against the voices in my head, I got myself ready. It was strange to dress in my work uniform after ignoring its presence for all this time. Holing up in the house meant I hadn't had to worry about my appearance. My clothes were stained and stiff with sweat. Today, that would have to change. I hopped in the shower, feeling better now that I was clean, and when I finally stumbled out to the living room to put on my shoes, my phone pinged with a message from Keaton. Stunned by the sound of me up and about, Mom emerged from her room, standing at the edge of the hall to stare at me.

"Were you talking to someone?" she asked.

"Yeah, Mr. Waters called. He wants me to come back to work."

"So soon?"

It seemed long enough to me. "Two weeks is enough. I'm going in. I already told him I'd be there."

"Well, it's good you're focused."

I scowled. She was only focusing on the positives to help avoid confrontation. I hated it. Hated everything about her passive aggressive attitude.

"Yeah, it's better than hiding from my problems," I said pointedly.

Mom either didn't realize the shot was directed at her or she chose to ignore it. "Would you like me to drive you?"

"No," I said quickly, voice sharp. Truth was, I didn't know *why* I was angry. "No, that's okay. The exercise will be good for me."

I couldn't quite tell if I had hurt her feelings or not. If I had, she wouldn't tell me anyway. She would wait until I left to find her pills. "Alright. Be careful, okay?"

"Okay."

That was something she never had to tell me. My anxiety made sure I was on guard, even when there was no danger. I slipped out the door, closing it quickly behind me.

"I didn't think you ever passed this point on your own," Keaton's voice said from behind me. I looked over my shoulder to see her. Her hands were tucked into the pockets of her green army jacket as she descended two steps to flank me.

"I'm going back to work today," I told her as we walked down the rest of the stairs together. I was pleased to see no reporters outside of the building. There were still pieces of trash and brown patches of grass where they had camped out. In a rare moment of bliss, I pulled my phone out and snapped a picture.

"It really is a beautiful sight," Keaton remarked and paused as we passed the parking lot, eyes on her car. "Want a ride?"

I considered it, but the feeling of freedom was large and welcome. I wanted to walk, to take the bus, to prove that I could still live my regular life after all the horrors. "No, I'm gonna walk today."

"You're sure?"

I thought about it for another minute. "Yeah, I'm sure."

"Suit yourself," she said. "Text me later, and let me know how it goes."

"Will do!" I called, watching her climb into her car before I continued on my way.

The walk was uplifting, like I was making the right choice by challenging myself. When I made it to the bus stop, that confidence drained away. I hadn't had to worry about taking a bus in over two weeks, and I didn't know how people would react to me. I had a moment of weakness where I wished I would've said yes to Keaton's offer, but I pushed it away.

If I were going to go back, I wanted to go back strong. I climbed up the steps and sat in the first available seat. The points and stares were muted. People noticed me—that would probably be the case for a while—but at least no one moved seats or openly insulted me.

So far so good, I told myself when the bus approached my stop.

I got off, readjusting my grip on my backpack strap as I made my way around the block. I stopped for coffee. Something I *never* did. When I stepped out of the cozy little shop, the Grocer's Way sign was a beacon. Standing outside the place where it had all happened made everything suddenly real. In the back of my mind came flashes from the day of the shooting— the crowd, me being led out in handcuffs, the sounds of the ambulances.

I blinked hard until the images cleared back to a normal parking lot. In all my pondering, my feet betrayed me, and I walked through the sliding glass doors before I was mentally ready to do so.

I expected the same kind of treatment from my coworkers that I always received—passing glances and harassment from Samuel. Carmine offered me a small smile, and Harlow openly waved, grinning wide. The other cashiers offered the same attention.

Gradually, my guard started to lower. Samuel couldn't convince *all* these people to be nice to me, right? These people were *happy* to see me, and I appreciated the warmth of belonging. Even if it was fleeting. And who knew, maybe it wasn't fake. Maybe they were generally appreciative for what I had done.

Samuel, standing at the end of the aisle nearest to the registers, did *not* greet me with warmth. A cruel malicious smile spread across his face as I tried to squeeze past him. "Well, well. Looks as if the prodigal daughter has returned. Oh, how I've missed you."

I didn't acknowledge his comment as I went to the employee lounge. It took effort to avoid looking at Mr. Waters' office on the way, and I forced myself to focus on the now.

There were no gifts from Samuel in my locker, but I attributed that to him not knowing I was coming back rather than a sudden change of heart. On my way back to the floor, I passed Mr. Waters who was heading toward his office.

"Good to have you back, Jessica," he said, clapping his hand on my shoulder.

"Good to be back."

Mr. Waters nodded as if I had said something profound and went about his way.

On any usual day, I tried to avoid eye contact at all times because I wasn't in the mood to be noticed. Today, though, I would be a fool to think I wouldn't be. My best bet was to meet the attention head on, to be *ready* for it. So, I did just that. I kept my head up, my eyes locking back onto whoever dared look at me. And surprisingly, it worked. People didn't look for long under my reciprocating gaze. When I didn't make my weakness apparent, I intimidated people. That was information I filed away, sure that I would be able to use it at another time.

I made the mistake of going down Samuel's aisle again. He stared as if he expected me to double back and go a different route. Any other day, I might have, but I had already come so far. I was here to make a point. My steps were slow and deliberate as I passed him, making sure to kick one of his boxes for added effect. He sneered and set down his can on the shelf before he reached toward me, hand caressing my shoulder.

"You must want my attention," he whispered.

I smacked it away, and he grinned. I backed down the rest of the aisle and watched from my peripheral when I turned my back to close the gap to the registers.

Taking my place, I spared a moment to watch him with his guard down as he went back to work. He looked so normal that even *I* had a moment where I doubted he was the one to take pictures of me, to send me vicious texts, to stalk me.

How much of the darkness did *he* possess?

Chapter Nineteen

THE DAY ENDED without incident. Every time I left my register to go to the bathroom or went to the employee lounge for a break, I expected Samuel to corner me or to find something foul in my locker, but he kept to himself. I hadn't known he was capable of such a thing.

I was happy. So happy, in fact, that I kept my head up all through the shift. None of the customers really commented much on the shooting, and I counted that as a win.

When closing time approached, the other cashier on the floor with me, Dawn, a newbie, crossed the front to stand beside me. She was a tiny thing with long limbs, short black hair, and heavy red lipstick. I finished ringing up my customer, pretending to not notice she was close. When my customer walked away though, it became harder.

I was almost certain she was delivering a message on behalf of Samuel. Why else would she insist on talking to me? "Hey," she said when we made eye contact.

"What's up?" I said, searching for paper towels to clean my register.

"I wanted to say what you did must've been hard, and I give my condolences for Oscar."

Condolences for Oscar? No one but his family had been willing to pass those along. Further convinced that this was a mind game that Samuel was playing, I said the simplest response I could, "Thanks," and walked away to work on something else.

Dawn took the cue and went to clean her own register. Needless to say, I was relieved when it was time to leave. After the entire day of taking on a different persona, I was worried it might stick.

As I started to walk home, I pulled my phone out and saw a few missed calls from Chelsea. I narrowed my eyes, wondering what else she could have to say to me that hadn't already been said in our last meeting. They wanted me away from the school, and I hadn't gone back. Chealsea calling now made no sense. She'd left no voicemail to boot.

I would have to call her back in the morning to see what she wanted.

The bus stop was quiet, and I stared up at the dark sky as I waited, wishing I could have a moment of peace, just one where I wasn't worried about something or angry.

The hairs on the back of my neck stood up. I had the sensation of being watched. I scanned the entire area around me, but there wasn't anyone else at the stop. For all the times I'd stood here alone, I had never stopped to consider that I might *not* be alone, that someone might be watching. It almost seemed ridiculous, but in the wake of all that had happened these past few weeks, I was willing to believe anything.

I glanced over my shoulder, into the shifting darkness. *It's all in your head,* I told myself. Before my paranoia could get the best of me, the bus arrived, and I shuffled on. There were only a handful of other passengers, but I made sure to pick a seat that was as far away from any of them as I could. I glanced out the window before I sat down, catching the outline of a shadowy figure moving behind the glass wall of the bus shelter. I fell to the seat with a thump, trying to settle my heart.

You're seeing things.

The ride was quiet, and I was the only one to get off at the stop near my apartments. Clutching the strap of my backpack tighter, I started to circle around the block and froze. That sensation of being watched was here too.

Something is wrong, my gut screamed at me.

Imaginary alarm bells ringing, I suddenly didn't care who could see me. I took off like a bolt of lightning, closing the remaining distance between me and home. I didn't stop running until I was up the stairs. Keys in hand, I hurried to undo the lock, and stepped inside, panting as I closed the door behind me.

Keaton was already here, sitting in the armchair in the living room with the television going. When the door slammed, she jumped up and rushed to me. "Are you okay?" she asked, moving a stubborn lock of hair that had embedded itself in the sweat on my forehead.

"Yeah, fine. There was a ugh…loose dog out." There was no way I was going to tell her I was playing games with my shadow. She was probably the last person who actually respected me, and admitting my own human weaknesses seemed like the kind of thing that could change that.

"Oh." She looked me over. "How was work? Samuel keep his hands to himself?"

"Work was fine." I paused. "I'm sorry, Keaton. I totally

forgot about grabbing something for dinner."

Keaton waved a hand and laughed. "Dude, you're fine. I went and got a burger an hour ago. But tell me everything. It was *really* okay? You're not just saying that?"

I let my bag slump to the floor. "Yes. It was fine."

"Fine?"

I scratched the back of my neck. "Okay. It was…*weird.* You know those dreams you have where it feels like an alternate version of reality? That's kind of how today was. Everyone was *treating* me differently. I kept thinking I'd wake up and none of it would be real."

"I'm sure you handled it just fine. But you should've let me drive you!" She swatted my arm. "I would've gone in with you for moral support."

I stared into her eyes. Before everything, that would've been my go-to move. Stressful situations were easier to tackle with Keaton by my side, but today went smoothly with me operating completely alone—except for the trip home of course. "It was okay, really," I insisted. "Nothing happened."

"Good," she said though the twinkle in her eyes made me sure she knew I was lying.

KEATON AND I talked for a while, and when it hit midnight, she finally decided to go home to get some sleep. I did the same, tossing and turning most of the night. I had the acute feeling that if I let myself drift into a deep sleep, I would have to struggle with my sleep paralysis upon waking, and I didn't know if I was ready for that.

I kept glancing toward my laptop in the corner of the room, thinking of the shadowy figure I had seen outside the bus. If Samuel had been following me, would he admit it? With tired eyes, I opened the computer, scrolling to the IM thread.

You think you can hide in the shadows? he wrote.

I wrote nothing back. I closed the laptop and got up, peeking through the curtain. I didn't see anyone outside, but I was too on edge to attempt to sleep again. Exhausted, I started my day much earlier than I normally would've. The apartment was quiet and dark as I drank the biggest cup of coffee I could make. I watched TV for a little bit then sought out my phone, staring at Chelsea's number without dialing.

I didn't think about the fact that it might be way too early before I hit the call button. I was too determined to get this over with. It rang and rang. I redialed every time it went to voicemail. After the first four or five calls yielded no results, I put the phone down and made myself breakfast as a means of distraction. I sat down in front of the television, the news on once again. There was nothing about me or Oscar or the shooting, and I was relieved.

When enough time passed, I gave Chelsea another call, this time getting a response.

"Hello?" she said at last.

"It's Jess, returning your call."

"Ah, yes, Jessica," Chelsea said, professionalism slipping over her exhaustion like a glove. "How are you?"

"Fine," I said, giving her the same automatic response I gave everyone. "Did you need something from me?"

"Yes, of course," she said. It sounded as if she were

ruffling through papers. "The Dean wanted to see if you would like to come back to class this week."

"Oh, yeah? Why now?" When college had been the last thing I had left to distract me from the horror show of my life, they hadn't wanted me there and part of me was still hurt by the decision.

Chelsea was silent.

Defeated, I said, "I'll be there."

"Okay. If you have the time today, I need you to come down to my office to sign a few papers first."

"Why? I didn't sign any to go *on* leave," I said, thinking vaguely of the confrontation in the cafeteria.

"Well, you were supposed to but..." she trailed off.

"Fine," I said again, not wanting to rehash my meltdown. I already had a good enough memory of it.

"Good." She paused then reluctantly added, "If it's too soon, I can tell the Dean next week."

After two weeks of being away, I was most likely behind in all my classes. Passing them now would be a difficult feat. Adding more time would only make it harder.

"No. I *want* to come back," I insisted. She didn't know what I needed. No one *truly* knew what I needed. They all made assumptions with nothing to back them up.

"Okay," she said, and the sound of shuffling paperwork came through the phone again. "Will two o'clock work for you?"

I glanced at the clock. I had work at three. I could do both, but that meant I'd have to drive.

I was facing everything else head on. Might as well do the same for this. I thought of the shadowy figure by the bus stop again. Driving would eliminate the possibility of being followed.

For today at least.

"Sure, see you then," I said and hung up.

Chapter Twenty

I T HAD BEEN a long time since I was last behind the wheel of a car. I was so nervous about having to drive that I didn't ask Mom if she had anywhere to be today. I did a full minute of breathing exercises as I started up the ugly red thing. On the road, my driving was sporadic at best, distracted at the worst, but I made it to campus without getting a ticket. I counted that as a win.

I didn't look forward to the meeting with Chelsea, but I reminded myself it would be ten minutes of my life. If I couldn't get through that without losing my mind, then I had some serious issues to work on.

I parked, a little over the line but not enough to make a scene or have someone leave a nasty note. Chelsea's office was on the outskirts of college grounds, near the library. It was really the only part of campus I enjoyed. Since it was much farther from the rest of the buildings, it had significantly less foot traffic.

Less people always made me happy.

I pushed my way inside her office. There was a tiny waiting room and Chelsea's desk separated from a flimsy plastic chair by a divider. When she saw me, she waved me over.

"Good timing, Miss Mills," she said, gesturing for me to

take a seat.

"Thanks," I replied, sitting down before she passed me a stack of papers through the gap in the partition. "Why so much?" I asked, thumbing through it. I made a show of checking the time. "This seems excessive."

"These are some class adjustments and financial forms."

I went to work signing as she explained each one. I put the top two packets aside and stopped at the third. "Liability waiver?" I asked and held it up. "What's this for?"

"Well, in light of recent circumstances, the Dean thought it best that the campus not be held responsible if well… if something were to happen to you."

My mouth went dry. "So, you're saying if I get hurt you won't help me?"

"No, no," she said, frantically waving her hands in a way that reminded me of a bird learning to fly. "We would help, of course, but we wouldn't be *responsible.*"

"Wonderful," I remarked, staring at the blank signature line. *Samuel himself couldn't have drafted up something more insulting.* "And what happens if I don't sign it?"

"Then I'm sad to say the Dean won't let you come back to the University."

"This is a joke, right?"

"No, Miss Mills, I'm afraid not. Those were the requirements passed to me."

I stared up at the ceiling in an attempt to calm myself down. "So…sell my soul or forfeit my scholarship? Okay." I angrily jotted my name on the line. "What next? You need me to sign in blood? Or maybe you need a kidney since I already sold my soul."

Chelsea took a breath, a mix of uncertainty and fear. "I understand why you're upset, but we're trying to take all necessary precautions. It's nothing against you."

I was dangerously close to breaking down, and if I let myself slip, I wouldn't be able to come back. "That's not how it feels," I said, but I didn't look at her again. I didn't think I had it in me. I forced my shaking hand to scrawl my signature on the rest of the documents, making sure to not read any more.

I was better off not knowing.

***

"THEY MADE YOU sign *what?*" Keaton's voice blared through the speakers as I drove from campus to work.

"A waiver. If someone happens to hurt me when I'm at school, they won't be to blame."

"That's terrible. As a student, it's their job to keep you safe," she said. "How could they think anyone would want to go to their school after being treated like that? Especially after what happened there last year."

I felt sick when I thought of Molly. "As of this afternoon, it's officially not their job. If Samuel wants to hurt me, all he has to do is come find me at school."

"They're wrong for that," Keaton said.

"Maybe, but what can I do?"

"I think you should do an interview and sway the public in your favor. Make people less likely to *want* to hurt you."

"I know. I know. We sent the email, remember? I never

got a response," I said, making a mental note to check my spam folder when I got home in case they *did* respond and in all my infinite luck it had gotten lost along the way.

"If I were you, I'd try a few other offers. Better than putting all your eggs in one basket."

"Yeah, maybe," I said, pulling into the parking lot outside of Grocer's Way. "But listen, I just pulled into work."

"Okay. Be careful. Talk to you later," Keaton said and hung up as I switched the engine off.

I sat in the car, staring out the windshield for a long minute before I worked up the courage to get out and go inside with my head down.

"Hey there!" Harlow called. I pretended to be happy to see her as she trotted up to me. She was tall and thin with hair the color of caramel cut short and spiked. I stared at it rather than make eye contact "How're you doing today?" she asked.

"Fine," I said, walking faster.

We zigzagged through the lines and that was when I saw Samuel glowering at us from a few aisles away. If he was that unhappy then he wasn't responsible for Harlow. I expected him to make an excuse to join us, to eavesdrop on the conversation, but as we passed, he continued to work.

I took note of that. I might not really care for Harlow, but she had never done wrong by me, and if she meant protection from him, then I could endure whatever conversation she wanted to had.

"How are you?" I forced myself to ask, not wanting her to leave.

"Great! My little brother and I..." Inside my mind, her

voice faded to nothing as she continued to babble. I glanced over my shoulder, expecting to see Samuel lurking in the shadows.

He didn't follow. I wanted to hug Harlow for this magic, but she wouldn't understand. I gave her a crooked smile that must've come off as strange, but she didn't comment on it. By the time we got back to the front of the store, Samuel was gone.

"I'll let you get to work," Harlow said, taking her own place at the register.

On instinct, I glanced to Oscar's favorite register and wondered when I would stop doing that, stop expecting to see some glimpse of him. I lost myself in work after that, glad for the monotony to keep me busy.

"Jess?" Harlow's voice drifted into my ears an hour or two later.

"Huh?" I asked, startling out of my thoughts.

"I didn't mean to scare you. I was wondering if you've seen Samuel."

"No."

"Huh, that's weird," Harlow said, pulling out her phone. "He was supposed to meet me for lunch."

"Weird," I said, voice flat as I tried to keep my true feelings from showing.

Harlow didn't notice as she typed out a message. "I'll have to get to the bottom of this."

I didn't bother to say that it didn't matter to me where he was or if he took her to lunch. I rang up another customer, and after she left, Harlow's phone beeped. She pulled it out of her pocket.

"I guess he went home," she said. "Claims he wasn't feeling too well. Oh, well. Do *you* want to come to lunch with me?"

My spirits lifted. Not at the invitation, but the thought that I had upset Samuel so much he couldn't think of a counterstrike. He'd had to disengage completely. While today might've had a shitty beginning, it was starting to look up.

THE REST OF the day went with no taunts, and it gave me a good insight into what my other coworkers felt toward me. Harlow stayed by my side, filling the spot that Oscar had once held. She paid for my lunch too, and I wasn't sure what the appropriate response was. I wasn't used to people showing me kindness.

One thing became clear though: my coworkers had never hated me. It had been my anxiety convincing me they did. Now that they had broken through my outside shield, I could truly see them. It was nice. *They* were nice. Maybe *Samuel* hated me, but they didn't.

I stayed at work later than I usually did, hoping to make up a few hours for all the pay I had lost over the last two weeks. I was the last one there, Harlow bidding me farewell at least an hour before.

"Time to call it a night," Mr. Waters called to me from his place by the door.

I looked up from the register I had been carefully cleaning, so lost in my thoughts that I hadn't been aware of how late it really was. "I can finish cleaning this if you want."

"Nah. You've put in a solid day," he said, pushing open the door.

"Okay," I said, setting down the spray bottle and rag right where I had stood. I grabbed my belongings from my locker and hurried outside. Mr. Waters locked the door behind us.

"Thank you for putting in the time today," he said as he walked beside me to the parking lot.

"No problem," I said. "Thank you for having me back. It couldn't have been an easy choice."

"You're joking, right? Jess, that was the easiest decision of my life."

"Really?"

"Yes, you're a godsend in today's day and age. It's never easy to be strong, but you do it well."

My bottom lip trembled as Oscar's words floated through my head. *Never change.*

"Have a good night, okay?" he added. I didn't move, unsure of what to do after a sentimental moment like that. Mr. Waters paused as if he wasn't sure he should leave me alone. "Do you need a ride?"

I glanced across the lot to the little red sedan. "No, I've got my mom's car. Thank you though."

"Okay, be safe," he said and climbed into his car.

He drove away, and I didn't think about his parting comment. Everything was looking up or maybe it was just that this was my first run with rose-colored glasses. Either way, I took my next step with my head held high. I felt bold, almost brand new. Tucking my hands into my pockets, I started to walk across the parking lot, observing the shadows on the side of the building when footsteps echoed behind me.

Chapter Twenty-One

I TURNED IN time to avoid a brick being lodged into the back of my skull. It clashed against the building, sending dust and tiny chunks of stone into the air. I hopped backward, brain rushing to process what was happening. In what felt like slow motion, my eyes moved from the brick, up the perpetrator's arm to the face—Samuel. His eyes were black under the brim of his hood, pupils wider than I had ever seen them. I recognized the glazed, distant look. He was under the influence of *something,* and that wasn't good for me.

"What the hell is your problem?" I demanded.

I was afraid, but I was also angry. So angry that the brick still in his hand, hanging at his side, wasn't taken into the picture. I didn't think about it as a source of danger, that he could swing it again at any minute and cave my skull in.

"You. You are my problem," he said, voice angry though his face didn't reflect the emotion. "You really think you're all that, don't you? As if it's not bad enough that you embarrass me by reminding me I wasn't good enough for you every day, now you're stealing my friends too?"

I stared, confused, trying to make sense of his delusional brain.

"I saw Harlow talking to you today," he sneered. "I think you went out of your way to make sure I did."

"So what? Doesn't mean she's going to be my best friend now. I saved her life is all. Saved *yours* too if I remember correctly. She's thankful. She's still *your* friend. She cried half the day about you ditching her for lunch."

"You're not content taking a man's pride. That's the problem with women. They think they can treat a good man however they want. Take his heart and crush it to a million pieces."

"Really? You think you of all people are a 'good man'?" I wanted to laugh until I cried.

"I know I am. Before you came into my life, things were perfect. I never…felt so much resentment."

"Your sense of entitlement is off-putting. Don't you get that? We could've been friends if you hadn't assumed that you deserved more. If you didn't think of me as some object, we could've been closer than that. But no, not you. You're not satisfied unless you stick your dick in everything. Amiright?"

He laughed. "I don't know what it is, but something about you brings out the worst in me. I have this need to make you suffer, to hurt."

"That's because you're a psychopath. Believe it or not, what you want to do to me has nothing to do with *me*. It's all to do with whatever screws are loose in your head. I did nothing to you, and if you can convince yourself otherwise, then *you* need help."

"No. I *need* something else ," he said and swung the brick. "I need you to disappear from my life."

I stepped backward out of the way. "If this is your attempt to scare me, it's not going to work. I'm not going to go away because you tell me to. I've been an outsider my entire life. I was bullied in middle school, high school, you name it. You think some pictures and threats are going to be enough to get me to uproot my entire life? I *thrive* on the pain."

"You were in on it. The shooting," Samuel said, shaking a finger at me. "You and that Oscar freak have always been fucked up. His sister was too."

The comment caught me off guard. "You knew Molly?"

Samuel ignored me, continuing his rant. "Everyone thinks you're a hero for what you did, well, they'll think I'm a God for what I'm about to do to you!" An animalistic sound ripped through his chest as he lunged toward me. While Samuel wasn't a *big,* big guy, he was still much larger than me.

Panic bloomed in my stomach as I dodged him. I didn't realize I had begun to back down the alley leading away from the parking lot until the walls appeared on both sides of my vision. If I wanted freedom, I would have to go past Samuel, and the only way I could do that would be to talk him down…or *take* him down. My eyes went to the brick. If I could disarm him, I could run.

"Why do you assume they'd cheer?" I asked, trying to distract him long enough to find a way out of this situation.

"I hacked your computer," Samuel said. I met his eye as he continued, "How did you think I got all those pictures? Uninhibited access to your webcam. You watch sick, sick shit. Everyone thinks you're this sweet shy girl, but you're not. I've seen *you,* the you that you are when you don't think anyone is around."

"What does it matter? I've never hurt anyone."

"Except Oscar, yeah? There's no telling if he was your first victim or not. You have skeletons, possibly real ones, and I am determined to get to the bottom of it."

"By killing me? Let me know how that works out."

Samuel lifted the brick. "Oh, sweetheart, it wouldn't be my first time."

My adrenaline surged, my mouth filled with saliva. I wasn't going to be able to talk him down. He was determined to go through with it.

It wouldn't be my first time.

My brain clicked. "It was you," I spluttered. "*You* killed Molly."

I'd assumed that Oscar hated Samuel for the way he picked on me and him. I'd never thought there was more to the story.

"And would you look at that? Now I have a *reason* to kill you," Samuel said, lunging forward to grab me by the shoulder as the hand with the brick came toward me. I grabbed his wrist before it could hit me, and he dropped it, shattering to pieces when it hit the ground. The hand on my shoulder pinched into my skin, and I screamed, letting go. Before I could do more than that, he grabbed me, fingers scratching my collarbone as he ripped my shirt, buttons clattering to the cement.

I gasped and tried to pull the knife from my pocket. The clip caught on my pants, and I tugged uselessly. Samuel was faster than me, taking the blade from my fingers and slinging it open with such precision that I wondered if he had practiced for this moment.

"What're you going to do with this?" he purred and laughed, pointing the blade toward me. "Thank you for making this easier."

I stared at the blade. The same one that had killed Oscar and thought how ironic it would be to be killed with it too. Samuel reared his arm back, and I jolted to action.

Fight knocked out of the equation, I tried to run. Maybe when it came down to it, I wasn't built for the whole serial killer thing. I was terrified, brain working hard to process my surroundings. I saw everything in a series of blacks and whites. Samuel's steps thundered behind me, but I started to think I would get away.

Somehow, someway, I *had* to. It couldn't end like this…not in a dark alley. Not by *his* hands.

Then the alleyway curved and ended, a sudden wall of stone blocking my path. Samuel's laughter blasted around the confined space, each beat in rhythm to the frantic pounding of my heart. He stopped running. I backed up until my hands patted the bricks, trying not to let my panic overwhelm me. He took steady step after steady step until he was only an arm's length away.

"Looks like it's you and me," he said. "Who's gonna save you now?"

Tears on my face, I forced my body to relax, waiting for him to come closer. Fighting would get me hurt. I was smart enough to know that.

Play the part, I told myself.

Against the voices screaming in my head, I stood still as

he sniffed my hair. He took another step closer, his body pressing to mine. Uncomfortable electric shocks rocked through me, each one a warning of impending danger.

He rested my knife against the side of my throat as the fingers on his other hand explored the waistband of my pants. I swallowed back bile, trying my best to seem compliant. I reached a shaking hand up to caress his chest, waiting to make sure he noticed it. When his lips pressed to the skin on my neck, I slid my hand back toward myself, taking the chance to slip the knife from my bra. Before he realized his mistake, I plunged the tiny blade into the left side of his chest, exactly where I had felt his heart beating a moment before.

At first, nothing happened, and I wondered if I hadn't pushed it in deep enough. He reached up with shaking fingers but didn't pull it out. His face went as white as the moon, blood dripping from his mouth.

I tried to take another step backward, conscious of the knife in his hand, but he didn't swing. He stood frozen, the trickle of blood a torrent that stained his shirt. I made eye contact with him as he collapsed to the ground, gasping for breath. Over the sounds of my stifled crying, it was hard to hear. I stared him down as he lay on the ground, puddle of blood around him. His breath grew weaker and weaker, but he managed to pull the blade out a second before the ragged gasps stopped altogether.

I could've called 911 at any time during that struggle, but I didn't. It didn't come to mind. All I could think was that I wanted the moment to be over, wanted to run away and never look back. I wanted him to die. If what he'd said was true, he *deserved* to die.

Samuel was dead.

I had killed him.

There was blood literally on my hands.

I focused on the lights buzzing at the far end of the alley. Everything was hyper real. Colors more vivid, senses more pronounced. The smell of Samuel's blood stirred something in me, the same monster from the shooting, and suddenly, any and all emotional thoughts were gone. The darkness was taking over again, but this time, I was glad. For all I had read about serial killers and murders, I was clueless when it came to firsthand experience.

Samuel's eyes were open, staring up at me, and I could've sworn that even in death he cursed my name.

I looked around. There were no witnesses as far as I could tell. The last person out of the store had been Mr. Waters, and he had left a considerable amount of time ago. I moved my eyes up and down the alley but didn't see any cameras. From what I could tell, it was me and a dead body.

My mind kicked into overdrive, listing every possible choice I could make next. It wasn't too late to go to the police. I could call them, tell my side of the story, and see what happened. I would be guaranteed a manslaughter charge at least, murder at the most. It was risky, perhaps *too* risky. I had acted in self-defense, but there were no promises the police would see it that way.

I couldn't *prove* it was self-defense this time. Not to mention that the work Samuel had done of breaking down my reputation would work against me. Who would believe me murdering two boys in a relatively short amount of time was due to self-defense?

Serial killers were often successful because their victims were strangers, people who had little to no connection to themselves. Samuel and Oscar had been known parts of my life. I could nearly *read* the thread on Samuel's website. It didn't matter how I looked at this, it ended badly for me. The question was, how bad did I want the outcome to be?

I crouched down beside Samuel, staring at the tick in his jaw. He had lived angry and died the same way. *Good riddance,* I thought, running my finger over the bulging muscle.

I could hide a body.

I had spent many years going through true crime documentaries. I knew the best and worst methods. Why was I on the verge of panicking? Hadn't I been preparing for this moment my entire life? It certainly felt like it.

I studied Samuel's body, debating the best way to move him. If I was going to get away with this, I needed to make him disappear, and I needed to do it *fast*. I grabbed him under the arms, the solid bulk of his muscles and the fading warmth of his skin meeting my touch. He was heavier than I imagined he would be. At first, I tried to pick him up, convincing myself that with the adrenaline coursing through my veins I could do it.

Distressed mothers have been known to lift cars. Surely, I could lift a twenty-four-year-old bigot.

I tried again to lift him, muscles straining. I didn't want to admit I wasn't strong enough, but Samuel was a big guy, and dead weight was worse. I wasn't going to be able to lift him myself. In a moment of desperate fury, I half dragged, half-carried Samuel to the end of the alley. I dropped him where he would be out of sight as I did another survey of the environment. It wasn't overly bright. A fact of which I was grateful. I stood there, forcing myself to count to twenty to see if anything would change. No cars passed on the road.

I glanced to Mom's car. The few feet that separated the mouth of the alley and the trunk of her car seemed to stretch into eternity. Could I really make it that far with no one seeing me? Would that be the best move I could make?

Samuel was bleeding a lot. Getting that inside the car would be all the prosecution would need to convict me. I thought of the things Mom had in the trunk—a towel from our last beach trip, a cover for the windshield, a toolkit—nothing I would really consider helpful. My best bet would be the towel though I knew how identifiable that could be. Hell, fibers from the carpet inside the car could be enough to link us.

I glanced back to the store wishing Mr. Waters had let me lock up alone. I became aware of my shirt, and I half-heartedly tried to rebutton the pieces that were left, but it did little to hold it together. I clutched the sides in my fist and ran to the car, heart pounding again. A little voice reminded me that anyone could come up at any time and see me, see *him,* and it'd be over.

Stay calm, I told myself as I fiddled with the keys.

It had the opposite effect as I pushed the button, popping open the trunk. With forcibly slow steps, I walked over to the back of the car, nearly squealing in delight. There was a tarp inside from Mom's last hiking trip.

Thank God for extroverts, I thought and pulled it out. I gave another glance to the road before darting into the mouth of the alley.

"Okay, Sammy," I said to Samuel as I began to wrap it around him. "Found you a nice blanket."

The thump of his body as I rolled him over and over came across louder than it actually was. I didn't slow my work until the tarp was safely secured around him. He laid on his stomach, and I was glad for that as I bent down, trying to lift him again. It didn't work. Uttering a silent prayer, I dragged him as quickly as I could out of the safety of the alley and into the open.

Then, I realized a new problem I had. To get him in the car, I would *have* to lift him. There was no way around it. It wasn't as if I could go out and ask someone to help. I wrapped myself around him, suddenly not caring how much of his blood I got on me. Clothes could be thrown away. The moment if I got caught could not. I stood up. Pain shot through me from the strain of my back muscles, and I feared I would drop him, but I fought against it and kept lifting.

Somehow, I thrust him inside.

I barely celebrated my success before I closed the trunk and rushed into the driver's seat. With him out of sight, I felt a bit better, but my heart refused to calm. How long could it pound this hard before it gave out?

I took a moment to really look at myself. I was a mess— shirt torn, skin covered with a mix of Samuel's and my own blood, and a chunk of hair missing near my part. I didn't remember him doing that, but I had been so out of my mind that I was sure plenty of moments from tonight would be lost. I did my best to clean myself up, but normal wasn't possible with the frenzied emotion in my eyes.

I wanted to cry. It wasn't the reaction I'd anticipated. Ever since our failed date, I had wished Samuel would disappear.

I should be *happy*. But I wasn't.

Not like this, I thought over and over again.

You don't always get what you want, that cruel little voice in the back of my mind reminded me as I slid the key into the ignition.

Chapter Twenty-Two

FINDING THE PERFECT body drop zone was a lot harder than I imagined it would be. Television serial killers made it look way too easy. On long car trips, Keaton and I had played a game where we would say "This could be a perfect spot to hide a body" anytime we went down a road that seemed particularly isolated or had a lot of trees.

Playing that game by myself with an actual body wasn't as fun. Sure, there were plenty of woods around us—a river too—and they were all spots I used to imagine could hide gruesome secrets, but I didn't like any of them. Now that I had my own secret, none of those places seemed good enough. If I wanted somewhere secluded, the ravine would be my best bet, but it got a lot of foot traffic this time of year.

I can't worry about that now, I told myself, glancing toward the backseat. Though Samuel was carefully tucked away into the trunk, I had the paranoid thought that I would somehow be able to see him.

I put the AC on high, hoping to keep the car incredibly cold, colder than necessary, to off put any possible smell. I drove as carefully as I could manage, doing everything by the book. The last thing I wanted was to get pulled over. I knew all too well how many serial killers were caught because of something small.

When I finally made it to an isolated stretch of woods, I pulled enough off the road to avoid being seen, but not deep enough into the foliage that I'd leave tire tracks in the mud. I maneuvered as close to a bush as I could, peering over the black leaves to the road beyond. I was pretty sure I was hidden here, but I would double check. Things had to be perfect; I'd only have one shot to make it right. After that, it wouldn't be wise to return.

Hyping myself up, I got out of the car and glanced to the road again. It was dead. I crept a few feet away, peering toward the bush and the car. From an angle, the moonlight reflected off the surface of the shiny hood, but for the most part, it could go without being seen. Encouraged, I walked back and knelt down, poking the ground. The recent drought had ensured the dirt was hard and crumbly.

Counting my blessings, I rose to my feet and stared at the trunk. Now would be the time to see how long things kept working in my favor. With a deep breath, and a silent murmur, I popped it open. I already knew what I would see inside, of course, but I still wasn't prepared for it. Samuel's blood smelt stronger in the confined spot—a warm iron that burned all the way up my nostrils. It became overwhelming as I leaned forward, trying to decide the best way to pull him out.

Eyes watering, I held the back of my hand to my mouth, wishing I had something to block out the smell. *This is your punishment,* I told myself before reaching toward the plastic. I was glad he was face down as I wrapped my arms around him. When

I'd put him in the car, I had been able to feel his warmth through the tarp.

Now, I couldn't.

Gagging on the smell, I tried to clear my mind of everything, to focus on nothing, but it was impossible. The ironic little voice in the back of my head said, *If you had touched him like this to start with, none of this would've happened.*

Shut up, I told it, so furious for the spontaneity of the thought that I hoisted Samuel up onto the lip of the trunk. A muscle popped in my back, but I kept going until he rolled out, hitting the ground with an unpleasant thump.

I closed the trunk and looked left and right, wary of witnesses. I wondered what would happen if I saw anyone— would they really notice *him* or *me*—but I didn't let myself dwell on the thought too much. Senses alert for any sound around me, I dragged him, plastic and all, across the leaves and twigs.

The dirt was hard, but the foliage would have a scar that I would have to ensure was gone before I left for the night. The longer I moved, the heavier Samuel seemed to get. I dropped him once on accident and sighed, glancing over my shoulder. In the darkness, it was impossible to see how much farther I had to go to reach the ravine.

Recuperating, I grasped Samuel again, his blood smearing all over my arms up to my elbows, but I ignored it and kept pulling, too emotionally spent to give another thought to what I was doing. I maneuvered him down a hill and through a particularly dense patch of undergrowth before I picked up the sound of rushing water. I pulled Samuel a few more yards before my feet sunk into soft mud. Up ahead, black water rushed past, and I dropped him. Glad for the loss of weight, I sat down beside him, staring up to the sable sky above.

In some weird way, I was at peace. There was something about the blackness that comforted me. It reminded me that in the grand scheme of things, this terrible night was one tiny moment of it. Life would go on. Not for Samuel, of course, but that wasn't a concern of mine.

I glanced to him again. His dead eyes stared up into the same blackness as me. The only difference was he was *part* of it. It filled him in all the places life used to.

"I guess hanging out with you isn't bad," I said, patting the edge of the plastic tarp. "But we've gotta wrap this up."

I gauged the distance of the bank by sound more than sight, and I crawled a few feet away from Samuel, patting the dirt for the softest spots. I plunged my fingers into it, digging up handful after handful of muck. My nails filled with mud, the roots scratching my fingers and up my wrist. Even when the repetitive movement started to hurt, I kept going.

It wasn't as if I'd be able to give him a proper grave like this, but I had no shovel. *Some* sort of burial would be preferable to none at all. After I dug a formidable pit, I dipped my hands into the river water, reveling in the way it felt to have the dirt and blood wash off me. When I pulled my hands out, they were raw, mistreated, and I wondered if the feeling of blood would ever go away. Fighting the exhaustion radiating from the core of my being, I trudged back to Samuel's side.

It's almost over, I told myself.

"This is it for you," I told him before I grabbed his shoulder and rolled him into the shallow grave. The tarp loosened a bit, and I saw his face. His black eyes were pits, accusing me with words he could no longer say.

"Why did you have to be such a creep?" I demanded.

His sightless eyes stared into mine, and I suddenly thought of another aspect—his identity. It's nearly impossible to charge murder if a body is never found, but if it is, delaying the identification of the person is the best way to go. It's harder to make connections if the police don't know who their victim is. Cutting off the head and hands would be the way to go.

I patted myself down, feeling the knife I'd used to kill him. There was no way it was strong enough to saw through a human neck, and it was the only thing close to viable I had. I groaned, considering running to town for a larger blade, but how suspicious would that look?

"I guess you get to keep your head. Ironic since losing your mind is what led to this."

I smiled into his lifeless eyes. There was something about the thought of him staring into nothing for eternity that made my creepy little heart happy.

Chapter Twenty-Three

BY THE TIME I got home, Mom was already asleep. I was grateful for that. I was dirty, covered in blood, and my clothes were in tatters. To be seen like this would've been the death of me. However, my blessing would also be my curse. Whenever I would be questioned by the police, I would need a solid alibi. Without Mom actually *seeing* me walk through the door, she couldn't verify what time I came home. Mom would lie for me though, that much I was sure of.

Exhausted, I went to the bathroom, pulling off my clothes and burying them at the bottom of the trashcan before jumping into the shower. I scrubbed my hair, studying the streaks of brown and red running against the white. I went through several layers of soap and shampoo but none of it was enough to get the clammy dirt off my skin. I shivered as the warmth ran over me, erupting goosebumps down my arms and legs. I scrubbed my skin until it was red, and the water was cold.

When I got out, I wrapped a fluffy towel around my chest, pinning it under my elbows as I wiped the steam off the mirror and stared at my reflection. There was a series of marks on my neck from where my clothes had dug into me and scratches down my collarbone where Samuel had made contact.

Under it all, I didn't recognize myself—there wasn't an ounce of humanity left.

I bundled up in layers of pajamas and sat on the middle of my bed in the darkness, hugging my knees to my chest and replaying the night's events. I couldn't quite grasp the reality of what I had done.

Samuel was *gone*. Forever.

There would be no more taunts, no more insults, no more glares.

I couldn't bring myself to believe it. I still felt as if the entire thing was a dream, a figment of my crazy imagination. I opened my laptop, waiting to see an anonymous IM, but there were none. I wouldn't have one from him ever again. The thought left a weird cold blazing through my chest.

I thought about what he'd said about Molly and felt worse. Could he have been telling the truth?

There's no way, I thought and picked up the computer.

I opened it and searched *Molly Rodriguez, 2018.*

Tragedy on Campus, the first link said, and I clicked on it.

Molly Rodriguez, a local nursing student, was found deceased in her dorm. Police suspect foul play and are unwilling to release details on her death at this time.

If you or someone you know has information that can lead police to her killer, please contact the Albany Police Department.

I set the computer down, digesting what I had read.

Police suspect foul play.

I clicked on a few more links, comparing the information

and came to the conclusion that police had never found her killer.

Her case was still open.

Samuel had been serious. He thought he'd been free to tell the truth because he was going to kill me, and it wouldn't have mattered.

Oscar must've figured it out, I thought. *And I stopped him from getting revenge.*

I was ready to close my laptop when I realized I had a new email. The reporter Keaton had encouraged me to reach out to had written me back.

Yes, thank you for the response. Sorry it took me so long to get back to you. Things have been crazy lately. If you're still interested, let me know when you're available, and we'll get things going.

I stared at it, the room filling with a squealing sound that I realized was my own choked laughter. I had wanted the interview to prove to Samuel, to the prove to the world, that I was innocent. But that wasn't true anymore. How was I supposed to plead my case knowing it was all a lie?

How's that for irony?

THAT NIGHT, I dreamed of blood and screams. I saw flashes of Oscar's and Samuel's faces mixed with the *bang* of a gun. At the end was a woman's screams. When I woke up, it was with the painful recollection of what I'd done. Every time I blinked, I could see Samuel's glossy eyes staring up at me in the alley. If ghosts were real, he was haunting me. And why not? He couldn't leave me alone in life so it made since he wouldn't leave me alone in death either.

My throat was painfully dry, and I gasped, feeling as if invisible fingers were digging into my skin. I opened my eyes, unable to sit up as I stared at the blackness of my room. The sleep paralysis pinned me down, making it impossible to move anything but my eyes. A gathering group of shadows at the foot of my bed materialized into a humanoid-shape. Someone stood there, concealed in darkness. The figure took a shambling step toward me.

Samuel leered down at me.

I screamed, the binds of my paralysis loosening enough for me to jump up. I scrambled to my feet, convinced there was an attacker, but no one was there. I wiped my hair off the sweat clinging to my forehead and made my way out of the room and into the kitchen. I scrambled to grab a glass out of the cupboard, fingers slippery as if they were still covered in blood as I filled it with tap water. I emptied it with a series of heavy gulps.

"What's going on out here?" Mom asked from the end of the hallway. Her hair stuck up on one side of her head, and it was obvious she had just woken up.

In any other situation, I would've laughed. Today, I hoped she wouldn't see the crazy in my eyes as I set the glass down. "I was thirsty."

"You sounded like you couldn't breathe," Mom said, crossing the living room. She glanced toward my room as if she expected to see someone else in the apartment. "Are you sure you're okay?"

No, I wasn't sure. In fact, I wasn't sure if I would ever be okay again. "My sleep paralysis again," I said, hurrying past her.

She didn't need to see me like this. No one did.

"Wait."

Against my better instincts, I stopped. "What is it, Mom?"

"How was yesterday? Everything okay?"

I thought about all that had happened—the meeting with Chelsea, the awkwardness at work, and the confrontation afterward. Not a single part of the day had qualified as *okay.* "Yeah, it was fine. Why do you ask?"

"I didn't see you come home," she said.

"Oh, I uh, stayed a little late to make up hours. I helped Mr. Waters lock up. When I got home, you were already asleep, and I didn't want to wake you."

"You have work today?" she asked as she got the coffee maker started. I listened to the normal sounds of the morning, thinking how they sounded now that everything was upside down. "Are you going to want a ride?"

I had to bite my lip to keep myself from barking out *No.* Truth was, I never wanted to be inside any vehicle again, let alone Mom's little red deathmobile.

"No, that's okay, Mom. My shift doesn't start for a few more hours. I was gonna get some more sleep," I said, jerking my thumb over my shoulder.

She made a face like she smelled something unpleasant.

I didn't want to draw out the conversation, but I couldn't keep myself from asking, "What?"

"You've been sleeping a lot lately," she said as she added a few spoonfuls of sugar to her coffee.

I shrugged, knowing what she was hinting at. "And?"

"I worry about you."

"You don't need to. I can take care of myself," I said, barely resisting the urge to roll my eyes.

"As your mother, I don't understand how you expect me to do anything else."

I wanted to argue. I wanted to remind her how much more she was worried about her pills and alcohol, about how many times *I* had to take care of *her*, but it didn't seem worth it. I wanted to disengage. To go to my room and stay there until the day after tomorrow.

"Okay," she said after a long minute of silence and wandered into the living room. She set her mug on the table and walked toward me.

I gripped the doorframe, unsure what was happening. Mom cupped the back of my neck and pressed a kiss to my forehead. When she pulled back, her eyes were intense, focused. I searched for some familiar sign that the pills were in her system, but there was no glaze.

She was lucid.

"I love you. You know that, right?" she said.

I forced my chin up and down, but I didn't know. Not really.

"Good," she said, smiling before she went to seat herself in front of her coffee.

And just like that, she left me in a worse mood than I had already been in. My paranoia was convinced that she somehow knew what I had done. That she was waiting for me to confess, and this was all a tactic to pull it out of me.

That's impossible, I argued back.

For the time being, *no one* knew. That thought left me feeling worse as I sulked back to my bedroom and opened the laptop. I had left it on the email, the one from the reporter, but I hadn't typed a response yet. *It would let you get your story out there. That way people have a chance to see you without Samuel's filter,* Keaton's words echoed in the back of my mind again. I stared at the blinking cursor hovering over the reply button.

Time for damage control, the little voice in my head said.

I still didn't want to do it. The interview would be hard, and if they mentioned Samuel, I would crack. How could I answer *anything* normally with the image of him dead and bloody sitting behind my eyes? Not to mention the confession he'd made.

Anytime is fine with me, I wrote back and clicked send before I could change my mind. I stared at the email, refreshing every two seconds to make sure it actually sent. After a few minutes of that, and no response, I let the tension out of my shoulders.

Today would be stressful enough without making it worse on myself. I hadn't lied to Mom about having work tonight, but I lied about my plans. Just because I *had* work didn't mean I intended to go. After what had happened, the last thing I wanted was human interaction, and in the scene of the crime to boot, but it couldn't be avoided, could it? If I didn't go in, it would certainly look suspicious when Samuel was reported missing.

I didn't want to be the first thought on everyone's minds. I had to pull myself together and do it anyway.

By the time I emerged from my room, Mom was already

gone. On instinct, I did a double scan to ensure she was really out of the apartment before I went to her room. I went through her drawers for any sign of a familiar orange bottle. I couldn't find one. Angrily, I slammed the drawer and admitted defeat. Today of all days I would've welcomed Mom's hobby, but we were never on the same page. About anything it seemed.

As I passed into the kitchen, I downed a cup of orange juice instead of eating an actual meal and slid my shoes on. I was a disheveled mess as I went out the door. I checked my email on my phone over and over again as I walked to work, refreshing it every minute or so. I had no replies from the reporter by the time I clocked in, and resentfully, I crammed the phone in my locker.

"Hi," Harlow said nearly as soon as I came up to my register. I wanted to pretend I hadn't heard her and go through my day, but she was stubborn. She stuck by my side, making eye contact before she said it again. "Hi, girl. You okay?"

"Yeah, yeah. I…didn't sleep well," I said, combing out my ratty hair with my fingers and trying to keep my bitter mood to myself. What had happened wasn't Harlow's fault. It wouldn't be fair of me to take it out on her. When the truth about Samuel came out, it might do me some good to have someone on my side.

Harlow was a good sport. She didn't take my standoffishness to heart, and I was glad for her mindless chatter because it made the day go by quicker. Without her, I would've been left alone to fight my thoughts. When lunch came though, she didn't go with me. She waited for Carmine. That sort of thing wouldn't have hurt my feelings before, but it did today.

I ate a few bites of a burger alone, trying to gather my thoughts and figure out where my life had gone wrong. How had I gone from my version of normal to this tangent existence where I was responsible for the death of two people and cared what other humans thought about me?

It was unreal.

I threw most of the burger away, finding that eating no longer interested me. Although Harlow hadn't gone with me, she was waiting for me when I returned.

"How was lunch?" she asked.

"It was good," I replied and typed my code into the register. "Have you gone yet?"

"No. Not yet. Carmine wanted to wait for Samuel, but I haven't seen him. Have you?"

The question choked the air from my lungs. "No."

"Hmmph. He's been taking too many sick days lately," she said, slipping her pink phone from her pocket, presumably to fire off another text he would never read.

I forced the air back into my lungs and said, "Yeah, no, that's weird."

Harlow went back to Carmine, and I was relieved. Pretending to be hard at work kept her from coming back. The time would come where I would have to talk about Samuel, but it wasn't going to be today.

When people began to gather in my line, I was happy for the distraction. I tried to do everything Mr. Waters expected of me—greet the customer, ask them how they were—things I normally dreaded because feeling like an ass was better than anything else I could manage to feel.

Despite my efforts, I could still hear it all. There were plenty of whispers about Samuel—why he wasn't here, and why he had taken so much time off recently. While they laughed it off today, blaming him to be hungover or into some other shenanigans, that wouldn't be the case tomorrow and the day after that and the day after that. The longer this continued, the worse it would become.

When the end of my shift came, I pulled the trash bag out of the tiny can beneath my register. It wasn't as if I was a suck up or anything, but I was so desperate for a distraction from myself that I would've gotten on my hands and knees and scrubbed the floor with a toothbrush if Mr. Waters asked me to.

I glanced up at the sound of footsteps to see Harlow hovering over me. "It's weird to not hear anything from him for this long."

I couldn't bring myself to tell her to *go away,* but I thought it. How was I supposed to escape my problems when she kept making me face them? "Maybe he needed a day off," I said quickly and hoped she wouldn't notice how ugly my voice sounded.

"Yeah, maybe he needed a break from all our glamorous faces," she said with a laugh. "Well, you have a good night, girlie. I'll see you again tomorrow. Same time, same place."

My body shook, and I headed to the employee lounge. Partly I believed it to be because my nerves were dealing with residual fear from the night before as the time approached that of the confrontation with Samuel. Desperate to get home, I got my phone and bag out of my locker. My first move was to check my email—still no response from the reporter—and then I realized I had a message from Keaton.

Everything okay, dude? Haven't heard from you in a little while.

I stared at the message. It warmed me in places that I didn't know could still feel. I wanted to tell her the truth, what I had done, and have her tell me it was okay, that *I* was going to be okay. I typed a message, deleted it, typed it again, and my finger hovered over the send button.

Anything I *could* say wouldn't make it better. I deleted the sad response and shut off my phone before I could change my mind. I kept my head down as I adjusted the strap on my backpack and left the store. I had class after this, but I wasn't sure I could handle it.

In the end, my paranoia convinced me to go, but I felt worse and worse during the bus ride. By the time I made it to campus, it was all too much. I had hit my limit, and I couldn't move past it. I never made it to class that day, instead opting to turn around and go home. The bus ride back was a lot better, my anxiety easing the second I rounded onto my block. I couldn't wait to go back to my dark fortress and hide from society.

When the apartment came into view, I started to jog, using my memories as fuel for every stride. I couldn't get away fast enough. I opened the doors to the lobby hard enough to slam into the wall and jogged up the stairs. I hardly recognized Keaton. She held an arm out to stop me, forehead scrunched.

"Hey, there you are. Everything okay? You never answered my text."

I stared at her the way I had the cursor. Except this wasn't a message I could delete or decide to deal with later. Whatever I said, I wouldn't be able to take back. Lucky for me, I couldn't say a thing. My tongue seemed to have doubled in size, choking me, and keeping any words from escaping.

"Why do you look like you've seen a ghost?" she asked, eyeliner-circled eyes stretching wide.

"I'm okay," I said and pulled her into the tightest hug I had ever given anyone in my life.

"Ooof," she said as the breath was knocked from her lungs. A second later, she let out a tiny chuckle. She didn't fight though, simply stayed like a giant ragdoll in my arms as I got through my emotions.

When I pulled away, I stared at this girl, the closest person to a friend that I had, and thought again about telling her everything I had done. Everything that had happened. If anyone could understand, it would be her. If I had called her last night, when I was in the thick of it, she most likely would've helped me bury the body. The problem with her kindness though was that I didn't want her to be dragged down with me. Not for something that wasn't her fault. That was why I *hadn't* called her last night, and that was why I couldn't tell her now.

The longer I looked into her eyes—my demons to her light—the more I lost all willpower. In the end, I said nothing, keeping all of the darkness to myself, and clapped a hand to her shoulder before I continued on my way upstairs, resisting the urge to look back though I could still feel her eyes on me.

Strangely enough, thoughts of my own life bled away as I unlocked the door to the apartment, and I was left thinking of an interview I had read somewhere with Edmund Kemper. He talked about the difference in realities when he attended a therapy session carrying a gym bag that had a head in it. He mentioned how odd it was to think about the contrast of both worlds, and that's how this moment was for me.

Keaton was most likely going out to meet Trixie and have an evening full of fun, light, and laughter, while I was heading to my fortress to seclude myself from the world and contemplate why I belonged there.

Chapter Twenty-Four

I LOST ALL sense of time after that.

I curled up in my blankets, staring at the tiny sliver of light that managed to sneak past my black out curtains, and pondered everything. I didn't know how long I stayed like that. One moment I laid down, and the next thing I was aware of was knocking on the door.

I didn't get up, not right away at least. Then my phone buzzed with a text from Keaton. *Girl, open the door.*

I didn't want to obey, but my feet betrayed me, swinging over the edge of the bed before I lifted my head. Agitated, I crossed the living room with deliberate steps, hoping that if I took long enough, she would leave, and I wouldn't have to explain myself.

She was too stubborn for that. When I finally opened the door, she stood on the other side, arms folded over her chest and foot tapping in an annoyed rhythm. "You weren't going to open the door, were you?"

"Guilty," I said, statement true in more ways than one.

Keaton muttered a string of curses as she pushed her way into the apartment. "Your mom home today?"

"She just left for work," I said, glancing up at the clock. I had no idea if that was the truth or not. I hadn't known that a full twelve hours had passed since I came home. Mom could be in the gutter scoring more pills for all I knew.

"Everything okay? You're…paler than usual," Keaton said, drawing her features tight as she studied me.

"Yeah…I…" I grasped my elbow across my torso, unsure how to finish that sentence. I didn't like being under a spotlight, especially when it came to Keaton. Everything *was* fine for the moment, but it wouldn't stay that way for long. My luck was bound to run out eventually. "I think I have a bug."

"Hmm, okay," Keaton said, going to the living room to give it a good once over. "Got any plans today?"

"I have work in about an hour," I said. Again, I wasn't sure if that was the truth or not. All the days in the week were beginning to blend together, and I hadn't checked my schedule recently. It could've changed, or I could have my day wrong. Either way, I wasn't planning on going, but I wasn't going to tell her that. If the conversation went south, that was going to be my ticket to escape.

Keaton accepted the answer, and why not? She didn't expect me to tell her anything but the truth, and suddenly, I felt bad for deceiving her. She deserved better, but I had started to accept that my lot in life was to infect everyone around me with my toxicity.

Keaton glanced toward my room. "No snacks visible. I'm guessing you've been holed up all day?"

I said nothing as I moved past her. If I told her I had been in my room the entire night as well she might force me out of the apartment. Keaton beat me to the bed, picking up the laptop before she sat on my covers.

"Let's see what you've got going on," she said, scrolling through my open tabs. "Anything new? Any love notes from Samuel?"

I cringed when she said his name, but she didn't notice. "No, haven't heard from him in a while."

Keaton peered at me over the top in an *I-don't-believe-you* stare before she continued to snoop. I could've stopped her at any time, but I didn't want to. If I couldn't tell her what was wrong directly, I hoped that maybe she could pick it up subliminally.

Stranger things have happened.

She clicked her tongue, apparently satisfied with her findings. My heart lurched with that sickening little bolt of anxiety that happened whenever something I wasn't going to particularly like happened, and I wondered if she had uncovered my research about Molly. "You didn't tell me you got a response from that reporter!"

"Yeah, she responded last night."

"And again this morning," Keaton confirmed, turning the computer toward me.

That was new.

I leaned down to read the email. *Can you meet today?* Beneath that there was a time and a date.

"Well?" Keaton asked. "You're still going to go, right?"

I continued to stare at the words, brain processing it like a complicated mathematical formula rather than a simple decision. My day could take two possible paths—the painful normalcy of work or the unpredictability of this new opportunity.

Keaton stared me down. It didn't seem as if I had much of a choice. "Tell her yes."

She beamed at me and typed up a response. She had a habit of sounding far more professional than me, and I wanted to seem like I had my life together. "Sent! You are all set up for the interview today." She set the computer aside and assessed my dirty grey sweater and pajama pants. "What are you going to wear?"

"I don't know." I squirmed under the intensity of her gaze. "Does it matter?"

"You know I'm anything but a girlie girl," Keaton said. "But in this situation, it does. Your clothes will make an impression before you open your mouth. You have anything business casual?"

I thought through my outfits. The closest thing to professional I had were the uniforms I had stolen from old jobs. "I have a pencil skirt and a blouse," I offered.

"Show me."

I summoned the outfit out of my closet and held it up for her to see.

"Hmm," she said, tilting her head.

"Too much?"

She looked from the outfit to me, considering. "No. No, that should be perfect. You'll look like an All-American Girl."

"But I'm not."

"They don't *know* that," Keaton reminded me. "Remember. It's *your* turn to make an impression. Don't let them define the way it goes."

It sounded simple, but in the heat of the moment I

would clam up. I always did in social situations. Spotlights and cameras, would only make it worse.

"You know what you're going to say?"

"I want them to know…" a flash of Samuel's dead eyes in the alley "…that I'm innocent."

She tsked. "Innocence is all a matter of perspective. You can't blurt out that you're innocent right off the bat or they'll think you have something to be ashamed of. Something not so innocent."

"I guess that makes sense," I said. I was severely out of my element with this.

"There will be hard questions," Keaton said. "You need to be steel when you go in there because they'll try to break you down. Don't let them get that upper hand."

I lowered the shirt and skirt to my sides. "How do you know about this?"

"I don't know much about *this* per se, but I have been arrested a few times for shoplifting. I figure the protocol is probably the same."

For some reason, that made me laugh, and pretty soon, we were both laughing. It felt good to do something so normal. I wondered when I'd have the chance again.

Chapter Twenty-Five

WE PLAYED TWENTY questions until it was time to start walking. Keaton offered to give me a ride, but I didn't want to do that. The bus strengthened me by getting me situated to being outside of my house and around strangers. Being in Keaton's car wouldn't cut it.

She didn't protest much about the idea of taking the bus. She walked with me and asked questions from the point of view of the reporter. It was an exercise to help ease my anxiety, and get into the proper interviewee mindset, but it had the opposite effect. I tripped on my tongue, sweated, and overthought every question. If I was like this with my friend, how much worse would I be with a complete stranger?

"Maybe I shouldn't do it," I said as we began to close in on the bus stop. The reality of what I was doing was beginning to sink in. The skirt didn't feel right, and I didn't like that this outfit meant I could only carry *one* of my knives. I felt exposed, vulnerable.

"Relax. You're going to do fine," Keaton reassured me as she dropped onto the hard-red bench.

"Easy for you to say," I said as I sat next to her. *You*

didn't spend an evening killing someone.

"I think you'll feel better after doing this. And I'll tell you what. To make it up to you, I'll buy you a big juicy steak."

I smiled despite myself. The key to unlocking a better mood in me was food. "I'm gonna hold you to that."

She winked at me as the bus pulled to a screeching halt. We climbed on, battling for seats. We got two together near the back and kept our heads close, conversation quiet as she continued asking questions. A man across the bus kept staring at us. Keaton noticed him before I did and greeted him with a middle finger.

"I can't believe you'd rather ride the bus with all these creeps than have me drive you," Keaton said, sounding offended when he finally looked away.

"After a while, you stop noticing," I admitted. I felt at home among strange people, more than I did with normal people.

Keaton gave me a weird look and pulled the string, leading the way off the bus. No one else got off with us, and Keaton sent another middle finger to the staring man as the doors closed.

The local news station wasn't big, but it was intimidating. There were plenty of people going in and out of the big white building.

A nightmarish place for somebody like me.

"Breathe," Keaton said, taking an exaggerated breath as an example.

"When we walk in it's not gonna be like …an ambush, right?" I asked, glancing at Keaton from the corner of my eye.

Keaton looped her arm through mine as we wove through the car in the parking lot. "What? You think they're gonna jump out and start making fun of you?" I knew the idea was ridiculous, but it didn't seem ridiculous enough for my brain to give up on it. My face must've told her that because she said, "Enough. It's going to be fine."

She marched me up to the door, only giving me a few seconds to prepare before we were through it and in the lobby. There was a woman at a desk and a few people with clipboards passing through. I recognized a few reporters from the ones who had been camped outside the apartment, but for the most part, they were strangers.

I couldn't decide if that was a good thing or not.

"Can I help you?" the woman at the desk asked, smiling pleasantly as we approached.

"Yeah, hi. I'm checking in my friend here. She was told to meet a Marissa here in about—" Keaton looked at the clock, "—ten minutes."

"Okay," she said, glancing at the papers before her. "And may I ask for your name?"

"I'm Keaton, but my friend here is the one Marissa is interested in."

The woman turned her wide brown eyes on me. I waited, spotting the exact moment I went from a nameless nobody to *somebody*. "Jessica, right?"

"Yeah," I said, voice stiff.

"Marissa is expecting you. Go right on back." She gestured over her shoulder.

I stared into the mouth of the hallway. I could imagine

taking two steps into the maze and getting lost. That would be the perfect way to start this off.

"It's the first hallway, go all the way down on the right," the woman clarified as if she could see my confusion.

"Thanks," Keaton said, setting her hand on my elbow to guide me.

We walked into the hallway, my skin buzzing. It branched and branched again, but we stuck to the right. I started to wonder if we'd gotten lost anyway when we passed a gold sign with Marissa's name on it.

"How fancy," Keaton said, rapping her knuckle on it.

I didn't comment, knocking as hard as I could which came as a surprise to Keaton only. I wanted this next hour of my life to be over as soon as possible and that couldn't happen without this woman. When Marissa came to the door, she was nothing like I imagined she would be. She was tall with obvious curves I could see through her suit. Her long red hair hung to her mid-back and her thick lips were covered in coral red lipstick.

Beside me, Keaton stared. I elbowed her slightly.

"Can I help you?" she asked.

"I'm Jessica," I said, holding out my hand.

"It's nice to finally meet you," Marissa said, and for some reason, I believed her. "Come on in and sit down."

Keaton and I obeyed, following her into the room. There was already a setup of cameras, lights, and people. In the center of it all, they had created a cozy set with two armchairs sat across from one another, each flanked by a table. Sweat started dew on my temples, and I wondered if Marissa and Keaton could see it.

"Go ahead and take a seat in one of the armchairs," she said to me then turned to Keaton. "There's a seat over there you can use to watch the interview."

"Awesome," Keaton said and patted my shoulder. "You've got this."

Awkwardly, I followed Marissa's direction and sat in the chair. It squeaked, and I stiffened, trying to ease the sounds. Under the intensity of the lights, I sweated more. The fear came that I would melt, be reduced to a puddle of nothing by the time the interview ended.

"Can I get you a bottle of water?" Marissa asked as she sat in the other chair.

Marissa called for one of her assistants to grab two bottles before I could answer. He came back a minute later handing one to Marissa and one to me. I almost downed it all in a few gulps, but I didn't feel any better. It was still too hot.

"So how does this work?" I asked.

Marissa set her bottle on her table. "I'm gonna run through a few basic questions about what happened the day of the shooting. Basically, you're going to tell me what you experienced. Don't tell me things you've heard from other people—I only want to know the things you yourself saw, heard, or felt."

"Okay, that sounds easy enough."

"If any of the questions are difficult or you find yourself not wanting to answer, let me know, and I will gladly move onto a different one. My goal here is to make sure you're comfortable while talking about your experience. If you're not, tell me immediately."

"I will," I said. I didn't know her from Eve, but something about the way she made eye contact and spoke softly told me that she really didn't want to upset me. Or maybe I was fooling myself.

"Let me know when you're ready."

I took another sip of water, distracted by the bright lights shining down on me. My heart pounded in my chest, and I was hyper aware of all the people in the room. I could've sworn I could hear them all breathing.

Keaton gave me a thumbs up.

Deep breath in, and out, and I said, "Okay, I'm ready."

"Roll camera," Marissa said.

The man behind the camera counted down from three, and Marissa sprang into her introduction. "Hello, I'm Marissa Tambini, and I'm here with our own local hero, Jessica Mills. Jessica, how are you today?"

I put one hand over the other in my lap, squeezing subtly to try and comfort myself. I wondered if the gesture would be visible on television. Then I wondered how close of a zoom the cameraman would do. "I'm okay."

"Good, good. There's been a lot of talk about what happened at Grocer's Way a month ago. There are some people who still believe that there were more than one shooter."

"There was definitely only one," I said.

Marissa sat up in her seat, leaning toward me slightly as she said, "Tell me what happened."

"It started as an ordinary day," I said, not realizing until then how much it hurt to think about the contrast of before and after. "I was at work, and I had just clocked out for lunch when

I heard the shots. It was chaos. People running and screaming, I kind of froze up."

"Did you try to run?"

I shook my head. "Not at first. Based on the sound of the shots, I guessed the shooter was midway between both the front door and the emergency exit."

"Did you know who the shooter was at this time?"

"No. One of my coworkers ran past me, and then I kind of snapped out of it. I hid in my boss' office. It's a little closet-like room right by the break room."

"So, what you're saying is you could've sheltered with your coworkers, but you didn't?"

"The room was closer," I said, trying to not get upset with the idea of where I believed her questions were going.

"Okay. You hid and then what happened?"

"I waited to see what would happen next. I kept hearing the shots so I didn't try to run. Then I heard footsteps in the hall."

"You knew he was close by?"

"Yeah," I said. "There was a crack I could kind of see through, and that was when I saw him."

"You realized it was someone you knew?"

I pictured Oscar's curly brown hair and black clothes as he turned toward me, eyes lighting with familiarity. "Yeah."

"How close would you say you were to Oscar?"

"He was my friend," I said, heart thudding as I decided the best way to explain myself. "He was there for me at work whenever I had a difficult customer or was having a bad day."

"Did you ever think he could be capable of what he

did?"

"I didn't think he'd hurt anyone, no. He was kind of a loner, but he made people laugh. He was a good person."

"When you saw the shooter was Oscar, what was your first thought?"

"I couldn't believe it. I tried to see where he was going and then I argued with myself about trying to run for it."

"That's when you noticed him going toward the break room?"

"Yes. I'd seen quite a few of my coworkers run past me so I knew there were people hiding in there."

"Did you think he had a specific target in mind?"

Samuel, I thought. "No, I didn't know what his plan was. When he was far enough away, I tried to run."

"But he heard you?"

I thought of the way I had approached him, the barrel of the gun in my face, and the tearful hug before he helped me drag the blade across his throat. "Yeah," I said, and my voice came out a croak that was barely reminiscent of my own voice.

I glanced to Keaton in the corner of the room. She was leaning her elbows on her knees, enraptured in my story.

One of Marissa's assistants hurried on screen to hand me a tissue, and she asked, "Are you okay?"

I dabbed my eyes. I wasn't okay. I *really* wasn't, but I hadn't expected to be. "Yeah."

"What happened next?" Marissa asked, slipping back into her interview voice.

"He told me to leave or he would shoot me. Then he put the gun in my face."

"That must have been terrifying."

It wasn't, I thought because all I could remember was Oscar's eyes as he did it. There was nothing scary there. Soul-crushing, maybe, but scary? No. He was a wounded animal backed into a corner. Not dangerous. *Desperate.*

"Yeah," I forced myself to say again.

"Did you leave?"

"No."

Marissa's eyebrows shot up. "What did he do when you refused to leave?"

"He said *please,*" I replied, and I felt dirty. Like I was exposing an intimate moment that should've died with me.

"Please?" Marissa echoed. "You think he was still trying to encourage you to leave?"

A tear ran down my cheek, and I wiped it away. "Yes."

"But you didn't?"

"No. I knew that if I left, he would go into the employee lounge. It was the last place he had to go."

"Wow. That must have been one harrowing experience." She paused to take a sip of water from her bottle. "What do you have to say about those rumors that you were involved in the shooting?"

"They're ridiculous," I said, trying not to let the sadness channel into anger. I didn't want the world to see that side of me. "Sure, Oscar was my friend, but I wouldn't have wanted him to do what he did. The truth is, I blame myself a lot for what happened. I feel like I overlooked some signs, and that if I would've been paying more attention and been a better friend that I would've seen it. Maybe if I had, I could've helped him.

Could've given him what he needed, and the whole tragedy could've been avoided. Or maybe not. Who knows?"

"Now that you think back on those days before the shooting, what were some of those signs you mentioned?"

Never change, his words echoed in my head again. I would never forget them. I didn't want her to know that part. I didn't want *anyone* to know. "There were little things," I said finally. "He stopped eating for example."

"And what else?"

"He stopped making jokes," I said, thinking of that last lunch we had spent together. How quiet it had been. How he'd been a shell of himself.

Marissa sat back in her seat, thoughtfully. "There are some sources who believe Oscar was avenging his sister's unsolved murder by going after the list of police suspects. What are your thoughts on that theory?"

The question was so unexpected it hit me like a physical blow. My brain went to static, and I thought I might throw up.

"I-I—" I struggled lamely for a sentence that wouldn't come.

Marissa must've realized it because she smiled at the camera and said, "Well, that's about all the time we have today. You are a brave woman, Jessica. Thank you for being here with us."

The lights faded to black.

"And we're done," the cameraman said.

I stared at Marissa until her smile fell away, and she asked, "Are you okay?"

"Why would you ask me that?" I blurted out, tone

harsher than I'd meant for it to be. "Who are these *sources*?"

Concerned, Keaton hopped out of her chair and made it to my side as Marissa said, "It's a working theory thrown together by a few independent investigators. I meant no offense by it. Truth is, no one knows why he did what he did and a huge part of the interest in this case is trying to figure it out."

I said nothing, trying to process my anger.

"Honestly, this theory makes the most sense to me," Marissa added.

It did. It *really* did. Coupled with Samuel's confession the night I killed him made it all too real.

"You never thought about it?" Marissa asked, bemused.

"I never knew Oscar had a sister," I lied and threw up all over my shoes.

Chapter Twenty-Six

EVERY WORST CASE scenario played in my brain as soon as we left the building. I was embarrassed in myself for puking, embarrassed that I had choked for the entire world to see, and perhaps the most embarrassed that I had operated under the assumption that a *reporter* wouldn't uncover the connection between Samuel and Oscar that I had.

Keaton tried to reassure me over and over that I had done great, but I didn't think I had. I had wanted the world to understand that Oscar wasn't always a monster, but instead, I had torn open different wounds.

"Elephant in the room here," Keaton said as we walked to the bus stop. "When were you gonna tell me the whole Molly thing?"

"I meant what I said to Marissa," I said. "I didn't know she was Oscar's sister. And I certainly didn't know she was involved with Samuel." *Until recently.*

"He never talked about her?"

"Not to me." I didn't mention that I had never asked about his family. A new wave of guilt went through me. Anytime we'd talked, I'd focused on myself. I used him to vent and never reciprocated for him. *Some friend you are.*

"Samuel being a suspect actually *doesn't* surprise me," she said. "I wonder what evidence they had to connect him and why they never arrested him."

I stayed quiet, worried that if I talked too much, I would spill everything I'd learned from research, and Keaton would know I was lying.

"You're worrying over nothing," Keaton said, but I wasn't sure.

The only upside to this entire ordeal was the fact that I'd received a thousand dollars for my interview. Otherwise, I might've spent the rest of the evening crying. I might still. The interview was a double-edged sword. It would help me tell my side of the story, but it would also rehash everything that people were finally starting to bury.

After Keaton and I parted ways, I went home and sealed myself in my room. I thought about Samuel's chat threads and drummed my fingers on the top of my laptop, telling myself I didn't need to go back to that site. That it wouldn't help anything if I did.

But I *had* to know what people thought of Marissa's new angle. I lost the fight and opened the laptop, scrolling through all the messages both old and new.

Did you see the interview today? someone had written.

Yeah, I did. She seems…cold. Like she's holding something back. She didn't even smile.

She sure didn't look *like a killer.*

Yeah, but they never do, right? Look at Ted Bundy.

Why would she talk about things now? Why bring it up again?

Some people don't want their fifteen minutes of fame to end.

Clearly.

What was that about Molly? She claimed her and Oscar were friends but didn't know he had a sister?

Somebody's lying.

The messages hurt, but I deserved it.

As much as I wanted to go to sleep, to put an end to this day, I couldn't. I kept thinking about Samuel's website, the comments, and *Samuel.*

I closed the laptop. How much longer would it be before he was officially reported missing, and I was labeled the prime suspect? It wasn't a stretch to imagine he had other pictures of me, ones he hadn't shown. I was sure there were still some in his apartment, and if not, he had digital copies for sure. Those would link me to him. I had the sickening feeling he'd hoped for that.

A plan started to form, and I sat up, plotting how to break into Samuel's place. I'd wear black gloves. I'd make no sounds as I stole everything that linked us. Then the only evidence of our relationship would be rumors.

I could look for evidence to link him to Molly too while I was at it. It stood to reason that if he was this obsessed about me, maybe he had been toward her also and documented her the same way. It was when I started putting my shoes on that I realized I was *serious* about doing this.

Now or never.

If I waited too long to do anything, other people would scour his apartment first, and I'd forfeit my chance.

I slipped out of my room. The apartment was quiet, the

starlight outside falling in thin lines on the kitchen floor. I slung on a hoodie, draping the hood over my blonde hair before I scooped up my bag, making sure it was empty. I didn't know how much storage I'd need, but I didn't want to come up short.

I left the apartment, closing the door behind me. I glanced toward Keaton's apartment, but there were no signs of movement. Seizing the opportunity, I slid all the way down the stairs, bag clutched tight to my side. I didn't want to appear suspicious, but there wasn't really a way to do this without giving that impression. The cool night air felt good in my lungs, and that was what I focused on as I traveled.

I had only ever been to Samuel's apartment one time, but it wasn't hard to remember the place. A shabby studio apartment on the bad side of town. My only saving grace was that at least I doubted anyone would call the police if they caught me breaking in. They would have too much to lose.

Like the apartment I shared with Mom, Samuel's wasn't on the ground floor. The irony of this entire trip was that the only way to get inside without arousing suspicion would be through the fire escape… as I'd thought he had done to me.

The fire escape was a rusty, unstable thing, the landings leaning slightly toward the street, but it was enough to get up to the third floor. I hauled myself onto the platform and ducked down, peering through the window frame. It was impossible to make out shapes and I couldn't tell if this was the right apartment.

I counted the windows around the building, doing the math in my head. This had to be it. I glanced down to the road below. It wasn't too late to call this whole thing off and go home.

No, I told myself and wedged my fingers into the window, easing it up. *I'm already here. Might as well get it done.*

It didn't take too much effort to get the screen to come loose, and I set it aside. Quiet darkness inside. I pulled myself over the frame, dropping to the floor beyond the window.

Samuel's place smelt odd—a mix of stale alcohol, male body odor, and cheap cologne. By no means was it pleasant, but it assured me I was in the right place. Creeping across the room, I sought out the light switch. I was in Samuel's bedroom, and it was exactly as disgusting as it smelled. There were old pizza boxes, dirty clothes, and beer cans. This place could've been abandoned a lot longer than a few days.

Had he really lived like this?

Scan quickly and go, I told myself, not sure how much I was going to be able to find in this mess.

My first bet was to search around his bed. It wouldn't surprise me for a shallow creep to keep his trophies close, but the only thing I could find under the mattress was a stack of girlie magazines. I moved from the bedroom to the front room.

Thankfully, the worst of the odor stayed there.

In Samuel's front room, there was a patch of wall covered in pictures. It was only when I got close to them that I realized they were all pictures of *me.* On a hook near them was a hat, a *familiar* hat.

"He kept a fucking *shrine?*" I screeched.

I stopped caring about finesse and started tearing down the pictures, shoving handfuls in my bag. Little white squares were left behind from the adhesives he had used, and when the last picture was free, I grabbed the hat too.

I stared at it, frowning. The vigil felt like forever ago. Another lifetime. Another *reality*. It was all the same to Samuel, like every moment between us had been documented. I had thought that what I would find here would be bad, but I didn't think it would be like this.

My next move was to seek out his laptop which was bound to be one thousand times worse than anything else I'd seen. His laptop was a shiny silver monster hidden between the arm of the couch and cushion. I closed my eyes as I plucked it free. I wasn't sure what the purpose of that was, but I didn't want to look at it directly. When I realized how silly I was being, I opened my eyes, but I didn't sit down. I opened the laptop. It was already on, and it demanded a password.

It wasn't hard for me to guess what it was. The same name as the website.

Then I was in.

I didn't know where to begin. *Files,* I thought and pulled it up. The little cursor hovered over the *photos* folder. I cursed out loud as I scrolled through the contents. Like I had feared, it was filled with copies of all the photos that had been on the wall joined with images I hadn't seen before. There were hundreds of them, maybe thousands—some of me at school, some with Keaton, some of me at *work*.

How could no one have seen him?

It was unbelievable.

Enraged, I found the strength to go to his browser, and it was worse. The history was filled with links to my social media sites and chat threads he had created about me. I didn't let myself study anything in depth. I would probably regret it if I did, much the way I already regretted this entire adventure. I crammed it in my bag.

The rest of the apartment didn't offer much to see. A kitchen that could use a good cleaning and a bathroom that was twice as disgusting as that. Confident that I had found all I needed, I snuck out of Samuel's apartment the way I had gone in. The fire escape creaked more with the added weight in my bag, but I didn't slow down until I was back in the safety of my room.

Mom didn't notice me come back home, but I locked the door to my room anyway. When I sat down on the bed, I took my findings out of the bag and systematically sorted them into piles. I stared at them, wondering where to start.

I lost interest in the hat first. It had the least amount of information to tell me, so it was the first that I tossed to the side. That left me with the laptop and pictures, the colorful squares documenting. They were good pictures that captured me smiling and sunny—pictures of the human inside the monster. Timestamps put them at all different times throughout the day. Morning, noon, evening, night, every hour had at least a handful of photos to fill it. As far as I could tell, he had been watching me since our failed date.

That was alarming. Of course, I had known of his antics at work, but I hadn't known how much deeper it all went. He had been following me for *months*, waiting for me to slip up. That's what this was. He wanted to be there when I fell.

He never got the chance.

I gathered the pictures, stuffing them into my bag when I

stopped. There was a picture *not* of me mixed in. I hadn't noticed it at Samuel's apartment. What caught my eye was the amount of red. I brought it closer to my face and almost dropped it when I realized what I was looking at.

A mutilated girl's body.

I stared at it until my vision blurred. This wasn't like any of the gore I'd seen online that featured a bunch of nameless nobodies. This was a woman I'd seen on the news. Heard stories about from her friends around campus.

She was a human being. The thought hit me like a sucker punch to the gut. This wasn't entertainment. This was sick. And the worst part? I couldn't call the police because I would have to explain how I'd found this picture to begin with.

They can't find it here, I thought and hurried into the kitchen for a trash bag. I threw everything in it and rushed downstairs and across the street to the woods. I dug a hole with my bare hands and buried it.

Chapter Twenty-Seven

THOUGHT THE burden of what I had done to Samuel would get heavier, harder to bear as the time passed. I found out that the opposite was true. After finding that picture of Molly, I felt more justified in killing him and certainly more like a hero than I had after killing Oscar. The longer I was allowed to live my life in peace, the more I began to question if what I had done was really such a bad thing.

Samuel had been a monster, and I'd stopped him.

With the pressure of the interview in the past, and the confidence that people would find no connection to me in Samuel's apartment, I started to look forward to what my life would become. Things weren't exactly *better*, but they were getting there. I got back into my old routine of work and school. Keaton and I hung out a few times, devouring pizza and horror movies. My commitment to the morning news continued, only now it was to keep an eye out for the day Samuel's body was found.

If I closed my eyes and wished hard enough, I could believe that everything was going to be okay.

Nothing gold can stay, said the persistent little voice in the back of my mind.

I never forgot about the picture of Molly. I considered

sending it with an anonymous letter to the police station, but they would be able to trace it back to me, so I stayed silent, waiting for Samuel's disappearance to hit the news. To find the perfect opportunity to tell them what I knew.

It took a week for the police to get involved. One unexpected absence from Samuel had resulted in whispers. *Five* was enough for people to grow worried.

"Did you hear?" Harlow asked one day.

My shoulders stiffened automatically, the way it did every time someone approached me. "Hear what?"

"Samuel is *missing*. He and his sister like to go to lunch together once a week to touch base, you know," she said, and I nodded along as if I *did* know when really I had no idea what his life consisted of. "When he didn't show up, she called the police."

"That's crazy," I said, scratching the back of my neck. "Do they know where he went?"

"The police are baffled. Between you and me, his place is a disaster. I'm not surprised they didn't find anything saying where he's gone."

This was inevitable, but I didn't like the thought of the police scouring for answers. What if I hadn't been as careful as I'd thought?

A few more days passed, and I started to feel okay. *No news is good news.*

Two days later, Harlow came at me in a different mood. Her hair was in a tight bun, and she had bags under her eyes as if she hadn't slept or showered in days.

"Are you okay?" I asked her.

"When was the last time *you* saw him?" she asked.

"Samuel?" I asked, playing dumb.

"Yeah," she said. "It just makes no sense. He was here then what? Fell off the face of the Earth?"

"I'm sorry," I said, unsure exactly *how* to respond.

I wasn't sure if she believed me or not. The longer Samuel's disappearance stretched on, the more people would speculate. I made sure to keep my human mask taped on tightly enough that no one would catch a glimpse of the monster underneath.

I went to work and school every day without complaint. Rather than secluding myself as I had a habit of doing, I would greet Harlow as soon as I arrived at work or ask Mark how he was doing in class. In the end, that might end up being *more* suspicious, but trying *something* felt a lot better than doing nothing at all.

I was at work the first time the police came in to question my boss. Detective Morgan passed me a subtle glance as she went to the back of the store, and I stressed for the rest of the day about what that gesture meant.

If the police came here, questioned *all* my coworkers, then it would only be a matter of time before they caught wind of the strained relationship between me and Samuel. Maybe they already had an idea. Either way, they would come after me again, and it would be with a lot less sympathy than they'd had after Oscar.

I held it together during work, but when my shift ended, I cried during my walk to the bus stop. There was no real reason for it other than stress, I suppose, but when it was over, I felt better. Numb and tired. It was bliss. My feet felt like solid brick as I lumbered through the lobby. As I was unlocking the door to go inside the apartment, Keaton opened her door and spotted me.

"Just the introvert I was hoping to see," she said, bounding to my side. "Did you hear?"

"Hear what?" I asked as I popped the door open.

"Samuel's missing."

"I know," I said, focusing on not dropping my keys as I tried to shove them back in my pocket. "My coworker told me."

"Aren't you happy?" she asked, swatting me on the arm as I led the way inside the apartment.

"That's one way of saying it."

"It's literally what you wished for."

"What's what you wished for?" Mom asked from her place on the couch.

"For a long and happy life," I said, crossing through the living room.

Keaton followed me to my room, and when I closed the door, the joy left her. "Dude, what's wrong? I thought you'd be ecstatic!"

I plopped down on my bed and buried my face in my hands. I thought about the pictures and laptop loosely buried in the woods. I'd thought I'd gotten all the valuable things out of his apartment, but what if I had missed something? I hadn't noticed Molly's picture until I'd been back in the safety of my own home after all. If I could miss something like that in the heat of the moment, I was sure there were other things I'd missed too.

"I don't want to talk about it," I said at last.

Mom opened the door, leaning in the doorframe as she observed us. "Are you okay, Jessica?"

"Yeah, a long day at work," I said, glancing at her through a lock of blonde hair.

"It's about the missing boy, right?"

"How'd you guess?"

"It's on the news today."

"Of course," I said, shooting a sarcastic glance to Keaton. "Things aren't an issue unless they're on the news, right?"

Mom folded her arms across her chest. She wasn't on the pills today, I could tell by the look in her eyes. She was agitated, and for some reason, that brought me joy.

"I appreciate you coming, Keaton, but can I be left alone, please?" I asked, keeping my eyes on the shadows in the corner of my room. I could sense Mom's mood would lead to a fight, and I didn't want any witnesses to it.

"Are you sure?"

"Positive."

"Okay," Keaton said, standing up. "See you later, dude."

Mom escorted her out, and I reveled in the silence left by the closing of the bedroom door.

WHEN DETECTIVE MORGAN came in Grocer's Way the next day, I kept my eyes down as I checked out my customers. I never went out of my way to make small talk, but today, I was withdrawn even by my standards.

"Carmine, can you come with me?" Detective Morgan called from the end of the nearest aisle.

Harlow's friend immediately logged off the register, sent a glance to her friend, and walked toward the Detective.

"What do you think that's about?" Harlow asked me once they disappeared from sight.

"Most likely, they're going to question all of us about our relationship with Samuel and see if we know anything about where he could've gone." I cringed after I said it, hoping she wouldn't think it strange how easily I had come up with an answer.

"Huh," Harlow said, blowing a bubble with her pink gum before letting it pop obnoxiously. "I won't have much to offer, I mean he barely said anything to me that last day. Last *few* days actually."

"Yeah, uh, me too," I said and flagged down a customer to end the conversation.

When Carmine came back, she kept her eyes down. In a way, this was like a worse version of being called down to the principal's office except the consequences were a lot more serious.

Harlow went next. I bided my time. Part of me suspected she would leave me for last to ensure that my nerves were on edge by the time she talked to me.

They won't get me that easily, I vowed.

When I was called, I glanced to Harlow. "It's not bad," she assured me.

For *her* it might not have been bad, but that guaranteed *me* nothing. When I walked, I tried not to let my tension show.

This was routine, something they *had* to do. There was no suspicion on me yet. I knew all that, but reminding myself about it didn't take away the panic. My hands clenched and unclenched, and I was sure Detective Morgan noticed.

It was her *job* to notice.

She smiled, calmly, patiently. "Jess, nice to see you again though I'm sad about the circumstances."

"Yeah…uh yeah," I said, eyes on the wall as we traveled toward the back of the store.

"How've you been doing? You looked good during your interview. Very professional."

I couldn't tell if that was a genuine compliment or if she was baiting me. "Thank you. It's uh… getting easier to deal with."

"This has been a hard month for you," she said as she held open the door to Mr. Waters' office. In leu of taking everyone down to the station, he had allowed her to use his space for questioning. I glanced around, wondering where he had gone and wishing we could go somewhere else. Every time I blinked, I flashed back to hiding in the crook of the door like a hunted animal.

"First Oscar and now Samuel," Detective Morgan said and tutted as she sat down on her side of the desk.

I didn't speak as I slipped into my seat, patiently waiting for her to say something else. I knew the strategy she was using—get me to speak to see if I incriminate myself.

I wouldn't fall for it.

She leaned forward. "Well, I'm sure you already know what I'm going to ask about."

I held my hand over my chest as if I were truly sorry for what had happened to Samuel. "Of course. I-I heard he was missing."

Detective Morgan raised an eyebrow. "For the record, you heard *who* was missing."

"Samuel. Harlow told me."

Her face twisted as if the second statement left a foul taste in her mouth. "Yes. We're here today to see if there's some angle we've missed in our search. How did you personally know him?"

"As you said, he's my coworker."

"Is that all?"

"Yes."

"Ah, well, based on my investigation from before, and what I've gathered today, there was more to your relationship than that, wasn't there?"

"He was nothing to me," I assured her and shrugged, careful to catch and hold her gaze while I said it. He was less than nothing actually but saying that wouldn't make me look favorable.

"I've been told by several witnesses that you and him went on a few dates."

An angry bubble blossomed in me, and I had to fight to keep it down. "When I first started working here, I went on one date with him. *One*. Not a *few*. And I never saw him again outside of work."

Detective Morgan seemed to consider that. "Why not?"

"We didn't click."

"So, the one date was the only time you two have hung

out outside of work?"

"Yeah."

"Then maybe you can explain a few things to me that don't make sense," she said and pulled out a photo…of *me*. It was in a sealed evidence bag. I stared at it, heart thudding. Was this one I had somehow missed or had I dropped it? Were there fingerprints?

Idiot, you wore gloves, the condescending voice in my head reminded me.

"We found this in Samuel's apartment. Any idea how or why he would have this if you two had basically no relationship?"

I stared hard at the picture. It was the one he had given me the day of the shooting. The one I had crumpled up and thrown at him.

He knew I would snap, I thought, sick all over as I pictured the shrine. *He wanted me to snap.*

My throat started to close on the verge of a panic attack, and I gripped my fingers around the arm of the chair. *Not here, not now.* "He had…an attraction to me," I managed to get out.

It was vague, but I didn't know how else to explain it. A dark obsession would certainly give me motive to hurt him, but it was the truth. He was the one who had taunted me, bullied me, *forced* me to acknowledge his existence. If it had been up to me, I never would've spoken to Samuel again after the date.

"How do you mean?" Detective Morgan asked.

The conversation was heading into dangerous waters. I pushed the photograph across the table and considered my words. *Anything you start, you have to finish,* I scolded myself. "He liked me, but I didn't like him. He did a lot to get my attention. Making comments in the break room and leaving me nasty notes. It's not just me either. He's also harassed my friend, Keaton." It was out before I could stop myself, and in the crudest way I could've said it. Not only had I presented them with a possible motive for murder, I've also brought Keaton into their midst who had no other connection to this situation than me.

"When you say *harassing*, what does that mean exactly? Was it verbal abuse? Physical? Did he do the same things to you that he did to your friend?"

I glanced at the table, careful of my words this time. "Ominous statements. Pictures of me and Keaton that mysteriously appear in random places."

"You've never seen him actually take a picture of you?"

"No, but he's given several to me personally."

"Do you still have them?"

"No…I threw them away," I said, thinking of the last picture Samuel had given me with a barely suppressed shiver.

"Are they all like this one?" she asked, tapping the plastic surrounding the picture on the table between us.

"Sometimes. Sometimes they're normal ones."

"He gives these to you? That's it? No other context?"

"N-no, none at all."

Detective Morgan's eyes narrowed to slits when she heard the tremor in my voice. I was lying, and she knew it. "You have no way to know *who* took the pictures for sure then?"

I thought of his smug smile when he'd handed me the photograph of me in bed. I'd say that was the smile of a guilty man, but no court in the world would count that as evidence. "No, I guess not," I forced myself to say. I thought about telling them Keaton's theory about him hacking my webcam, but they might want to see my computer. And what if I hadn't scrubbed it as clean as I'd thought?

"Do you have witnesses to the times that Samuel gave you one of these photographs?"

I blinked, trying to dislodge a piece of hair that suddenly found its way into my eye. "The first time he did it, he put it in my locker at work. I don't know if anyone saw him do it, but they saw me give it back to him. That's why it's all crumpled up."

"Who's they?"

"His friends." I gave a quick list of their names that Detective Morgan promptly jotted down.

"Interesting. So, regarding the incident that reporters picked up a few weeks ago, the confrontation between you and Samuel where he ended up with a broken nose…"

I said nothing as I waited for her to get to the point.

"What happened there? Was it another picture?"

"Yes. It was one of me, my friend, Keaton, and her girlfriend, Trixie. It was after the shooting, and things were already tense for me. I didn't break his nose, by the way, just made it bleed. People were shouting and throwing things at me anytime I tried to leave the house. When I saw Samuel outside, I thought about the photograph he had shown me, and I asked him what he was doing there."

"Did he have a reason to be around your apartment?"

"No. He said there wasn't anything I could do about it. I

told him to leave and tried to walk away, but he wasn't having it. He grabbed my wrist, hard. I don't like to be touched…I…"

"Defended yourself?" she guessed.

"Exactly."

"Did he say anything else before you hit him?"

"Remember the other day in the break room? When you said I'd regret whatever I do to you? I haven't yet, and you…you keep making it easier. It's almost like you enjoy the torment."

"Is that really what you think?"

"I don't know what to think, honestly. You don't bother to tell anyone about our little interactions, and at first, I had to wonder why. Then, the shooting happened, and it occurred to me that you haven't sought out help because you're hiding something. You don't want to risk it being exposed."

"I-I don't remember," I lied. I wanted to tell her the truth, I did, but everything had gotten so twisted I couldn't separate one string without everything else unraveling.

By the way she stared into my eyes, I could tell she already knew there was more to the story.

Chapter Twenty-Eight

ETECTIVE MORGAN DISMISSED me, but I had the feeling things weren't over.

"How'd it go?" Harlow asked as soon as I made it to my register.

"It went okay, I guess," I replied, typing my code into the computer.

"What'd she ask you?"

I typed slower, considering how much I should tell her. How much of Samuel's fascination with me did Harlow know? Did she know about the pictures? The notes? The IMs? *Molly*?

"She asked me about my relationship to Samuel because she heard me and him went on a date."

Harlow's nose twitched. "I've heard that too," she admitted, reaching up to poke at her orange-blonde spikes of hair. "What *were* you two?"

These were the type of questions I had known were coming. Yet I still had no answers.

"Harlow! Back to work!" Mr. Waters called when he saw the line at her unattended register.

"Oops," she said, hurrying back.

Saved by the bell.

I felt like I had a rock in my stomach for the rest of the

shift. Part of me wanted to throw up, but the rock wouldn't move. When the rush died down, Harlow tried to find her way back to me, but I did my best to pretend I didn't notice. My shift would be over soon, and I didn't want her to have the chance to ask her question a second time.

I rang up a few customers, pretending not to see Carmine's points and gestures as she talked to Harlow. I wasn't close enough to hear what they were saying, and for that, I was grateful. The past few days I had come to think of Harlow as a sort of friend. She hadn't given me any reason not to, but today was different. I had to remind myself she had been friends with Samuel.

I couldn't wait for my lunch break for the chance to escape. I didn't eat, finding my stomach wasn't interested in anything I could offer it. I wandered around the store, trying to keep hidden as I eavesdropped on my coworkers' conversations.

"That girl from the ice cream shop. What was her name?" One of the stockers asked another. I ducked behind the shelf to listen.

"Who? Pamela?"

"Yeah, that one. Samuel was hanging around her a lot those few days."

"Think she had something to do with it?"

"It's possible."

It seemed that no one trusted anyone. For now, we were all in the same boat. Next time though—and there *would be* a next time—the detectives would have narrowed perspective on who they suspected.

WHEN THREE O'CLOCK came, I left without gathering my belongings from my locker. I didn't want to stay any longer than I had to. My senses stayed on alert during the walk from the store to the bus. Against my better judgement, I glanced across the parking lot as I passed it, eyeing the mouth of the alley. In broad daylight, I almost felt crazy for remembering what had happened in that exact spot.

Look away.

It was hard, but I managed, picking up my pace to ensure that I didn't get the sudden urge to investigate. The bus didn't take long to pick me up, and when I sat down, my nerves began to calm. Tomorrow, anything could happen, but for today, I was safe.

Despite my shot at optimism, Samuel was everywhere in my mind. I thought of the confrontation by the fire escape, the anonymous IM's, the photographs, and I wondered what else I missed. How long it would be before the police issued a search warrant? How long would it be before they issued a warrant for my arrest?

At the apartments, I rushed through the lobby and up the stairs. I barely recognized Keaton as I passed her. This time, she didn't let me breeze past her like I had been hoping to do. She held an arm out, stopping me in place. I thought about ducking under it, but she would grab me, and I would lose whatever sense of self-preservation I had left.

"Jess, you're avoiding me. Stop and talk to me. What's going on?" she demanded.

I played the same clueless game with her that I had with

the police. "Whatcha mean?"

"You haven't been the same since Samuel disappeared," she said. "And when I see you, you try to rush past me like you don't know who I am. What happened?"

"Nothing."

"Well, why did an officer come to talk to me not an hour ago? Asked a lot of questions about you. Any idea what that's about?"

"No clue," I said dismissively and tried to brush past her again. I couldn't have this conversation. Not now, when things had looked so clear.

"Not so fast," she said, catching me by the arm.

It was hard, *too* hard to stay detached from her when normally she was the one I told everything to.

Not this, I warned myself when the crack in my armor grew larger. *Never this.*

"What happened to Samuel?" she asked, eyes boring into mine.

I grasped her hand back, staring into her eyes and said what words could not. The look was filled with emotions and theatrics, and when she finally blinked, breaking the intensity between us, I had the weird feeling that somehow, she *knew* exactly what I had done.

She nodded once. I might not have noticed it if I hadn't already been staring right at her. Wordlessly, she pulled me into a hug. When she pulled away, it was to look me in the eyes again. I nodded back at her, a subtle lift and drop of my chin. Then, she let me go, and we continued our opposite paths up and down the stairs as if the interaction had never happened.

When I went into the apartment, Mom was seated on the couch, staring at a mostly untouched mug of coffee on the table. I would've been more curious if I didn't already know what this was about. If the cops had questioned Keaton on my behalf, it made sense that they would speak to Mom too. She barely recognized the fact that I stood there, staring at her. Her eyes were glazed over, and I made a mental note to check her prescriptions later.

"Are you okay, Mom?" I asked as I crossed the kitchen to go into the living room.

She wiped her eyes, clearing away some of the haze, before she took a small sip of her likely cold coffee. "Yeah, I'm sort of out of it. Some officers stopped by today. Wanted to know some things about you. There's a missing boy, and you're a suspect?"

My heart pounded like a caged bird desperately trying to escape. I had known this moment was coming, but Mom's face made it worse. She looked *traumatized,* and I could guess that whatever the cops had said hadn't been good.

"Why is this happening again, Jess?" she asked after a full minute of silence. "I thought the stuff with Oscar and the shooting was over, and now…"

I carefully considered how to make this approach. I didn't like how evasive she was being. Usually, I could play with my mother's emotions and thoughts and get her to do whatever I needed her to. This mood she was in was a rare one, one where she felt for someone besides herself. I couldn't tell if she was hurt by the possibility that I could've killed someone else or if she was beginning to give up on me. Either of those wouldn't be good. If I planned to get away with this, I needed her full support. As far as alibis go, Mom was the closest thing that I had that night. The evil part of my brain reminded me that her addiction could come in handy for that.

"What did they want to know?" I played dumb for the third time that day as I sat in the armchair. The act was tiresome, but I would have to keep it up for the rest of my life.

"Just what kind of person you are. If everything has been okay at home, and where you were about a week ago. They asked about your connection to some boy named Samuel. I told them you didn't know anyone by the name, but they made it pretty clear that you did. Now I feel like I don't know my own daughter. I thought the secret keeping was over, but I guess not."

A dangerous smile found its way to my lips. It wasn't an expression of happiness, but something primal—something dark. Mom wasn't trying to attack me, she was expressing her feelings, but the darkness in me didn't like it. "He was someone I worked with."

"And he's missing," Mom said the words pointedly slow. *Was that an accusation?*

"Yeah," I said simply, watching as she scrambled to get a hold of her mug. "My coworker, Harlow, said his sister called it in."

"So, you *did* know him?"

"*Know* is a strong word, Mom," I said. "I knew *of* him. Like I said, I worked with him. I work with a lot of people, but no, I didn't *know* him, know him."

Mom's nose twitched, and she set the mug down again,

the brown liquid threatening to swish over the side. "If you don't mind my asking, how close *were* you to Samuel? The police seem to think you two had some kind of connection. Something personal."

The feral smile came back. Mom didn't meet my eyes as she waited for me to speak, and I let the silence rule the moment as I considered my next sentence. I had never wanted to tell her about Samuel, and the fact that I *had to* made it worse. If I lied now, she would lose whatever faith in me she had left.

"We talked occasionally, but I mean, I talk to everyone at work in passing."

I could've been honest and ended the conversation, but when I thought about telling her about him, it made my stomach crawl. I had always done a good job of separating my home life from my life outside of the apartment. Telling Mom about Samuel was a breach in that strategy, one that could topple everything.

"Why do they think there's more to the story?"

"Supposedly they found things in his apartment."

"What kind of things?" I asked. My tone was demanding instead of curious. I *needed* to know what I had left behind, the mistake I had made.

As I stared at Mom, she finally pulled together the courage to look back up at me. Her eyes were red-rimmed, and I couldn't tell if that was from the pills or if she had been crying. Something tugged at me, and I wondered if it would be so bad to tell her the truth—not *all* the truth of course, but enough about what kind of a person Samuel was, or had been.

I clapped my hands and said, "Photographs. There was a

little more between us than just coworkers, but he was weird, Mom. We tried one date, but it didn't end well. Things have been…tense…ever since."

"Tense?"

"Yeah, he picks on me a lot."

"Oh, sweetheart," Mom said, jutting out her bottom lip.

Then I remembered *that* was why I didn't like to tell her things. I never wanted *anyone's* sympathy, and I hated having hers now. She acted as if I were a victim, a fragile helpless little thing who couldn't fend for herself.

Don't say it, I warned myself when the words began to burn like acid on my tongue. *There are other ways to prove your point.* That may be so, but none of them would be as satisfying as admitting that I wasn't someone who needed to be looked after.

"No, Mom, don't do that," I said. "Don't patronize me."

"I'm not *patronizing* you," she said, sitting up a little straighter at the anger in my voice.

"Then why does it sound like you think I can't deal with it? I have been this entire time."

"I never said you couldn't," she said, relaxing back against the couch as if that answer had satisfied her. "You've always been a strong, independent girl. Even when you were little you acted as if you never needed anyone to look after you."

That's because no one ever did, I thought, staring at the glaze over Mom's eyes. *I* had always taken care of *her.*

"If that's really all you two had between you, I'm sure they'll clear you soon."

Mom might brush it off as nothing, but the police wouldn't. I had motive, as far as they were concerned. At least more than anyone else with the exception of Oscar's family. With Samuel's laptop hidden, I wondered if they would be able to access all the secret IMs that had been sent between us.

"Yeah. I'm gonna go lie down," I said, ending the conversation before Mom could stop me.

I needed to be far from everyone and everything. I patted my thighs and rose to my feet, hurrying through the doorframe which separated the light of the living room from the darkness of my room. I put myself into my usual cocoon among the blankets and pulled my laptop toward me.

Like every other day, I argued with myself to leave it off. Scouring the internet would not help me feel better. Also like every other day, I lost the internal battle and powered the computer on. The first thing I did was stare at the old IM messages from Samuel.

"Goodbye, Samuel," I murmured as I deleted them.

Before the link was gone for good, I maneuvered to his website, to the discussion boards.

Now the only one who questioned her is dead, the top thread was titled.

Someone commented, *There's no proof he's dead. He's been reported missing.*

Something about it still doesn't add up. I mean has everyone forgotten that she broke his nose? She's not the sweet thing she pretended to be in her interview. If anyone was responsible for his disappearance, it was probably her.

Yeah, finishing up what Oscar couldn't.

That was enough for me.

I deleted my profile, trying to clean my digital fingerprints the best I could. If the police decided to check my laptop, it wouldn't matter much. They would be able to find it all. They probably already thought it strange they couldn't find Samuel's computer. It would look bad if mine went missing too.

What was done, was done. It was too late for me to go back.

Chapter Twenty-Nine

THE REST OF the day passed without incident. That wasn't surprising considering I didn't leave my room for anything except bathroom breaks. I wondered how long it would take of this total isolation before I lost what was left of my mind.

When I woke in the morning, I wanted to stay in bed. This wasn't going to be a good day. I didn't know why I thought that, but I couldn't make the feeling go away. The only thing that lured me out of my room was the premise of coffee. A cruel caffeine headache worked at the front of my head, but at least this was one problem I could fix.

I went to the kitchen, slamming things around as I got the coffeemaker started. Mom was still asleep, or she wasn't home. Hard to tell for sure. I hoped for the latter of the two though.

When the coffee was finished, I poured it into my mug without my usual dosage of sugar and creamer. Wary of spilling it, I moved back to the couch and sat down. The first sip of liquid burned my mouth, but I was glad for the sensation. It made the next sip easier. In a way, it was like life. Things happened to strengthen you for the next terrible thing that would stumble across your path. The incident with Oscar as a prelude to Samuel told me that.

I shivered and took another sip, wincing. It was then I remembered yesterday, the absent look on Mom's face as she sat in this same place with this same mug. I wondered if I was doing more harm than good to the people around me by staying here after what I did.

Before Oscar, it hadn't been unusual for Mom to hint that it was time for me to move out and try to make it on my own. What if she was right? Living by myself with no Keaton upstairs? I didn't know if I could handle that. I might not be actively happy with Mom, but somehow, the thought of living without her left a bad taste in my mouth. If I was going to go anywhere without her, it would be prison.

I tried to imagine what my mom could've been like if she'd had a different kid, one who was normal.

One who didn't have blood on her hands.

As if she had heard my thoughts, Mom's door clicked open. I closed my eyes, listening to her footsteps as she trudged down the hall. She stopped at the entrance of the living room, and I could feel her staring at me.

Eyes squeezed tight, I asked her the heaviest question at the front of my brain. "Is it because of me?"

She was silent, and I opened my eyes to make sure she was still there. Mom looked more confused than she had in a while, and that was saying something since I'd seen the disorientation her highs brought her.

"What?" she asked.

"The pills. Are they because of me?" I repeated, really studying this woman. She was cloaked in her baggy pink robe and matching slippers. She seemed to shrink in on herself. The drugs were making her lose weight again. She was taking too many. In my opinion, one pill that she didn't need was too many, but Mom had to be taking double her usual dosage for the effects to be visible.

Mom said nothing for a minute. Then, she stepped over the threshold and sat beside me. "Why would you think that?"

"You're high right now, for starters," I said, voice equal parts patience, sadness, and anger.

Mom was silent. I hadn't expected her to try and defend herself, and she wouldn't. Not when she was confronted directly.

"Before the shooting, you were doing better," I said. "You did good for a little while after too. Then yesterday with the police…and now, things are bad again. It's like you don't trust that you know who I am anymore."

Tears bubbled in her eyes. "It's been a hard year for both of us," she said. "But never blame yourself for what I am. This is a demon I've grappled with long before you were born."

I stared down at my hands. Seemed as if everyone had a hint of darkness inside them, but it was the way they chose to spend it that defined who they were. Mom was an addict, Oscar a murderer, and Samuel? I hadn't figured his out exactly. A mix and match of demons?

"Okay," I said and left Mom alone in my room. As if on cue, my phone began to ring from where I'd left it on the table next to the couch. "Hello?"

"Are you awake?" Keaton asked.

"Obviously," I replied, barely containing my agitation. "What's up?"

"They're rounding up search parties today for Samuel, and there are *hundreds* of people ready to help."

"Where are you?"

"I went to get breakfast with Trixie and saw people gathering in the park. We passed it less than ten minutes ago."

I tried to cap my panic without alerting Keaton or Mom to the fact that it was there to begin with. "Why are you telling me this?"

"I thought you should know."

She hung up, and I was left staring at my phone, a dozen questions bounding through my head. The most prominent— *Did she know?*

I went to my room for my laptop and settled in bed, Googling what Keaton had told me. Search parties were scheduled throughout the week to scope for signs of him "dead or alive." They were planning to search the woods and the ravine.

The ravine, I thought, chest tightening.

A clock ticked in my head, each second an insistent pounding at my temples. I was on the verge of a stress-induced migraine that would only grow as the day continued. I tried counting to ten and back down again to wrangle my thoughts into place. Panic wouldn't help me. I needed a plan. For now, Samuel was a missing person. No one could say the "m" word until a body was found.

With shaking fingers, I did something that I didn't want to do—I signed up to join Samuel's search party.

I QUESTIONED EVERYTHING about myself as soon as I finished filling out the form, but it was worse as I approached the park. There were people there I knew. Of course there would be. Why hadn't I thought of that? I wouldn't be a nobody here.

Carmine and Harlow were there as well as Mr. Waters and a few regular customers from the store. The stockers I had eavesdropped on were there as well as the girl they had been gossiping about. When I approached, they all looked at me the same way though no one said a word.

What are you doing here? that look told me, and I didn't know.

This would be a mistake, I was sure. Even if I could potentially steer anyone away from Samuel's final resting place today, I couldn't do it forever, and now the police had one more connection between me and him.

"Hey, friend. I didn't think we'd see you here today," Harlow said, running up to me.

"My friend told me this was happening, and I wanted to do my part to help," I said, trying to keep eye contact. With Harlow's t-shirt displaying a picture of Samuel under the words *Have You Seen Me?* it was a challenge.

Harlow's face blazed with an approving smile, and I was surprised to see there was no trace of suspicion. If I could keep this act up, I might be in the clear.

"We've been here for a while," Carmine said, peering at me through her huge sunglasses.

I interpreted it as a shot for almost being late, but before I could respond, a guy with a megaphone called the group to attention.

"Thank you, everyone, for volunteering today! I'm sorry to announce that we may be searching for a body, but we must consider all options in Samuel's disappearance. Now that we're in groups, you'll be given an assigned area to search. When you're out there, be careful of any potential hazards like snakes and be sure to keep hydrated. At the end of the day, report back to me, unless of course you find something sooner, then alert someone immediately."

Chattering sprung out around the clearing, but I pretended not to hear it. I was paired with Harlow, Carmine, and a few strangers. I crossed my fingers as maps were handed out with particular areas circled in red. When the man with the megaphone approached our group, he handed the map to Harlow.

I peeked over her shoulder to see our circle. The area covered a span of woods not far from Samuel's dumping ground. I had no doubt that some other group would have that part of the ravine. This was bad. What could I do if someone from my group stumbled over him before I could move him…or someone from another group found him instead?

I'll get to him first, I vowed as we set off on our grim journey.

Chapter Thirty

HARLOW AND CARMINE were far more upset about Samuel's disappearance than I could pretend to be. As we walked to the woods, they exchanged memories of him, laughing and crying. A few times, Harlow tried to include me in the conversation, but I walked faster, pretending I hadn't heard her.

Maybe that was suspicious, but my anxiety made it impossible for me to decide how else to act. I didn't have warm memories to share with them. All my memories were as cold as his body. I wanted today to be over with because it held two distinct possibilities at the end of it—life would go on as normal or I would go to prison for the rest of my life.

When we reached the trees, I glanced to Harlow who glanced to the three other girls in our group.

"How are we going to do this?" Carmine asked.

"He said to make sure we stay about an arm's length apart as we search," Harlow said, reading the notes jotted into the corner of the map.

"What happens if we get separated?" Carmine asked, staring into the copse of trees.

"Meet back up here," I suggested.

The other girls glanced at me for an uncomfortably long moment before Harlow said, "Works for me," and tucked the map away into the pocket of her short shorts. "To the ravine first. Here's to hoping we *don't* find him out here."

I muttered *Amen* under my breath.

All five of us walked far enough away from one another that we would seek out different ground, but not close enough to overlap. Keeping restraint on my pace was one of the hardest things I had ever done. I wanted to run ahead, leaving them in the dirt, but that wasn't something I could explain away. I had to keep my place at the end of the formation, walking step after slow step, waiting for the perfect moment as we approached the trees. I brainstormed possible ways to break away from the line. Would they accept a bathroom break as an excuse.

You're fucked, that little voice declared in the back of my head. *You just don't know it yet.*

Don't count your chickens before they hatch, I argued back.

Harlow was the first in the trees, the rest of the group a moment behind her. The uneven ground made it difficult for us to stay in perfect formation, and the trees didn't help much either. The deeper we went, the farther we had to spread out until I could no longer see Harlow or any of the other members of our party through the foliage.

That's lucky, I told myself, heartbeat speeding up with opportunity.

This would be my chance to look on my own terms, but the spot I needed to get to was still a good ten minutes away. If I disappeared for that long, would they notice?

You're not going to have a better chance, the singsong voice warned.

The stirring of indecision in my gut made me dizzy, as if my intuition suspected this moment would lead to something bad, something I couldn't take back. I pushed it away and ran. I couldn't tell if the girls were still close enough to hear the crunch of foliage as I bolted through the trees, but I didn't let myself dwell on it. I ran and ran until the burble of the river sounded in the distance.

The ravine looked different during the day, and I wondered if I would be able to find Samuel's resting place easily. When I had been in the moment, I'd been sure that I would never be able to forget it, but now? Everything was in a haze as if the fog wanted to keep me safe by concealing the worst parts of myself from being accessed.

In the soft mud around the edge of the river, my feet sunk deeper and deeper as I glanced up and down the coast. I didn't see anything from here, and that left me both relieved and worried. If it was this hard for *me* to find him, at least it would be challenging for anyone else in the area. I swallowed roughly, glancing to the right, the direction I was sure the rest of my group had disappeared to. Had they noticed I was missing yet? If they did, were they looking for me?

Don't worry about that yet, I thought and decided to run left.

The pebbles and mud under my feet made it hard, and for all the effort I put in, I barely got a few feet away from my original position. Against my racing heart, I forced myself to walk, to tread the edge of the riverbank carefully. In my mind's eye, I pictured Samuel's grave again. It had been a huge hulking mound of mud, the dirt thin in some places.

If nothing else, animals might've found him by now and moved him. When I finally spotted the mound, it was smaller than I remembered as if the darkness of the night had exaggerated it. Or maybe that had been the direct result of my guilt.

Fluttering blooms of red covered it. Blood. It was blood.

I lifted a hand, blocking the worst of the sun's glare as I closed the distance. The red spots moved in a wave of color, and I realized what it was.

Butterflies.

His grave was covered in butterflies. At least a dozen of them, maybe two. I took a step closer, unsure what to do. They didn't fly away, not at first, and I had to put effort in to get them to move. They were like a beacon, a spotlight, a target. My head whipped from side to side as I scanned again for any of the other groups.

I turned back to the grave, thrusting my hands at the dozens of tiny insects. At last, they took to the sky as one giant swarm, but I was unsettled, convinced the butterflies had been trying to signal Samuel's final resting place to passersby. Almost as if it were Samuel himself spiting me from the other side.

That's ridiculous, I told myself.

It didn't make the goosebumps go away. Especially when all I had to do was look down to see the pale dead skin of a corpse. Some of the dirt had chipped away where animals had attempted to dig their way to him. I clamped my hand over my nose and mouth, trying to drown out the smell. It was sweet and musty, the unmistakable smell of rot. On reflex, I gagged and rushed to kick a clump of dirt over the exposed spot. That wouldn't be enough to fix this. That smell would draw other scavengers, and tomorrow, he could be exposed again. I needed a new plan.

I glanced from him to the rushing water of the river and back to him again. My plan was risky, but so was leaving him here on the bank where any hungry animal could expose my evil deeds to the light of day.

"Okay, asshole, change of plans," I said to him.

With the sun drying the dirt, it came away from the mound easily, a thin layer left to dust Samuel's bloody form. His eyes had gone milky, his skin ashen. Trying my best to breathe without smelling or tasting, I reached into the pit, grabbing him by the shirt. The crusted blood scratched my palms, and I closed my eyes as I hoisted him out.

This would all look bad once he was gone—the hole and the drag marks—but the sooner, I disposed of him, the sooner I could clean it all up. Puffing my cheeks with the strain of his weight, I pulled him to the edge of the burbling river, wading in a few steps, not enough to be knocked off balance, but enough that the water rushed over my shoes.

I used the momentum of the water to move him over the slight drop, closing my eyes when I heard the thud and the splash of his body. There might be other groups searching this side of the woods, but hopefully they would either back away before reaching the river or would happen to miss Samuel for whatever reason.

I made sure there were no signs of gore on me. Passing inspection, I hopped out of the water and dropped to my knees, scraping the dirt into the grave and over the drag lines. By the time I had finished, I was sweaty and muddy, but at least the ground appeared to have never been disturbed. I hobbled up to my feet, walking back in the direction that Harlow and the rest of the group had disappeared to about a half hour prior.

I need an excuse, I said, glancing around.

They would ask where I had been. I'd been gone too long, and I'd be stupid to think they wouldn't have noticed my disappearance. Cold sweat ran down the side of my face. "I got lost" wouldn't cut it.

I needed something they *couldn't* argue with.

By the edge of the trees, a bit away from the riverbank, there was a large root sticking out of the ground. The twisting brown vines left a tiny loop above the mud that would be easy to get caught in if someone weren't paying attention to where they were walking.

I wiped my clammy hands on the side of my shorts as I approached it. What Samuel needed was time for his body to drift away. Time was something I could buy—today at least. I approached the root, circling it like an alley cat about to get into a brawl over territory. I had never broken a bone before. I didn't know what to expect beyond the obvious: it was going to hurt like Hell. I sat down, tucking my ankle underneath the rim.

Above the line of my sneakers, the rough surface of the Earth pricked my skin. The sensation was easy to ignore in the thought of the pain that would replace it momentarily. Gently, I moved my foot from side to side, seeing how tightly the root would hold me in place. I couldn't move much, but it was still too much for this to work. I slid closer. The root dug into my ankle.

Breathing out, I looked up at the sky, the mesh of branches overhead dissecting the sunlight into a thousand slivers, and pulled my ankle violently to the side, audibly cracking my own bone. I didn't hold in my screams. I let them out, long piercing wails until I was sobbing.

For good measure, I repeated the movement, yanking it in the opposite direction until the pain was so intense I thought I might pass out. Through the agony, I tried to pull my foot free of the trap which proved to be just as painful. Now that it was in there, the root didn't want to let go. My face was soaked in tears by the time I scooted completely out of contact with the branch.

Shouts started in the distance, but through the delirium of my pain, I couldn't tell if they were real. I thumped onto my back on the forest floor, trying to count the branches as the screams grew louder. I couldn't tell which were mine and which weren't.

"Jess! Where are you?" It was Harlow.

I didn't respond. I moved my useless leg, using the fresh stab of pain to free another scream before footsteps sounded on the nearby foliage.

Her hand touched my shoulder before she knelt down beside me. "Oh, my God! Jess! What happened?"

"I-I got separated from you guys, and I tried to backtrack to where we split up. I guess I wasn't watching where I was going as well as I should've—" The rest of the group began to converge around Harlow "—and my foot caught on something. I fell, and I think I broke my ankle. It hurts, Harlow," I said, putting as much emotion into my eyes as I could. Since the wound really *did* hurt, it wasn't hard to pull off this act.

Harlow's bottom lip trembled as she studied the mass of bone jutting awkwardly against my skin. "Let's get you to the hospital," she said and sat me up, hoisting an arm under my shoulder. She glanced to Carmine to do the same.

Between all three of us, walking was manageable though I was uncomfortable with the close proximity. I hated being touched, especially by strangers. *You brought this on yourself,* I reminded myself.

"What should we do?" one of the extra girls in the group asked. Ruth, I thought her name was.

"Go tell the guy what happened," Harlow said.

The extra members of our group filtered away to make a report as Harlow and Carmine led me to their car. For now, it was impossible to tell if my plan was the right move or if it would come back to bite me in the ass later on.

Chapter Thirty-One

CARMINE LEFT WHEN we got to the hospital with the reason that she wanted to touch base with the event organizer before going home for the day. Harlow kept her arm looped under my shoulders as we went into the waiting room. I took my time filling out the admission paperwork, but Harlow didn't seem to mind.

"How's your ankle?" she asked as I passed her back the clipboard.

"It still really hurts," I said with a small laugh.

"I bet," she replied, taking the clipboard back to the receptionist.

When she sat down again, she looked down at my awkward leg, and I wondered what she thought. She didn't seem impatient or upset. When a nurse wheeled out a chair, Harlow helped me get into it. She saw me settled into my room and my ankle tended to before she had to go. As I laid in the stiff bed, watching her leave, I almost thought what a shame it was to live in this universe where I was *me* and considered her to be someone non-vital to my existence. On another timeline, perhaps, she could've been a good friend.

I rested my head and closed my eyes, trying to adjust my

uncomfortable ankle in the sling they had put it in. Though they had given me plenty of pain medication, it still somehow wasn't enough to block out *all* of the pain. When I heard footsteps, I cracked open my eyes to see Keaton. She folded her arms over her chest, eyeing me from head to foot.

"You look like shit," she said and plopped down into the hard, black chair beside the wall.

"I shouldn't. I only broke my ankle."

"I've never broken any bones, but I'm guessing that wasn't fun," she said and leaned toward me. "What happened?"

I ran my hand across the starchy white blanket slung over my hips. "It was an accident."

"How do you accidentally break your ankle during a search party?"

"I wasn't watching where I was going," I said. "Pretty simple. It's not as if I was familiar with that particular stretch of woods."

Keaton made a noise in the back of her throat and rolled her eyes. "You've been in those woods before, right?"

"Once or twice. You've been in them too," I reminded her, cutting her a sideways glance. "What's your point?"

Keaton's face went tight with thought. She was weighing the pros and cons of something. That wasn't like her. Usually, she blurted out whatever came out then thought about it later. "Nothing, I guess," she said at last.

That wasn't what she had *wanted* to say. There was a gleam in her eyes, something haunted, that told me she wanted to say something else, that she *knew* something she wasn't saying.

"I don't know if I believe you," I replied.

"That's on you," she said and stood up, circling the bed. She poked the white bandages on my ankle. "How many places did you break it?"

"I think they said two," I replied, trying to shift my position to get rid of the growing numbness in my lower back. "Where's Mom?" I asked, hoping to steer the conversation away from the destructive path it had been on.

"She's working," Keaton said. "I told her what happened, but she still has an hour or two left of her shift then she said she's going to come visit."

"Oh," I said. I wouldn't be surprised if she simply went straight home to her wine. Part of me almost wished she would—at least that way, I would get to avoid playing twenty questions.

"What is it?" Keaton asked, narrowing her eyes at me.

"How'd you know I was here?"

"It wasn't hard. I went to the store looking for you and your coworkers said you were in the hospital."

I stared down at my blankets, skin scorching under her intense glare. With my nerves and anxiety already high, her visit felt like a trap, like I couldn't trust anyone.

"You know you can tell me anything, right?" she asked.

Absently, I said, "Yeah. Of course. Best friends forever." I lifted my fist to pump it into the air sarcastically.

"So, if you know, why aren't you telling me everything?"

Carrying my own version of a haunted stare, I said, "Because there's some things you're better off never knowing."

Chapter Thirty-Two

KEATON NEVER QUESTIONED my strange comment. She accepted it, and life moved on. The next week of my life proved to be a bizarre one. While I was allowed to leave the hospital, my foot and ankle were bound in a cast, and I was advised to not walk on it, or it would take it longer to heal. Mom scraped up the money to get me a knee crutch, but it was awkward, and I could see myself getting further injured trying to use it.

At first, I had expected Mom to help me understand the thing she had put all her money into, but she basically left me to my own devices. It was silly to expect anything else. Keaton put more investment into my healing than Mom did. Like usual. She helped me to practice with it, and after a few days, I was managing properly. While I had wanted to use the broken ankle as an excuse to hole up in my room and never emerge again, Mom wouldn't have it. Keaton either.

Of course, those days where I was still learning meant time at home, out of the loop of work and school. After the show I had made in front of Harlow and Carmine, I couldn't tell if not being around them was a good thing or not. If I knew them, they had gossiped about the day over and over, thought it was strange and probably stranger that I hadn't bothered to call in. Part of me hoped I'd be fired for missing the time because at least that way, I would have an excuse not to see them again.

Being cooped up in the house offered me stress that it never had before. I kept thinking about Samuel's hulking body being carried steadily down the river to God knew where. The river was huge, cutting across multiple counties, and I couldn't remember if it emptied into a lake or the ocean. That was something I could Google, but I didn't want anything to link me to Samuel's dumping spot.

According to the news, search parties went out every day with more and more volunteers each time. I was sure Harlow and Carmine went back whenever they could. After a week though, there was still no sign of him. Detective Morgan paid me two more visits over the course of that time. She didn't have anything new to tell me, but rather, she wanted me to tell *her* about how I'd gotten hurt. I wondered how the news had traveled to her and if someone had gone out of their way to report it. I thought of the way Keaton had been directed to the hospital the day it had happened, and I suspected Carmine to be behind it.

Detective Morgan wasn't a fan of mine. I could tell she hoped that the frequency of her visits, the repetition of her questions, would make me nervous enough to trip up on my story and mess up some crucial detail so she could run and tell the rest of the police department that I was lying. But I gave her the same speech. Every time she left, she seemed more frustrated than the last. As long as I kept up this routine, kept telling her this story, I would get away with what I had done.

Having the knee crutch meant Mom wouldn't let me

walk and take the bus so I was subjected to her awkward car rides when I needed to go somewhere. That made my already slim desire to go outside reduce to zero.

When I went through the doors at Grocer's Way, Harlow was the first to notice me in my awkward struggle across the front of the store. "Welcome back!" she cheered, running up to me to throw her arms around my neck. "How's your ankle?"

"Better, I guess," I replied, glancing down at the contraption subbing in for my all but useless leg.

"Ew," she said. "How long do you have to wear that?"

"Doctor said about four to six weeks—however long my ankle takes to heal. It was either this or traditional crutches and at least this way, my armpits won't hurt."

"That's true," she said. "I would've thought you'd take some time off though."

I laughed. "Yeah, me too. Science says otherwise."

"Well, I'm glad you're back," she said, glancing toward her register when she noticed the customer there. "Talk soon!"

Walking the hall to the employee lounge was hard. This place of a thousand memories only lit up with the darkest of them. I limped along, seeing the puddle of blood from Oscar's final resting place in my mind's eye.

Wrapped in my thoughts, I didn't notice Mr. Waters until he clapped a hand on my shoulder. "Jessica! I'm surprised to see you."

"Yeah, Mom got this thing for me so I can still move around. It didn't make sense to miss time I didn't have to," I said.

"Well, it's good to have you back," he said, going on his

way into the store.

I went to my locker, tossing my stuff inside and returned to the front of the store, trying not to think too much into the comment. I took my place at the register, doing my beset to comfortably situate myself. While my other coworkers, the ones who didn't speak to me, stared at me from their various places across the store, no one asked about my injury or the device I was using to compensate for it. I attributed that to Carmine and Harlow who had most likely filled them in. I didn't let myself wonder what exactly their story entailed because the more I wondered, the more likely I would be to ask.

"What happened to you, dearie?" an older lady with sparkling white hair asked me as she began to pay for her items.

"I uh, broke my ankle," I said, counting out the crisp bills as she handed them to me.

"Hope it gets better soon," she said.

I thanked her and passed her back her change. Nice customers were rare. Customers who took a moment to realize the person behind the register was also a person were even rarer.

When lunch came, Harlow and Carmine were already on theirs, but neither of them invited me to sit with them. They ate at a corner table in the Burger Joint, and when I entered, they looked up at me from their yellow wrappers. For perhaps the first time in my life, I was floored. I hated social interactions, but I had somehow come to think of Harlow as a friend.

Wounded by the quiet rejection, I ate nothing, clocking back in early from lunch. Harlow made no apologies when her and Carmine eventually came back, and I did my best to stay a good distance from them both for the rest of the shift. If

Harlow had anything to say to me, she would.

When I clocked out a few hours later, I said nothing to anybody. I clambered to my locker, got my belongings and went outside, patiently waiting for Mom to pick me up. I hated this new routine of depending on another person. I wasn't used to it. For as long as I could remember, I had been my own knight, rescuing myself again and again.

When I had broken my ankle, I hadn't realized what type of commitment I was really making. I paced back and forth, not wanting to catch anyone's attention. I made my way into the parking lot and passed the alley. I told myself not to look, but I couldn't help it and glanced down it, imagining a river of blood pouring out, covering my shoe, the scent filling my nostrils.

Glancing casually left and right, I checked my surroundings to see if anyone had noticed me. Cars moved along with the bustle of a workday afternoon, but from what I could gather, I was at no one's focus. A couple walked to their car on the other side of the lot, but they didn't glance at me.

Heart pounding, I ducked into the shadows, annoying knee device scraping the cement in a way that left chills down my spine. I didn't go far, enough to gawk at the place where Samuel's body had landed. There was no trace of blood, and I felt dumb for acknowledging this place where *anyone* could see me do so.

I went back into the street, head down. When Mom finally pulled up, I was so ashamed by my decision, I didn't see her right away. She yelled my name loud enough for everyone in the vicinity to stare. Face glowing in embarrassment, I climbed into the passenger seat and slammed the door, wishing I could escape all my problems so easily.

Chapter Thirty-Three

OM DROPPED ME off at the apartment and went to work. My first move was to sit on the couch and take the torture device off my leg. Someone knocked on the door, and I called for whoever was there to come in. Thankfully, it was Keaton and not a serial killer. Though the odds of there being two killers in the same place would be astronomical. I bit back the sarcastic smile that thought caused as she joined me in the living room.

"Just get home?" she guessed.

"Work was interesting."

"How so?"

"People acting as if they were glad to see me."

Keaton twisted her face. "How do you know they weren't? Believe it or not, you're not as bad of a person as you think you are."

I laughed at that. We spent the next few hours binging horror movies and eating junk food. Keaton volunteered to make dinner. By the time Mom came home from work, the table was set, and there was a meal ready.

"Girls, this is a surprise," she said, hanging her purse on the hook by the door.

"Thank Keaton," I said from my place in the living room. If she hadn't come to help, Mom would've come home to nothing. It was what I was used to receiving.

"Thank you, Keaton," Mom said as she took a seat.

Hobbling, I managed to get up and make my way to the table. I refused to put the walking crutch back on for the rest of the night. Mom frowned at me, and I knew she was thinking about how much money she had paid for it, but I didn't care. We ate mostly in silence. Since Keaton had cooked, Mom volunteered to do the cleanup. That was when Keaton helped me to my room.

"Sure you don't want to bring your thing with you?" she asked, glancing over her shoulder to where it sat on the couch.

"No."

"Suit yourself," Keaton said, helping me the last few steps into my room. "You should come out with me tonight," she added as soon as I sat down. "We'll go to the theater, like old times."

I glanced down to my cast. "I think I'd rather stay in if that's okay with you."

Keaton tapped her foot twice. "Even before you broke your ankle, you'd say that."

"Yeah, but I don't feel up to human interaction. Today was kind of exhausting as it is."

"That's also something you'd say. Well, let me know if you change your mind." She planted a kiss to my forehead and left.

I sat in silence, listening to the blood pounding in my ears. Part of me wanted to hang with her, and I wasn't really sure why I had turned her down. I wanted my life to continue as if I had never done anything wrong, but it couldn't. I would be trapped in this limbo, this waiting for bad news, until the news actually came.

I waited until the sounds of movement from the kitchen went silent before I limped across the room and out into the living room. I sought out Mom's wine bottle, chugging what was left before I laid down in a drunken stupor. For a little while at least, the world didn't look so bad.

***

IF I HAD known that was going to be the most peaceful sleep I was going to have for the rest of my life I would've slept in longer, much longer. But as life would have it, I would be woken early in the morning. My phone rang and rang beside my head. I silenced it, but that didn't stop it from vibrating over and over. When I finally cracked open my eyes to see who was disturbing me, I realized it was Keaton.

She had never called me like this before. If something was on her mind, she would come over, tell me in person. *Something must be wrong.*

"Hello?"

"Let me in," Keaton said. "I'm outside."

I pulled the phone away to glance at the time in the corner of the screen: *3:30*. I must've been blacked out and not heard her. Or was she was trying to avoid waking up Mom.

"What? Why?" I groaned.

"Please," she said. "You need to hear this."

"Fine, I'm coming," I said and hung up.

I looked for my knee crutch beside the couch and got it hooked to my leg as quickly as I could. With the pounding at the front of my forehead, it took me a few tries. I took in a deep breath against the swirling nausea in the pit of my stomach. Trying to make little sound, I crossed through the living room to the door. I peered through the peephole, catching a distorted Keaton waiting on the other side.

I cracked it open. "What's wrong?"

"Let me in," she hissed, pushing against the wood.

I stepped out of the way to allow her to come inside. She closed the door behind her and leaned against it, staring at me.

"What is it?" I asked, almost annoyed by her silence. If it was an emergency, why wasn't she speaking?

"They found him."

"What?" I asked, half-asleep and not wanting to be sure of what I heard.

"Samuel. They found him."

My eyes stretched wide. "Really?"

"There's a bunch of cops by the woods not far from the old Melville house. Trixie said they have the area roped off with caution tape."

I didn't want to believe her, but she wasn't lying. Not about this. Keaton plucked her phone out of her pocket, reading a text message before she glanced up at me. "They're saying foul play."

I said nothing to Keaton as I made my way over to the couch and sat down, staring at the blackness of the television screen.

"Jess?" she asked, following me. "What is it?"

I held my tongue.

"What did you do, Jess?" Keaton said.

I wanted to give her the same lie that I had used from day one—that nothing had happened and everything was fine—but the words wouldn't form. Speaking would damn me as easily as silence. Keaton approached, crouching in front of me until I was forced to look into her big blue eyes, and I had a moment where I hated her for doing this.

Then, it dissolved away.

I used to think my hate made me strong. For so long, I had used it as a shield to distance myself, to keep the world at bay, because things were easier that way. Or so it seemed. I hadn't understood that, in reality, my hate made me ugly, it made me *weak*. Seeing the soul inside of my best friend told me how much that hate had cost me. She pulled me into a hug, and I broke down in tears.

Chapter Thirty-Four

I CRIED AND cried, but Keaton didn't leave. She held me, saying nothing as I let it all out. Despite my show, I didn't tell her the words I needed to say. She stayed in the apartment as the pink rays of the sun broke out over the horizon as if she was waiting for me to inevitably break the rest of the way. I switched on the news, waiting for the story. Footsteps announced Mom's presence at the end of the hallway.

"Jesus, Jess. Keaton. It's early," she said, holding a hand over her heart as if we had startled her awake somehow though we hadn't talked in over twenty minutes.

"Yeah. I couldn't sleep," I said quickly.

Keaton bowed her head, politely staying out of the conversation.

"Want some coffee?" Mom asked as she walked into the kitchen.

"Yes, please," Keaton said.

I didn't chime in.

There was silence as Mom got the coffee started. I stared at my fingers as she distributed a cup to Keaton and one to me before she went back toward the hallway, pausing. "You work today?" she asked me, setting a hand on the wall to balance herself.

"Yeah."

"Okay. Let me know when you're ready to go, and I'll drive you."

"Okay, Mom."

She went back into her room, closing the door behind her.

Keaton tilted her head. "You know I'd be happy to give you a ride if you don't want her to."

"I don't want to put you off like that."

Keaton laughed. "Are you kidding? It's no trouble. Your job is only like a block from mine."

"Yeah, I know," I said, but I wouldn't ask her.

"I am sad to report that the search efforts for a missing twenty-four-year-old man have ended," a reporter declared.

"Here we go," Keaton said, turning up the TV.

"A local man walking his dog came across a gruesome discovery along the Hudson river this morning. What at first he believed to be pieces of logs and rock were the remains of missing local Samuel Black scattered along the river bank. Authorities at this time are unsure how the young man came to this unfortunate end, but they are ruling the case a homicide."

I couldn't bring myself to imagine what pieces of Samuel's body must've looked like after all the time in the elements. Against my will, my brain flashed back to him in the shallow grave, the chew marks from the animals who had stumbled across him, and I had the urge to vomit. Bile pooled at the back of my throat, and I remembered what he'd smelt like. My stomach got the best of me, and I hurled all over the floor.

"Jesus!" Keaton said and hopped up to rush to the

kitchen, grabbing the roll of paper towels. As she laid them systematically over the pool of vomit, her eyes scorched the side of my face.

I kept my eyes glued to the television as they panned to images of Detective Morgan. "The news we have come to learn today is unfortunate," she said amongst a chorus of screams and flashing lights from reporters. "But whoever is responsible, we will bring to justice."

She stared into the camera, and I felt as if she could see me through it. Shivering, I picked up the remote and turned off the television.

"Are you going to tell me what happened now?" Keaton asked at last, standing to her feet with the paper towel roll still in her hand.

"No," I replied and struggled to copy her. I didn't care when my foot touched the paper towels soaked with my vomit. I needed to get away.

"Jess!" Keaton called behind me, her voice a mix of surprise and pain. She followed me halfway across the room. "You can tell me. You don't have to go through this alone."

I didn't reply. I went into my room and closed the door.

Chapter Thirty-Five

I EXPECTED KEATON to follow me, to whip open my door and demand I talk to her. She did neither. I waited, counting the minutes in my head. After a good ten had passed, I got up and pressed my ear to the door. It was silent. I risked cracking it open.

Keaton was gone.

I was glad for the silence, but the voices in my head weren't kind. I thought of Oscar. I'd thought less and less about him since his memorial, but now, he entered my mind. I had the sudden need to be close to him.

I slid my shoes on and moved out of the apartment. I kept my head down and my hood up as I moved out of the building. Outside, it was raining and dark with the morning before dawn, and I counted my blessings. At least I wouldn't be as conspicuous dressed like this. I tucked my hands into my pockets, listening to the soft *patter* of water hitting the cement.

At the cemetery, I hurried across the wet grass to the columbarium. Thankfully, there was no one else inside. The residual memories of my last trip played in my head, but as I approached Oscar's niche, they faded away.

I set my hand to the plaque with his name and bowed

my head as I whispered, "Hey."

It was easy to imagine him beside me, greeting me like he used to do at work. I ran my finger over his engraved name and thought through all the laughs and good times. I couldn't wrap my brain around the fact that those memories had somehow led to this reality.

"I miss you," I told him.

I didn't like to think about the afterlife and what may or may not be waiting on the other side, but I thought about where Oscar could be, and if he knew what I had done to Samuel. If he would haunt me or if Molly would.

"I did it," I whispered. Tears misted my vision, and I blinked them back.

I thought of the feeling of stabbing my knife into Samuel's chest and his lifeless eyes afterward. If the afterlife was real, were Samuel and Oscar in the same place? Or had Oscar been reunited with Molly?

"I don't know if you can hear me," I said, "but things aren't the same without you. I think I made a mistake…doing what I did to you, but I'll never really know for sure. Either way, I can't take it back, and I'm sorry."

You…did what you had to do. My Oscar he…he was troubled…and you set him free, Oscar's mom had said.

I closed my eyes as a tear leaked free, and in my mind's eye, I could see his smiling face. That was the image I held onto as I dropped my hand from the plaque. I looked at Molly's for a second and said, "I hope you're finally at peace," before I turned away to go back home.

BY THE TIME I made it to the apartment, I was more mentally exhausted than physically tired, but I fell asleep without meaning to. Mom was the one to wake me.

"What time do you have work?" she asked.

I yawned as I studied her. She was already dressed in her uniform with her hair and makeup done. She was ready to go out the door, to get on with her day, but I was not. This was the day I had been dreading, the day that in a perfect world, would've never happened.

I glanced at my phone, seeing it was close to noon. "I don't have work until two, but you can drop me off on the way."

"Are you sure?" she asked. "You won't be bored?"

There will be plenty of entertainment, I'm sure, I thought. "No, I'll be fine. Give me a minute to get ready."

"Okay," Mom said and ducked out of the room. "What are all these paper towels?"

I winced, pretending I hadn't heard her. I had a message from Keaton. *I'll be here when you need me,* she had written, and my eyes welled with tears.

I wasn't proud of the way I had treated her over the past few days, but it seemed important to keep her at a distance. I tried to keep myself from feeling anything as I got dressed and pulled my hair into a ponytail. I reminded myself that this might be the last time I got dressed on my own accord. Next time, I might be put into an orange jumpsuit.

"Ready," I said to Mom as soon as I stepped back out into the living room. The mess on the floor was gone.

"Is everything okay?" she asked, eyeing me.

"Yeah, I'm fine."

"You don't look it."

"I have a little bit of a bug," I said, fake coughing lightly. "That was why I was awake early this morning."

"And why you left your vomit on the floor?"

"Yeah, that too."

Even for the device on my leg, I moved faster than her and avoided eye contact as we climbed into the car. The drive to work was as tense as I had expected it to be with Mom asking me every two minutes if I was sure I was alright and if I really wanted to go to work. Of course, I didn't *want* to go. I would've rather been hit by a bus or broken my other ankle, but today of all days, I thought it to be important to show my face.

People would be looking for it.

"Have a good day at work," Mom said to me.

I didn't reply as I got out of the car. Usually, when I got to work early, I hung around outside to avoid my coworkers. This time, however, I migrated to the employee lounge to hear what they had to say about Samuel. As predicted, there were plenty of whispers about him, theories as to what could've happened.

"It was a fishing accident," one of Samuel's stocker buddies said. "He waded out too far and the current swept him away. Case closed."

"There's no way to tell for sure though, is there?" his friend countered. "If he was as mutilated as the news said, how could they tell what actually killed him?"

I had to restrain myself from jumping into the conversation. *You're here to observe,* I had to remind myself. *Not guide.*

Detective Morgan appeared to question us again about ten minutes before I was supposed to clock in. When she came into the employee lounge, her eyes immediately went to me, and I wondered if she had been seeking me out.

"Jess, it's good to see you again," she said, then her eyes dropped to the cast on my foot. "How's your ankle?"

"Pretty much the same as the last time we talked."

She nodded along as if she hadn't really cared about the answer but had used it as a conversational ice breaker. "Are you on the clock?"

"No, I'm about to clock in though."

"Can I ask you a few questions first?" she asked, but we were already walking toward Mr. Waters' office so it was clear the question was rhetorical. As soon as the door closed, she was much more serious, more grim, which I hadn't known was possible.

"I don't know if you've heard," she began.

Once again, I stuck to my whole say-as-little-as possible trick. "I saw the story this morning on the news."

"Then you know this is no longer a missing person case. This is a homicide investigation."

That word echoed in my head, resounding with all the times I had thought it since that night. *A murder.*

She stared at me, stared hard. I didn't know what she was looking for, but the frustrated crinkle at the bridge of her nose told me she hadn't found it.

"If there is anything I can do to help, please let me know," I said, threading my fingers together in a way that I hoped appeared careful, thoughtful.

"There is actually," Detective Morgan said, pulling out a notebook to set on the table between us. "Run me through the night of Samuel's disappearance again. What were you doing around midnight?"

At this point, I wasn't worried about fudging on the details. It was a well-rehearsed script. Every time I said the same sentences, same words, they were etched deeper into my brain. Maybe Detective Morgan had the same thought.

"Are you sure that's the time you left the store?" she asked.

That was new. She hadn't bothered to ask for *detail* details—the superficial information I had given her up to this point had been enough. Now though, we were in the nitty gritty, stakes raised due to the discovery of Samuel's remains.

"Yes, I am. My manager can verify," I said, and Detective Morgan nodded again as if that answer satisfied her.

"Now who can collaborate the time you arrived back home?" she asked.

"My mom," I said without missing a beat.

"Hmm," Detective Morgan said, staring me in the eyes before writing something in her notebook.

"Is something wrong?" I asked, trying to keep my tone as innocent as I could, but it came out forced and squeaky. I was going off script.

Thankfully, Detective Morgan didn't jump at the opportunity. She said, "No. Tell me a little bit about your accident."

I furrowed my brow. "Why? I already told you what

happened."

"It happened while you were involved with a search party for Samuel, right?"

"Yeah, what about it?"

"According to the organizer of that event, the part of the woods your group was supposed to scout out wasn't too far upstream from where Samuel's remains were found."

My palms went sweaty, and I wiped them subtly on my pants thinking *This is it.* "That's…unfortunate," I choked out. "Maybe if I hadn't hurt my ankle, I could've found him."

"Did you or anyone in your group find anything suspicious before you fell?"

"No," I said quickly, maybe too quickly. "I got separated from the group, and I ended up falling down a hill which led to me breaking my ankle. I was taken to the hospital after that. I don't know if my group continued on without me or not. Carmine and Harlow came to the hospital with me, but the rest of them stayed behind."

"Don't worry Miss Mills, I intend to ask all of them."

When the silence became awkward, I asked, "Is that all you need from me?"

She leaned forward, elbows sliding on the desk as she tried to get a bit closer to me. "Why don't you tell me?"

I hid my nervousness behind a scoff. "That's all I know."

"Right," she said, dropping the pen onto the desk as she sat back up straight. "Thank you for your time."

I smiled a tight-lipped bitter smile. "My pleasure."

Chapter Thirty-Six

TODAY, CLOCKING OUT wasn't much of a relief because I had class right after. Wandering across campus with my device was embarrassing, and I wondered why I hadn't skipped today like I had most of the week.

No suspicion, the voice in my head reminded me.

When I made it into forensics, the class stared. Of course they would, I looked ridiculous, but the only one who seemed sympathetic was Mark. When I took my seat, he peered at me for a full minute before he asked, "What happened to you?"

"Broke my ankle trying to help in the search party," I said, tossing my backpack to the floor.

"For that Samuel guy?"

I muttered, "Yeah."

"I heard they found him in the ravine…or what was left of him anyway."

"Yeah, that's what I heard too," I said, pulling out my textbook to hide my face.

"It's crazy to think you can be alive one moment and gone the next," Mark said, sounding genuinely amazed by the concept.

"If it wasn't for death, we wouldn't have possible careers," I reminded him, tapping on the cover of my textbook.

"I suppose that's true."

I kept my eyes on him after the conversation was over. Mark had never talked to me this much before, usually ending our communication after he pilfered another of my pencils. It was strange for him to start now, but people *were* strange. It was almost as if they got some sort of thrill from talking to me because I had been on the news.

Class started, and I leaned forward in my seat, pencil posed over my notebook to start writing. Our professor didn't speak at first. He stood in front of the room with his hands folded together, staring at all of us. "I don't know if you've seen the news today, but one of our own was found deceased."

"Yeah, they found pieces of him," someone from the back of the class called.

"According to the official statement, the remains were greatly disturbed by wildlife," the professor agreed.

"Can they tell how he died?"

"The torso was found, although badly ravaged, and it will be enough to perform an autopsy though if it'll be able to produce conclusive results is yet to be seen."

I closed my eyes, trying to bite back my comments, but I was unsuccessful. "I thought it was illegal to talk about an open investigation."

"Ah, it's illegal to *interfere,* but we are not, Miss Mills. We are simply pulling a real-world example of forensics into our curriculum."

"Right," I murmured, studying the lines in my desk. *Why*

didn't I stay home?

THE REST OF the class was a hotbed of debate about Samuel. Apparently, he had a few friends in my class who believed his death to be murder. They couldn't fathom what he would be out there doing in the woods and insisted that he wasn't the outdoors type. Regardless of what anyone else said, they wouldn't back down. They believed that he was in need of "justice," but I thought that was overstepping boundaries a bit. The only kind of justice Samuel had been owed was divine retribution from karma which he had earned.

I couldn't understand the version of Samuel they had known, the one who caused them to want to run to his defense, to fight in his favor. He had been such a horrible self-involved human being that the thought of anyone seeing positive traits in him baffled my mind. Especially knowing the darkness he was capable of.

I kept that thought all throughout the rest of that night and into the next day. When I went to work, Harlow greeted me, though not as excitedly as she had before the search party incident, and I returned the sentiment. I didn't say more than one or two words to her until about half the shift was over. When she clocked out for lunch, she hung at my register, waiting for Carmine.

I studied her profile and couldn't help but ask, "Do you miss him?"

"Who? Samuel? Of course. Not a day goes by where I don't."

I asked the question that burned at the back of my brain. "Why?"

A little surprised chuckle fell from her lips. "What do you mean, *why?*"

"I mean what about him do you miss?"

Harlow considered the question before she said, "I don't know."

I thought she was joking, but based on the look on her face, it was clear she wasn't. She really didn't know why she missed Samuel, she simply believed she did. That was interesting. Was that how *everyone* felt about Samuel, and they were too invested in the drama of his loss to realize they let the mob mentality determine their feelings?

Chapter Thirty-Seven

WHEN MOM PICKED me up from school, she didn't say much. At home, she had a moment where she stared at me as I ambled across the kitchen and into the living room. When I sat down on the couch, she followed into the room, sitting down beside me.

"Is everything okay?" she asked.

"Just peachy, Mom, why wouldn't it be?"

"For one, you're watching nothing," she said, gesturing to the blank television screen and the remote on the other side of the room. "Second, I saw the news. They found that boy."

"Yeah, I know," I said, running a palm across my forehead. "Everyone's been talking about it."

"Everyone but you, it seems."

"He wasn't my friend when he was alive, I'm not going to pretend otherwise now that he's dead," I said and forced myself to my feet.

"You've been spending a lot of time mourning for someone who didn't care about the person who died," she said.

I looked at her over my shoulder. "I'm not mourning. I'm resting to heal my ankle."

"Well, what about before you broke your ankle?"

"Why are you needling me with questions?" I snapped.

"I'm not trying to bother you, but things don't make sense to me."

I could've approached her rationally, this was a tense situation for everyone, but I was falling apart at the seams. I had been sure that no matter what, Mom would be on my side. I hadn't considered that she might *not* be.

"You don't believe me?"

"It's not that. I love you. Of course, I believe you, but I…I want some clarity."

"I went to the search party because everyone else at work went," I said slowly, struggling to keep my anger under wraps. "He was one of us, and it wouldn't have been right for me to *not* go. Just like the vigil. I didn't feel right at the vigil either, but I went because I thought I should."

"Did you want him to be found?"

"Mom…" I said, tone almost whiney like a petulant teenager. I didn't want to answer. I wanted to snap my fingers and be somewhere and someone else and have this conversation end.

"Yes or no?" she asked, voice more authoritative than I had heard in years.

"No," I replied at last and let a sarcastic chuckle free. "Alright? Is that what you wanted to hear? No, I *didn't* want him to be found. He was a selfish, arrogant prick who got what was coming to him, and I wish he would've rotted away to nothing alone in the woods."

Mom said nothing. She stood and straightened out the bottom of her shirt before she disappeared into the hall, the slam of her door a moment behind.

THE REST OF the day, I was uneasy. Usually, I would've gone to Keaton to cheer me up, but I was alone. To distract myself, I started thinking about serial killers, and how I compared to them.

Berkowitz, or the Son of Sam, was one of my favorite serial killers because his patterns, his story, didn't seem to fit the guidelines for what was known of other serial killers. Where the others had a type of victim, he did not. He was guided by a feeling deep in his gut that warned him he wasn't like everyone else. Essentially, that was my M.O. I didn't lure victims to my car to knock them out like Bundy, and I didn't serenade them and lure them back into the quiet of my home like Dahmer. I killed people I knew, people who knew me, because some fundamental part of me told me it needed to be so.

I could've let Oscar live. I could've called 911 for Samuel, but those hadn't been my choices. I could only guess what Mom thought of me. She probably thought about all the horror movies I obsessed over, the video games I played, and blamed herself for not seeing the signs like I did with Oscar.

It wasn't her fault. It was no one's fault but mine. At any point in my life, I could've made a choice that would've changed everything, but I had not. I'd let my future decay away.

Numb, I watched the news, hoping to see some update on the Samuel situation. I didn't have to wait long. They had the autopsy results, something that had been heavily debated in class. Death by exsanguination. He bled to death which was ironic to me. For all the times he had made me emotionally bleed, all it took was one wound for his bleeding to turn fatal.

Chapter Thirty-Eight

WHEN I finally got around to pulling it open, Detective Morgan was on the other side. I stepped aside to let her in. It seemed as if every time Samuel was mentioned, I would get a visit from her. Now the two were a synonymous event.

She took her usual seat in the armchair, and I took my time hobbling over to the couch. I could've gotten there much sooner if I had wanted to, but it was early, and I was still too groggy. Detective Morgan's eyes stayed on me the entire time. In the first few days of having her around, that would've been enough to make me nervous, but I was used to it. No matter where I went, the police were nearby.

Or maybe I really *was* paranoid.

"Sorry if I woke you," she said.

"I was awake anyway," I lied, wiping my eyes in an attempt to clean away any remaining traces of sleep.

"The autopsy results on Samuel came back," she said, folding her hands in her lap.

"Yeah, the news said he bled out," I replied.

Detective Morgan glanced toward the television. "I don't know how those reporters are getting this info."

I didn't either, but I was glad they did. At least this way, I couldn't be caught by surprise.

"Well, whatever the case, I'm asking this to everyone who knew him—do you know any enemies he might've had? Anyone who would've wanted to see harm come to him?"

I didn't believe these were questions she was going to ask everyone because they were questions she had already asked them and come back with one answer—me. I was the most well-known enemy he had.

"No, I don't," I said, somehow maintaining eye contact without giving anything away.

She stared back as if she knew the truth was there *somewhere,* but when she finally spoke again, it was just to say, "Okay."

***

MOM LEFT AROUND noon without asking if I had anywhere to go. I had work and college but no energy to try and limp my way around the world. I called in sick for work and skipped my classes. I could've asked Keaton for a ride, but I liked the excuse Mom had given me better. While I had thought sitting alone in the quiet of the apartment was what I wanted, it ended up being too much. I stared at my phone, eventually breaking down and contacting Keaton.

Hey, I texted after four hours of debate.

She didn't text back right away, and I had the paranoid thought that I had messed up our friendship for good and that she *wouldn't* write me back.

Then, what felt like hours later but was really less than two minutes, came her response, *Hey, dude.*

Wanna come over for dinner?

The knock on the door came before a text ever did. I got up, thinking Mom was home early, but it was Keaton. I opened the door, staring down at Keaton's black and white checkered Vans. "I think I owe you an apology."

I heard the smile in her voice as she said, "You don't owe me anything." With a reassuring hand on my back, she guided me to the kitchen table. "Do you *have* anything for dinner?"

I opened and closed my mouth, feeling stupid. How could I invite her for something I didn't have? "No…I…I didn't have the chance to cook. Mom didn't tell me she was—"

Keaton held up a hand. "Say no more. Sit. I'll make something." I didn't obey as she started to rummage through the cabinets, pulling out various things to line up on the counter. "Sit down."

"But *I* should cook for *you*. I invited you."

"I don't mind," Keaton said, running her finger along the labels of her gathered ingredients. "Besides, you're crippled right now."

"Fair enough," I said, falling back into my chair.

I stared at the table as Keaton moved around the kitchen. I envied how easy life seemed to be for her. Nothing made her mad or upset. She went with the flow.

With the food simmering on the stove, Keaton pulled out the chair beside me and sat down. She grabbed my hands and held them tight, stroking the skin with her thumb. "What made you finally reach out?"

"I missed you, Keaton," I said. No point in hiding that fact. "And I can't do this alone anymore."

"Do what alone?"

"Live with the guilt. Ever since Oscar I…" I paused to swallow. "I feel like I'm a different person and then Samuel—" I was ready to confess, to hear the words out loud, but they lodged in my throat.

Keaton squeezed my fingers. "I understand," she said and gave me a heartwarming smile wide enough to see the gap between her teeth, the kind that used to reassure me everything was going to be okay. It didn't do the trick now. It made me ache instead. When I was in prison, her smile would be one of the things I'd miss the most.

Keaton got up and finished dinner. I gave up on conversation and watched her work, wondering if she could feel the love and appreciation that I felt for her through my stare alone. At last, Keaton put a plate on the table in front of me then an identical one in front of her own seat.

"This is good," I said after taking one bite.

It had been forever since we'd really spent any quality time together. And that had been my fault entirely.

"How's college been?" she asked to break the silence.

The bite of food I had taken stuck in my throat as I remembered the debate about Samuel's remains, and the food lost all flavor.

"What is it? What happened?" Keaton asked, lowering her fork.

"They…debated Samuel in my forensics class," I said

after gulping down half my glass of juice.

"People will always make someone else's tragedy their own if it gets them attention," Keaton said, stuffing a bite of food into her mouth.

"So I've learned."

Silence passed while we finished our meal. When I put the last bite into my mouth, Keaton caught my eye. Whenever she said something I didn't like, she got a certain glint in her eyes, and it was there now, *looming*.

"Samuel's funeral is this weekend," she said.

Of all things to tell me, that wasn't it. I didn't want to know when his funeral was. It had been wrong of me to go to his search party, but it would be downright inappropriate of me to go to his funeral.

I set my fork down, pretending I had already known that information. "That's fast, isn't it?"

She stood up, gathering her empty dishes and mine before she said, "Maybe, maybe not. Honestly, I think his family wants to put the entire thing behind them."

That was something I could readily agree to.

Chapter Thirty-Nine

ANOTHER WEEK WENT by and life went into an odd sort of normalcy once again. Mom got up the nerve to start talking to me as if our last fight hadn't happened. The mood between us wasn't the same though, and I doubted it ever would be again. At least she had come to terms with the situation, and it seemed as if part of her had accepted me for all the horrible things that I was. I let her keep doing what she needed to do to get through this, and I would do the same. Everyone else cut me off like a diseased hand—Harlow, Carmine, and even Mr. Waters kept their distance—but Keaton was still there for me.

I was getting dressed for work when the pounding at the door came. Mom, in her usual icy fashion, said nothing as she walked over to it, pulling it open to reveal Detective Morgan with two officers behind her.

This wasn't like any of the interviews she had conducted. This had a much more serious vibe, and the sight of all those people on the other side of the door flared up something awful in me. When Detective Morgan stepped across the threshold, all of them moving in sync, I knew it was over. She didn't greet me as she pulled out a pair of shiny handcuffs, holding them up enough to reflect a bit of light.

It's funny how in the days after that, the handcuffs would be the thing I remembered the most. Not the arrest, not the pride in Detective Morgan's voice, or the shame building deep in my stomach. No, it was the damn handcuffs.

"Jessica Mills, you are under arrest for the murder of Samuel Black," she said.

Mom started crying in the corner of the room. I didn't let myself look at her for long. I didn't know if that was a reflex intended to protect me or her because in the end, it would do neither. The noise Mom made was loud, and the commotion got Keaton's attention all the way from her apartment. She stood on the stairs, tears brimming in her big wide eyes as one of the burly officers led me down the stairs, and into the lobby. I glanced at Keaton as I was pushed past her, and a tiny smile touched my lips. I wanted her to know that it was okay, that *I* was okay, because there was no use in her being sad over me.

I didn't remember much else about that walk until they put me in the police car. I was almost catatonic, barely aware of my head missing the roof on the way in. That ride could've been a few minutes or a week. Time was meaningless. When we got to the station, it was more of the same fog. They didn't speak to me as they maneuvered me through the building, and some of the officers who were seated looked up as I passed. There was something equal in all their gazes that deflated me a bit—hope and joy. They already knew they had their man, and I knew better than to argue then.

What would be the use?

The officer who was moving me onward opened the

door to a small interview room and gestured me to go inside. I had flashbacks to the day of the shooting, my shirt sleeve covered in Oscar's blood, and in place of the panic I had felt then, there was an odd sense of bliss. The officer seated me before leaving the room, and I tried to pretend that I didn't know the shiny wall on the other side was one-way glass.

When the door opened again, Detective Morgan stepped in. She wasn't smiling, but her features seemed somehow *lighter* than I was used to. She sat across from me, setting a stack of paperwork on the table between us.

Before she could say a word, I looked into her hardened silver eyes, and asked, "How did you know it was me?"

That was a question I would've assumed would catch someone off guard. Detective Morgan's face didn't change expression. "Getting a clear picture of what happened to him wasn't easy. However, we found enough. Under the nail of one finger there were skin cells with traces of your DNA. That evidence mixed with the CCTV footage of you arriving home on the night of Samuel's disappearance were enough for a warrant for your arrest."

I had done everything in my power to disconnect myself from the murder except destroying his hands. I thought about the scratch down my collarbone when he ripped my shirt, the way his nails raked my skin, and wondered how I could have forgotten such an important detail.

Detective Morgan didn't threaten me with jail for the rest of my life or frying in the electric chair. She stared at me with those deep silver eyes as if she could see something in me that I couldn't see in myself before she asked, "Why'd you do it?"

The door burst open and a man in his fifties with a bad combover came in. "Don't answer that," he said sitting beside me. He threw his briefcase onto the table in such a way that I didn't like him. It spoke of arrogance, a heightened sense of self-importance—a perfect metaphor for myself.

I didn't look at him even when he stared straight at me.

"Don't answer anything you don't feel comfortable answering," he said and handed me his card. "It's nice to meet you. I'm Damien, your attorney."

"Thank you, Damien, but I won't be needing your help," I said, tossing his card onto his briefcase before I looked back to Detective Morgan. "Here's what happened…"

I answered her question in full, telling her the truth about the past Samuel and I shared filled with his threatening pictures, the IMs, the chat threads, and the confrontation that the reporters had taped. I told her about breaking into his apartment, and the photo I had discovered. Detective Morgan listened patiently as I laid it all out on the table before her.

"That's quite a history," she said and clicked her nails on the table before adding, "How'd you kill him?"

Damien patted me on the arm as if he thought I had forgotten he was there. "Don't answer that," he said again.

I ignored the advice. What good would it do me? I was tired of holding onto my secrets. Talking about it made me feel lighter than I had in a long time. "He attacked me," I said. "He backed me down this alley and grabbed me." I pulled down the line of my shirt where the faintest hint of the wound he had inflicted was still visible on my skin.

"You stabbed him?" Detective Morgan asked.

"I stabbed him," I echoed.

My lawyer slammed his hand to the table. "That's enough," he said, but there was nothing he could do. I already put it out there.

"But he didn't die right away, did he?" Detective Morgan asked.

I had let him die, like I did with Oscar, and that didn't have to be the outcome. "No," I said at last. "He laid in the alley for a long time before he…before he stopped breathing."

"Did you attempt to call 911 at any time during this period in which you had him subdued?"

I opened my mouth, but Damien had had enough of being ignored. "That's an unnecessary question," he said and held up a finger to Detective Morgan. "Give me a minute with my client, please."

Curtly, she gathered her things and left. Damien was a wall of stone. "Are you trying to go to prison?"

"Do I have any other options?" I asked. "They have what they need to send me away. I killed a man."

"If you're willing to confess, I can most likely get you a plea deal based on what you claim to know about Samuel's involvement in an open murder investigation. But for that to work, I have to have a chance to talk to the Judge. If you tell everything there is to tell now, I can't help you."

I didn't particularly think I deserved any type of mercy, even that of a plea deal, but if there was a chance I could redeem some of my life, shouldn't I try to take it?

"Okay," I conceded.

Chapter Forty

THAT NIGHT, I was escorted to my jail cell. Thanks to my notoriety, it had been determined I'd be safer without a cell mate. I sat down on the stiff bed, staring at my bright orange clothes, and thought about my life. So far, prison really wasn't bad. I heard rumors of a television in the common room. In a way, this existence wasn't much different from my original one.

I wondered how Mom and Keaton were doing. Keaton was most likely handling it better. I thought about Mom, how she was already dependent on her narcotics to get her through the day, and wondered if her addiction would only get worse from here. At least now, she had an excuse.

I wasn't tired, but I laid in bed, staring up at the black ceiling. Angry shouts and arguments were all around me. I should've been frightened, but I felt nothing. It was as if my cell was in a separate plane of existence from the rest of the prison.

Tomorrow, I wouldn't have that option.

I WAS WOKEN up bright and early by a guard.

"What is it?" I groaned, holding up a hand to shield my eyes from the beam of light being shone on my face.

"Time for breakfast. Up and at 'em," she said. I didn't say anything as she grabbed me by the elbow, walking me to the cafeteria. "Here you are."

Without any sort of crutches, movement was hard. My eyes studied the rows and rows of tables filled with women in orange suits. Some of them were eating while others stared daggers at other women across the room. The oppressive feeling of anxiety washed over me, and I had a hard time deciphering between the present and the memories of meals in my high school cafeteria. My throat seemed to have shrunken down to the size of a pinhole so every breath I tried to take was a struggle.

My vision dotted with black spots as I approached the line. I wasn't expecting to get anything good, and the slop given to me on a silver tray met that expectation. I grimaced at the bowl of muck that was supposed to be oatmeal and hoped the carton of milk didn't look as gruesome once it was opened.

I hobbled around the cafeteria three times, searching for the best place to sit without standing out. With my gait, it took a considerable amount of time, and my standoffishness had already drawn the attention of a few women.

"Run along, new girl," one of them hissed at me, but I didn't dare look in their direction to see who had given me the warning.

While I might not know the ins and outs of this place yet, I had learned plenty about prison life from videos about gang violence. It wasn't uncommon for inmates to stab one another over the smallest things, and that wasn't how I planned for my day to end. The end of the week…maybe.

Eventually, I found a seat by the least threatening girl I had seen here. She was thin, much thinner than me, with long dark hair and skin that matched. Her eyes were focused on the plate before her. When I sat down beside her, her gaze didn't move. I had to give it to her for her commitment to the bit. I could hardly tolerate the smell of the food from a distance.

She shoved another bite of the oatmeal into her mouth. "Be careful what friends you make here," she said, setting her spoon onto her tray with such force that a blob of the creamy food splashed up, landing on my cheek.

"Huh?" I asked as I wiped it away.

She gave no response as she stood up and tried to leave the cafeteria. The guard who had brought me in stopped her, taking her somewhere and leaving me to ponder what had happened.

The already unappealing food lost whatever glamour it might've had. This was a whole new world, one I simply did not understand, regardless of all the time I had spent researching it. Outside of prison, I might've thought I was invisible, but being here, among humans who were as despicable as myself, I started to realize that harm could easily come to me.

And most likely, I would never see it coming.

I forced a bite of the horrid food into the mouth. I hadn't eaten in almost a day, but the slop still didn't pass for anything I would willingly eat. I grimaced and set my spoon down, trying not to let myself cry as I gulped my tiny milk, desperate to get rid of the foul taste.

An officer crossed the room toward me, and I panicked. Had I done something wrong? Something I didn't know I *could* do wrong?

"Your attorney would like to have a word with you," she informed me, and I was escorted to the interview room by the elbow. I wasn't happy for the way she manhandled me, but there was little to do about that. I waited until we made it to our destination to glare before I took my place at the table.

Damien stared at me over his folded hands. "Here's what your options are," he said without greeting and opened his folder. "You can take a deal pleading guilty to voluntary manslaughter due to self-defense and take a sentence of ten years in prison or try your hand at going to court on first degree murder charges."

I didn't particularly care for either of the two options, but I would be an idiot to not admit that one sounded wildly better than the other. "Ten years for self-defense?"

"Ten years because you went out of your way to hide the body. Most people who kill out of self-defense don't do that."

I told myself this wasn't the place to be emotional. I needed all my wits here. "But you don't understand."

"It's not my place to understand," Damien said curtly. "It's my job to make sure you're not jailed for a crime you didn't commit, but you've made it clear that you *did* commit this crime. Now I'm trying to figure out how to get you the least amount of time possible for it."

The choice was easy. I had already told them everything, and if I hadn't trusted my *mother* to believe me, why would these complete strangers be any different? If I went to court, they could easily charge me with first-degree murder. Between hiding the body the first time and going out of my way during the search party to hide it again, there were red flags everywhere.

I bet Samuel's chat threads are loving this, I mused as I remembered that I wouldn't get to see for myself for a long time.

"Part of the plea deal is that you need to give them the evidence you took from the apartment. Anything that can help them show the judge the extent of Samuel's behavior toward yourself and other women. Especially Molly Rodriguez."

Ten years. Approximately 1/10 of my life.

Better than all of it, the little voice in the back of my head reminded me.

"Well, Jessica?" Damien prompted. "What's it going to be?"

"I'll take the deal," I said.

Real serial killers didn't go gentle into that goodnight, but for me, this had been my destination all along. Not going to court would mean keeping away from the limelight, and I was grateful. The world had seen enough of me to last a lifetime.

Outside of these walls, I was a spectacle and probably would be for a while. I could gauge that by keeping track of how long it would take Mom to make her first visit…if she bothered to visit me at all. Deep down, I hoped she stayed far away in the perfect little bubble she had built for herself. This place wasn't for her or for Keaton.

It wouldn't make me feel better to see them anyway.

Epilogue

I GIVE KEATON a small sad smile through the glass. "And that's the story."

"Wow," she says, clutching the phone tighter to her ear. "I can't believe you kept all that inside you."

"I told everyone I thought there was darkness in me, but no one believed me." I think of Oscar. He used to say no one took him seriously either. *We showed them.*

"They have to now."

I laugh. "Yeah, I guess that's true."

She smiles again, but then it fades so quickly that I wonder if she really smiled at all. Her voice drops to a whisper as she says, "You could've told *me*. I mean, you hinted at what you had done, but if you had *told* me, I would've done everything in my power to make sure this never happened."

"I believe you," I say, "and that's part of why I *didn't* tell you. I deserve, to be here. Not you."

"You don't though. What Samuel did to you and Molly was wrong. *He's* the real monster."

In the back of my mind, I could still hear the condescension in his voice during our last talk, the hate he had carried to his final moments, but ultimately, I had won our little fight. I'm still alive, and I brought his evil deeds to light. At the very least, the Rodriguez family can finally have peace for their lost children.

"You're going to be in there forever," Keaton whispers, and her entire face goes downcast.

"Ten years isn't that long," I point out. "By the time we're proper adults, I'll be out. It could be sooner with good behavior. Who knows?"

"It's going to be hard doing anything without you to keep me company," Keaton admits.

"You can visit any time. I'm not going anywhere," I say. I mean it as a joke, but she doesn't laugh.

"It's still unfair."

I'm not sure what to tell her. "Don't do the crime if you can't do the time, right? But really, you don't have to worry about me. You never did."

"Maybe, but don't you get it? I'm going to worry anyway. You're my best friend. I'll never meet another person like you."

Not much stings me emotionally, but that comment might as well have been a knife directly to my heart. "You're right. You'll find better people out there. People who can offer you things I never could. I love you, Keaton. Please, go live a long happy life, and don't waste another minute worried about me."

I hang up before she can reply, catching my last real glimpse of her through the plexiglass window as she tries to speak into the phone. When I stand up, she bangs her fist against it, but I tune her out. She might've been the person I was closest to, but she's better off without me. There's still light in her, such a beautiful chance at life. I don't want to ruin that, to corrupt her with my darkness.

Ten years isn't long, and yet it's forever at the same time. In ten years, Keaton might be married with kids and a high-powered job, and I will finally get to resume the life that I put on pause. She'll always be lightyears ahead of me, and what kind of person would I be to not want that for her? For everything she's ever done for me, she deserves nothing but the best, and without me weighing her down, she'll achieve it all.

As I'm escorted back to my cell, I have a weird moment of depersonalization. This body that I'm in doesn't feel like mine and neither do the decisions that I've made in it. With two kills under my belt, I didn't officially earn the title of *serial killer*, but people know who I am.

The days pass slowly, but for as solemn as I am in my tiny cell, I'm never truly alone with thoughts of Samuel and Oscar at the front of my brain. I think about Oscar more than Samuel, but it's interesting that I think of Samuel at all.

If the police had never connected Samuel's murder to me, would I have gone on to live a normal existence, washing my hands of the darkness deep inside of me? Or would it have come out to play full force? I think about Ted Bundy picking random victims to kill and wonder if I would've reached that point eventually, perhaps picking off people who looked like Samuel? People who acted like him?

I'll find out when I'm released, I suppose. The past few months have proven that I'm capable of far more and far less than I ever thought possible. No one ever plans to be this, a killer. It's not some career people choose when they're little like a firefighter or a doctor.

No. It's born from something deep in the psyche. Perhaps the scariest part is that *anyone* can become this, can become *me* if the need arises because killers aren't born.

They're made.

About the Author

Kayla Frederick is the new pen name for established author, Kayla Krantz. A little neurotic and a huge lover of Halloween, she enjoys creepy stories.

Other Works By the Author

8 artists.
1 art residency.
1 chance to leave alive.

Art is pain. Or so they say.

As a struggling artist in New York City, Ira is desperate to get
her shot at the big time. When an invitation to a week long art
residency on a private island in the Bahamas drops in her inbox,
she leaps at the chance.

But something is off about Turquoise Bay and its owner, The
Curator.

When Ira and seven other artists end up locked in an
underground bunker, the only way out is to play the Curator's
games.

Will they survive?

Or will they die for their art?